OTHER TITLES BY NICK SPALDING

Dumped, Actually
Dry Hard
Checking Out
Mad Love
Bricking It
Fat Chance
Buzzing Easter Bunnies
Blue Christmas Balls

Love . . . Series

Love . . . From Both Sides
Love . . . And Sleepless Nights
Love . . . Under Different Skies
Love . . . Among the Stars

Life . . . Series

Life . . . On a High
Life . . . With No Breaks

Cornerstone Series

The Cornerstone
Wordsmith

LOGGING OFF

NICK SPALDING

LAKE UNION
PUBLISHING

Published by Lake Union Publishing, Seattle

www.apub.com

Amazon, the Amazon logo, and Lake Union Publishing are trademarks of Amazon.com, Inc., or its affiliates.

ISBN-13: 9781542017480
ISBN-10: 1542017483

Cover design by Ghost Design

Printed in the United States of America

I'd like to dedicate this book to everyone who follows me on social media. You clearly all need something far better to do with your time. Try knitting.

Chapter One

GOTTLE OF GEER

Oh my God.

This is *amazing*.

Why haven't I *seen* this before?

It's an app . . . that records your bowel movements!

Its name?

HowUPooing.

Yes, that's right. It's called HowUPooing.

Genius.

I already use several health-checking apps that let me chronicle my blood pressure, cholesterol levels, weight, sleep patterns and BMI, but I've never had one that lets me note down (in exquisite detail) each and every bowel movement!

It's *amazing*!

Particularly useful for somebody like me – cursed with the joys of rampant irritable bowel syndrome. One day I'm bunged up like someone's shoved a cork up my bum, the next I'm an upside-down brown fountain. At least with HowUPooing I can maintain an overall picture of how things are going in my digestive system, so I can tell my doctor all about it the next time I visit him.

This morning, I have to chronicle in my shiny new app (which was only 99p to boot) that I am once again as constipated as a dog that's eaten a pound of plasticine. I'm also dog-tired – to continue the canine analogy – as I slept very badly last night, waking up at 2 a.m. in the legendary cold sweat. Snoregasbord – the sleep app I use – told me I got less than two hours of decent REM sleep. Terrible stuff.

I'm not surprised by either of these things in the slightest, as I have an important presentation to give today, and am feeling decidedly nervous. Sleep always goes out the window under such circumstances.

When it comes to nervous bowels, however, anybody else would be pooing like a mad thing, but my bowels don't work like that. They are contrary bastards, and like to do the opposite of what everyone else's do.

Having carefully noted down the ongoing fight with my inner digestive workings, I have a shower and a shave, and take a quick look at Twitter while I wait for the kettle to boil.

It's the usual cavalcade of nonsense opinion and trending hashtags that conspire to make the world seem like even more of a madhouse than it really is.

Today, people are up in arms about something that happened on a TV show about other people with weight problems. It's not a programme I watch, but I appear to be in the minority, as #FatChance is right at the top of the Twitter trends, and people are very angry about something Sandee has done. I have no idea who Sandee is – and, judging from the way people are speaking about her, I don't think I want to.

I then spend another few minutes looking at all my favourite movie and TV stars, to see what they're up to. Robert Downey Jr. has taken to wearing a unicorn onesie, I see, and Ryan Reynolds continues to make appalling jokes about how bad Blake Lively is at cooking. Ricky Gervais has managed to insult the entire Catholic world this morning, and The Rock has just bench-pressed Mount Everest.

Everything seems quite normal, then.

After all that, it's time to take a look at what my favourite Instagram influencers are up to – especially Lucas La Forte, who is just about the coolest bloke I think I've ever seen. Lucas is the same age as me, but his life choices have been somewhat more success-ful than mine – to say the least. He's a millionaire, has the kind of smile that can remove underwear from a hundred paces, and wears expensive suits in a way that I never could, even with a lottery win and about half a mile of run-up.

He's also extremely good with the old motivational speaking – something I am severely in need of this morning, with my presenta-tion looming. Today, he's telling me I should always focus on my goals, but learn to love the little things in life – all from the driver's seat of his Porsche 911.

The fact that he doesn't live all that far away from me makes me cooler by geographical association, I'm sure you'd agree.

With my tea made and all influencers present and accounted for, I flick over to Facebook and spend a constructive ten minutes having an argument with Jerry Pimbleton on the local news forum, about the proposed plans to build houses on the old, disused dairy farm on Cobb Street.

This argument between us has been ongoing for months now. I think the new houses would be a very good idea, as we're bursting at the seams around here. Jerry thinks otherwise.

Mind you, Jerry does live on Privett Road, so he has a vested interest in not seeing it chock-a-block with lorries and dumper trucks for the next two years. To be honest I can see his point, but I'm thoroughly enjoying the discussion, and have more or less taken up this opposing position just to keep it going.

I have to force myself to end this latest confrontation, because I really do have to make sure everything is ready for the meeting later today.

This involves putting down my iPhone, and picking up my iPad.

On it is the presentation I intend to give to the people at Fluidity this afternoon – along with several carefully picked examples of my work to show them once it's concluded.

Fluidity designs the kind of clothes I wouldn't be seen dead in, as I am not twenty-one and barely in control of my own faculties, but they do seem to have a lot of money to throw around.

I intend to be the graphic designer they throw some of that money at, when I wow them with my skills. I am convinced I can do a great job designing the visuals for their next spring promotion, and that's why this presentation needs to be absolutely *perfect*.

I should probably move to the iMac to make any last-minute changes, but there shouldn't be too much to alter at this late stage, so the iPad will do the job fine, I'm sure.

I regret this decision about half an hour later, when my neck starts to throb again. Staring down at an iPad while you're slumped on a couch is not the greatest way to work.

And yet, I still don't get up off the couch and make my way over to the desk. I'm so engrossed in making minute alterations to page four that I just put up with the pain, until it finally becomes unbearable.

Never mind, I can always pop a couple of ibuprofen – and I think I've definitely made page four sing about as loudly as it can. The discomfort is worth it just to get the damn presentation right.

I have it on good authority that the guys at Zap Graphics are also pitching to Fluidity, and I desperately want to beat them. They've swiped a good two or three contracts out from under me these past few months, and I don't want that to happen again!

I pop the iPad into my rucksack and look at my watch. I still have an hour to kill until I call the Uber to take me over to Fluidity's office.

Hmmm.

Maybe I'll play a little *Candy Crush* on the toilet. I'm so close to level 3,000 now, I can almost taste it – and maybe if I park my bottom on the loo for a while longer, my bowels might get the bloody message and start functioning again.

Unfortunately, this does not happen, but I do indeed manage to reach level 3,000 – so it's not a complete loss. I also answer a couple of emails, check Twitter again, as well as Facebook (Jerry hasn't responded to my last message as yet; he must be at work), and then pop on to the PlayStation Reddit forum to see if anyone has completed *Death Curse Intransigent* yet.

Death Curse Intransigent is a Japanese horror game that came out two days ago, and is as baffling to play as the title is to understand. Even CrackdownCharlie is having problems with it, and CrackdownCharlie is one of the greatest gamers I know. Without him, I'd never have finished off the Spaghetti Kid in *Steel Revolver*, and would still be up to my arse in goblins, playing *Gates of Torment*.

I've been umming and ahhing about buying *Death Curse Intransigent*, and was rather hoping Crackdown would have put his review up by now. He tends to finish games within days of their release, such is his commitment to his craft – but this game has confused and frustrated him as much as anyone else.

I think I'll hold off on buying it for a while. I don't need any more frustration in my life right now. Not with Zap Graphics stealing jobs off me, and my bowels refusing to work properly.

I don't recognise the Uber driver who's taking me across town. He must be new. I use the service so much that I've become pretty familiar with all of the drivers in my local area.

Mustafa drives a rather nice Mercedes, I must say.

I tell him as much as I climb into the back seat.

'Thank you very much, sir! It's a wonderful car to drive!' he tells me enthusiastically, before pulling away from my block of flats and beginning the twenty-three-and-a-half-mile journey to Fluidity. According to the Uber app, we should get there in twenty-nine minutes, so I sit back and try to relax as much as I can, with a little more *Candy Crush*.

During the journey, Mustafa tells me all about why he decided to buy the Mercedes over the Audi, and I pass another five *Candy Crush* levels. I also receive a text from my friend Fergus, reminding me about the drinks party he's holding to celebrate his promotion at work, and also telling me that I have to watch season three of *Kill Space* on Netflix, as it's literally the best show he's ever watched. I reply, telling him that I will of course be at the party, and will also watch the show.

In actual fact, though, I doubt I'll get around to it any time soon, as my watch list is already longer than my arm.

My watch list on Amazon Prime Video is only slightly shorter. There just aren't enough hours in the day!

After that, I take a quick look on Tinder, as you never know when the future love of your life might pop up on your phone screen. I end up swiping left seven times, and right once, on a particularly pretty black-haired girl with a set of lovely green eyes, called Grace. I don't hold out much hope that she'll also swipe right on me, but Tinder is more about the fantasy than the reality, in my experience.

'We have arrived, sir!' Mustafa tells me in a happy, excited tone. He must be angling for the coveted five-star review.

'Thank you,' I reply, and gather up my rucksack, checking that the iPad is still plugged into the bag's inbuilt charger. I breathe a sigh of relief when I see that it is. I never want a repeat performance of what happened at Spinnaker Sails. Everything was going so well until the bloody battery ran out. I'm pretty sure that was one of the main reasons why they chose Zap Graphics over me. It's a little hard to show off your graphic design skills when all you have to work with is a pen and one of their napkins. The K1425 Smart Rucksack cost me a small fortune, but I'll never turn up to another business meeting with a battery on less than 100 per cent again.

As Mustafa drives away, I thumb in a five-star review on Uber, before swiping it away and checking my emails one final time. I'm still waiting on a response from McGifferty's Pies about whether they want me to pitch for their new shop logo. My teeth grind together as I see that there still isn't one. Paul McGifferty promised he'd get back to me within one week, and it's been nearly two.

Never mind.

That's not important now.

I have to concentrate on getting across the line with Fluidity. That's all that matters. Like my Instagram friend Lucas La Forte says – you have to focus on your goals! He has a Porsche, and a haircut you could eat your dinner off, so he must know what he's talking about.

I feel my stomach flip over and hear it give a little gurgle as I walk into the enormous glass office block that contains the Fluidity offices on the twelfth floor.

These kinds of meetings never go down well with my internal workings – be they the ones in my gut or the ones in my head. Being a self-employed, freelance graphic designer is not easy on the mind or body. Especially not when the spectre of Zap Graphics is constantly looming over one shoulder.

During the ride in the elevator up to the twelfth floor, I note that Jerry Pimbleton has replied to my last comment on Facebook, with another lengthy diatribe about how the lorries will kill off his begonias. I'll have to read it and respond later.

I also check the weather for this evening, choose the Chinese restaurant I'm going to order my dinner from on Deliveroo, and look at my DeviantArt page. On the last, I'm pleased to see that the illustration I drew last night of Imiko from *Death Curse Intransigent* has gone down a storm. I may not have bought the game yet, but that doesn't mean I'm not buying into the hype. So far, the picture has over seven hundred likes, and I've gained thirteen followers. A warm bloom of happiness swells in my chest as the elevator door bings open.

I walk down the rather nondescript corridor, and arrive at the main door to Fluidity's offices. These do not look nondescript. Not in the slightest.

In fact, if there's some great universal scale on which nondescript is at one end, then these offices must be at the other. They are *super*descript. *Mega*descript. There's so much descript going on here, you could bottle it and sell it at a car boot sale.

I would say a riot of colour hits me as I walk through the doorway and into the offices proper, but that wouldn't do it justice. This isn't a riot. It's a bloody thermo-global nuclear war.

Fluidity designs clothes exclusively for Generation Z. And Generation Z really loves a lot of colour. I know this because I googled it.

I'm thirty-six now, and am therefore completely disconnected from the youth of today, but the world's most popular search engine has told me all that I need to know about Generation Z's fashion choices. They largely consist of bits of multicoloured material, sewn together haphazardly before being torn to pieces by a hyperactive badger.

The interior decor of the Fluidity offices apes this approach to an alarming degree. No two walls are the same colour. Hell, no two square yards of wall are the same colour. It's headache-inducing.

But I dutifully sit down on one of the brightly coloured plastic chairs in the reception area, having been directed there by the receptionist, who gave me a very funny look for daring to be over the age of twenty-five.

While I wait for someone to come and get me, I have another look at Twitter, to see that *Fat Chance* has been replaced at the top of what's trending by the latest shenanigans in Parliament. I generally ignore everything to do with politics, as in recent years it's become abundantly clear that those who work in it roundly ignore everything to do with me.

I also read Jerry's Facebook post properly, and find myself grinding my teeth at his selfishness. There have been no additional comments on my latest DeviantArt picture in the last few minutes – which is rather disappointing, as I really thought I was gaining traction.

Then I pull the iPad out of my rucksack, and have one last-minute read-through of the presentation. I absently rub the back of my neck and my shoulder as that familiar aching pain reappears. I should probably get something done about that.

'Andy!' a clipped voice says from off to my left. I look up to see someone dressed in Fluidity clothing coming towards me. I wish I was wearing sunglasses.

This must be Pikky – the person who arranged this meeting with me.

No, I have no idea what Pikky's real name is. I haven't had the courage to ask.

All I know is that Pikky is one of the three founding members of Fluidity, and is something of a rising star in the fashion industry.

Pikky is of Asian heritage, and requires a pie in his life at the earliest possible convenience. He's incredibly skinny. The colourful, badger-assailed clothing I mentioned before hangs off his frame in all the wrong places.

Mind you, I have no idea what all the *right* places are, so who am I to judge?

I get up from the plastic chair, wincing slightly as I do. I really must get my neck and shoulder seen to.

'Good morning, Pikky,' I say to the thin man, as he sashays over and holds out a skeletal hand.

'Oh please, Andy. Call me Piks. Everybody else does,' he replies happily.

'OK . . . *Piks*. It's very nice to meet you – and thank you for inviting me here today.'

Piks waves a hand. 'Oh, it's no trouble. We're keen on seeing as many designers as we can for this job.'

This makes me involuntarily grind my teeth again. I was rather hoping they wouldn't have many people competing for the tender. Realising I probably have a lot more competition than just Zap Graphics is irritating.

'Shall we go through to our touch zone, and see what you've got to offer us?'

'OK,' I say, slightly confused.

What on earth is a *touch zone*? I don't think I want to go into something called a touch zone with a complete stranger wearing baggy multicoloured clothing. Things may happen. *Strange* things.

But Pikky has already started sashaying away from me, so I'd better follow – and hope nothing untoward happens to my touch zone in the coming few minutes.

Pikky leads me through a small office space full of brightly dressed individuals, all sitting behind brand-new iMacs. None of them appear to be doing any work whatsoever, but this doesn't appear to trouble Pikky in the slightest.

One of them, a woman who would probably be stunningly beautiful if it weren't for the blue hair and three inches of thick make-up, smiles at me as I walk past. There's pity in that smile. Pity for the old man clutching his rucksack as he walks in fear through the valley of the shadow of the eyeliner.

I try to smile back, but the ongoing assault of colour from all angles has rather discombobulated my brain, and the smile looks more like a grimace of terror.

What the hell am I doing here?

These people aren't going to want me to design their spring campaign for them. They all have computers far better than mine – and actually understand the people they're trying to design fashion for. What possible input could I realistically have?

Run away! my thirty-six-year-old brain insists.

Yes! Do that! my thirty-six-year-old bowels agree.

I try my best to ignore them and scuttle off behind Pikky as he walks out of the office area and into a room that makes the rest of Fluidity's offices look positively boring.

Every wall in here is covered in fabric. A thousand different samples of a thousand different materials, all stuck to the wall . . . and just waiting for someone to give them a poke.

'Welcome to the touch zone,' Pikky tells me as he walks over to where two other individuals are sitting on a gigantic sofa. The sofa is also a patchwork of materials, and therefore blends into the wall behind it like an upholstery chameleon.

Sitting on the long sofa is a woman wearing a see-through shower curtain. Sitting next to her is a cowboy.

Look, I'm sorry, but I'm not making this stuff up.

That *is* a shower curtain she's wearing. I can see little plastic ducks on it. The ducks are multicoloured, so they're very on-brand for Fluidity.

The cowboy . . . is a bloody *cowboy*. What more do you need?

The cowboy hat is white – if that helps – and the chaps are brown leather. The waistcoat is as black as the handlebar moustache. I'm pretty sure the moustache is fake, though, as the person beneath it looks about sixteen.

'Andy Bellows, please meet my partners in fluidity, Winery Smalls and Tex.'

No, that's not a typo you see there. I deliberately didn't give Fluidity a capital letter when Pikky said it, because I just know he wasn't referring to their company name, but a state of mind that they all share. There's fluidity going on here, all right. Fluidity between bizarre and cheerfully insane.

'Hello, Mr Bellows,' Winery Smalls says, inclining her head. As she does this, the shower curtain rustles.

'Hello,' I reply, trying not to look at her skimpy underwear beneath the shower curtain.

'Howdy,' Tex drawls, tipping his cowboy hat slightly. The drawl is slightly ruined by the fact it's in a broad Lancashire accent.

'Yes . . . and to you,' I tell him. 'Howdy, indeed.'

I would like nothing more at this point than to ask why they are both dressed like that.

Is it a bet? I want to enquire.

Why is her name Winery Smalls? Is that her real name? And, if so, how much did her parents enjoy alcohol?

Why is he a cowboy? Is his real name Tex? Is the moustache actually fake? Is the Lancashire accent real?

I want answers to all of these questions, but it's quite apparent I'm not going to get them, because Pikky, having made the introductions, doesn't look like he intends to follow them up with any kind of explanation.

'So, Andy, we have a smart screen at the end of the room. You'll find it underneath that large square of hessian,' he tells me. 'You'll just need to Bluetooth it to your iPad and you should be ready to go, as we agreed.'

'Oh . . . OK,' I say, still unable to quite get my head around the shower curtain and cowboy hat.

'Please feel free to run your hand across the wall on your way,' Winery Smalls tells me. 'The tactile sensation should calm your second soul.'

Second soul?

I'm not entirely sure I have a first one, and now this shower-curtain-clad woman is telling me I have a second one?

There's a part of me that is starting to think this entire thing is either a massive wind-up, or a fever dream brought on by too much *Candy Crush*.

Turning slowly away from the three fashionistas, I do as I'm told and run my hand along the wall as I make my way to the hessian-covered smart screen at the end of the room.

'Ooh,' Winery Smalls says, almost orgasmically, as I reach the velour.

Nobody has felt this good about velour since 1978.

It certainly doesn't feel particularly good to me as I drag my fingers across it, and I'm quite relieved when I hit sponge on the next panel.

I like sponge. I have three of them in my bathroom.

Giving it a final little poke, I move away from the tactile wall and lift the brown hessian to reveal a reassuringly boring smart television screen. It's lovely to see something so solid, straight and black after all that eclectic colour.

'Pull the hessian away, Andy,' Pikky tells me. 'It's attached with Velcro.'

'Velcro,' Winery parrots, rolling her eyes with pleasure.

I do this, trying to ignore Winery's small, ecstatic moan at the sound of Velcro strips pulling apart. These are some very strange people I'm dealing with here.

It takes me only a few seconds to link my iPad to the screen, and within moments I am ready to start my presentation.

'Good morning,' I say formally to the three people sitting with expectant looks on their faces. 'I am very pleased to be here today, to pitch you my ideas for your newest campaign.'

'Excellent!' Pikky says, clapping his hands together.

'Divine,' Winery Smalls agrees.

'Tarnation,' Tex remarks.

I'm not sure he understands what that word actually means.

Nevertheless, I have to present to these people, so ignoring their idiosyncrasies is paramount if I'm to get through this. I can't spend the next ten minutes worrying about why a young man from Lancashire feels the need to dress like a cowboy.

I launch into the presentation as best I can.

To begin with, it seems to be going well. My Google research about Fluidity appears to have paid dividends, as I get a lot of nods and smiles from my audience as I talk about what I think their vision for the company going forward should be, and how my graphic design sensibilities can work for them.

I then show the three of them some sample text images I think would be appropriate for the upcoming campaign's wording. I've created some truly awful fonts for this. All jagged edges and over-blown serifs that most people would reject instantly . . . but this lot seem to think are right up their street.

It's actually going very well, until Winery Smalls drops a bombshell.

'It's so nice to see how different people can come up with the same idea,' she says, interrupting me as I'm trying to explain how the eclectic fonts I've created will complement the badger-ravaged clothing they want to sell to poor, unsuspecting members of the Gen Z population.

'Pardon me?' I reply, a bit nonplussed.

She leans forward. 'I just think it's *wonderful* how the creative process works.' Her hands go to her chest. 'I'm in awe of it. That two people, entirely unrelated, can come up with graphics that look *so similar*. It really must mean Fluidity has a strong and clear message that you've both understood so well.'

'Both? Similar?' I say, now completely confused.

'What Winery means,' Pikky interjects, 'is that the work you're showing us is very similar to the designs Zap Graphics presented us with yesterday.'

My jaw muscles instantly tighten, and I can feel my teeth wanting to clench themselves together. 'Is it?'

'Yes!' Winery crows happily. 'Isn't that a wonderful, *majestic* thing?'

'Majestic,' I repeat, barely able to get the word out.

'It really is quite amazing,' Pikky continues. 'A real wonder how you can both provide such similar proposals without having worked together on it.' Pikky's eyebrow arches with the last few words, indicating that he doesn't believe for a second that Zap Graphics and I haven't colluded on this project.

But that's not true!

I don't even know the guy's bloody name!

The only way we'd have the same kind of work to show off is if one of us had copied the other, and I know for a fact that it wasn't—

Oh, *bloody hell.*

15

Is that it? Has Zap Graphics somehow hacked into my computer and nicked my ideas?!

Yes! That's it!

The *bastard*!

My stomach flips as the horror of it envelops me. I have been hacked and ripped off. No doubt about it!

'Are you going to continue, Andy?' Pikky says expectantly.

Oh, Christ. Now I have to finish this damn presentation? Knowing that some bastard – whose name I don't even know – has stolen my work?

'Yes, yes!' Winery exclaims, bouncing up and down on the chair and making her shower curtain rustle loudly. 'Please carry on! I'm so interested in your creative process!'

'Y'all keep going, y'hear?' Tex comments, sounding like someone who owns a whippet while looking like someone who owns a cattle ranch.

The world has gone mad.

'Er . . .' I say, looking down at my iPad.

I should continue.

Just because they've already seen Zap Graphics doesn't mean his stuff is actually better than mine. I could still win this.

Focus on your goals, as Lucas La Forte would no doubt remind me, if he were here.

Christ, I wish he was here. Winery would probably go and lick his expensive suit, thus taking some of the attention off my shoulders.

'Er . . . let me move on to what I want to do for the online placements you mentioned in your tender.'

'Oh, excellent!' Winery says, far too excited about this whole thing for my liking. 'I bet that'll be the same as the other Andy's work as well!'

'What?' I spit, not able to help myself.

'Why, don't you know?' Pikky says with a smile. 'The man behind Zap Graphics is also an Andy. Andy Roan, I think his name was. Lovely chap. Very handsome. Very talented.'

Oh, for fuck's sake.

I'm dead in the water here.

I grind my teeth together, sending a sharp stabbing pain up through my right temple.

Just. Get. Through. It. And. Get. Out.

'So, the online adverts then,' I say from between gritted teeth. 'Here's what I think you should do.'

I flick my iPad screen to reveal the layout I've designed.

'Oh yes! So similar again!' Winery cries with happiness. 'Magnificent!'

If I grind my teeth any more, I'm going to turn them to powder.

I don't look at any of them, instead just concentrating on the two months of work that's on the TV screen.

'If you look, you can see that I've gone for an eclectic design that really shows just how vigrant and gold I think we can make the campaign.'

Pikky looks confused. 'Gold? I don't see any gold in there, Andy.'

'Nope! No gold on that advert, Andy Number Two!' Winery agrees.

I didn't mean gold, though, I meant *bold*.

'No, no . . . not gold . . . *gold*,' I tell them.

Now Pikky's look of confusion deepens. 'There's no gold in that design, Andy.'

'Gold! Gold!' I try to say, but the word isn't coming out right. The stabbing pain shoots up into my right temple again, and my hand flies to my head to hold it.

'Are you all right?' Pikky asks.

''Es. I'm fine,' I reply, lying through my teeth.

17

I have to lie through my teeth, *because I can't open my mouth.*

'Are you sure?'

''Es! No progem at all!'

Oh, Christ on a bike, I can't open my jaw! It's locked tight! What the hell is wrong with me?

'Are you OK to continue?' Pikky says, looking concerned.

Just. Get. Through. It. And. Get. Out.

''Es! I can carry on. I'm gerfectly vine!'

I'm clearly not perfectly fine. Far from it.

But, not wanting this crisis to turn into a disaster, I try to ignore the sharp stabs of pain that continue to pulse through my temple, and look back to the TV screen.

'Der cloves you make are vigrant, gold, exciting and mogern. My gravic designs revlec' dis.'

Jesus Christ. I sound like a ventriloquist trying to do a Jamaican accent – and failing miserably at it.

'Fluiggigy's style is gold and very grave, so I wanted to make sure—'

'We are not very grave!' Winery interrupts, looking displeased for the first time. 'We are very happy here! All of us!'

'No! *Grave*,' I try to say. ''O know! Grave! As in a comgany dat's gig, grave and gold! You're a vigrant, new comgany dat's really grave with what you design! Grave!' As if to further clear up the confusion, I start to flex my muscles. That's how you'd do 'brave' in charades, isn't it?

'Are you feeling all right?' Pikky says, now with no small degree of fear in his voice.

And who can blame him? There's a man in front of him trying to flex like Arnold Schwarzenegger, for no apparent reason.

''Es! I keeg delling you I'ge fine!' I try to reply. The pain in my head is getting worse, and now the locked jaw is starting to throb too. 'I gust need to get frew the res' of dis prezentation. I 'ave a lot more for you to look at!'

'Do you?'

''Es! I 'aven even got to der gest gart, yet!'

'The guest gart?' Pikky now looks positively terrified.

''Es! The gest gart! The artwork for your augum winner zelecshun!'

Pikky stands up. 'I think it might be a good idea if we ended this here.' He looks down at Winery. 'I think Miss Smalls is getting a little perturbed.'

I look at Winery, and have to do a double take as I realise that she's crying like a busted fountain. Her make-up is now smeared down her cheeks. How anyone can lurch between emotional states like that is beyond me.

'I'ge sorry!' I wail. 'If I gan jus' 'ave a vew migits, I can gum gack and figgig!'

Now I'm speaking in a completely different language. There's every chance Winery Smalls thinks I'm trying to raise some evil spirit from the depths to come and eat her shower curtain.

'Please stop!' she wails, burying her head in Tex's shoulder.

Tex, for his part, looks entirely bored to tears by proceedings. But then I guess if you're a twenty-something Lancashire cowboy with a fake moustache, there's probably very little in this world that can faze you.

Oh God . . . It's all gone wrong! It's all gone so horribly wrong!

My stomach, which has been periodically making its presence felt all day with the occasional nervous flip, now rolls over like a tidal wave crashing on to the shoreline.

'Oh Gesus!' I remark in horror as I clutch my stomach.

Pikky walks towards me, arms outstretched. 'Are you all right, Mr Bellows?'

I've become Mr Bellows now. Not Andy any more. It's a sure sign I'm not getting anywhere near that contract.

''Es. 'Ike I said, I'ge agsoluley fine!'

Except the sudden need I have for the toilet.

Any toilet.

NOW.

''Air's your toilet?' I cry in desperation, through my still-locked jaw.

Pikky, showing a remarkable level of foresight and self-preservation, steps back a bit. 'It's across the office floor, over there,' he tells me, pointing at the door that leads away from the touch zone.

It certainly is a touch zone, now.

People come in here to touch cloth all the time, and that's definitely what I'm currently doing.

'Dank you!' I wail, and scuttle off as fast as I possibly can towards the toilet.

As I hurry past all of the Fluidity staff, holding on to my bottom for dear life, I feel tears of frustration and horror in my eyes. This meeting could not have gone any worse if I'd simply introduced myself, squatted down in front of every single Generation Zedder in here, and relieved myself all over their latest summer collection.

The toilets (unisex, just to add to the misery) are pretty much where Pikky promised, and there's fortunately no one in them as I barrel through the door.

Gratefully, I just make it to the cubicle before the world falls out of my bottom. And when it does, it's incredibly painful and *extremely* unpleasant.

For a few minutes I can't think about anything other than the obvious destruction being wrought upon my backside. It's horrific.

My poor anus has never done anything to deserve this kind of treatment.

Quite why my bowels would feel the need to put it through such a trauma is beyond me. You'd think they'd want to work together to make life as easy as possible, but – as I've said before – my bowels are contrary bastards, and smooth cooperation with the other facets of my digestive system are not their priority.

Having said that, nothing like this has ever happened to me before. Sure, the irritable bowel syndrome has always caused me a bit of grief and discomfort, but I've never had to rush to the toilet like this. Especially not when I've been bunged up like the M25 at rush hour a mere hour or so earlier.

This is new, horrible and not a little worrying. Especially the awful *pain*.

. . . Which has turned into an unpleasant throbbing now the worst of it is over.

I think – I hope – that I've managed to evacuate everything I need to. I'm sure my anus is hoping the same thing, given that it's been through an assault upon its person that it may never recover from. Not without many, many soothing creams and a long bath.

Gingerly, I wipe myself and slowly stand up. For a moment my legs don't want to support me, but eventually I get them to behave. I pull up my jeans, flush the loo and wash my shaking hands in the basin just outside the cubicle.

Taking several deep breaths, I steady myself internally by the door to the toilet. All I want to do now is gather up my belongings and get out of here as swiftly as possible.

Yes. That's it. Just get out quickly, and try to put this entire miserable experience behind—

JESUS!

I've swung the main toilet door open to be greeted by a sea of anxious faces on the other side. It looks like the whole of Fluidity is standing there . . . waiting to see if I've survived my own period of extreme fluidity.

At the front of this stationary gaggle are Pikky, Winery Smalls and Tex. Pikky looks concerned, Winery looks distraught, Tex looks bored.

I am painfully aware that from behind me, a smell that is as vast as it is abhorrent is emanating from the toilet and heading towards the crowd.

'Everything OK?' Pikky asks.

'We were quite worried about you,' Winery adds.

'Yup. You took off like a steer that's been spooked by a rattler,' Tex says, still in his broad Lancashire accent.

For some reason, even in the middle of this terrible farce, I have to ask.

'Why are you dressed like a gludy cowgoy?' I ask Tex, as slowly and as clearly as I can, trying to ignore the stench of my disgrace as it wafts across the room.

Tex looks extremely taken aback by this, as if it's the first time anyone's ever asked. Of course, it could also be that he can't understand what I'm bloody saying.

'Lionel is channelling the Old West this week,' Winery says, by way of explanation. 'He's looking to be inspired by the rugged sensuality of the American frontier.'

I'm dumbfounded.

His real name is Lionel?

''Ight,' I reply, blinking several times.

This place is insane. And I have contributed to its insanity more than enough for one lifetime.

'Can I 'ave my rucksack and iGad, glease?' I ask the crowd, hoping that somebody can understand and help me.

A sea of blank faces greets this, until Winery holds up her hands. 'I think he's trying to ask for his rucksack and iPad,' she says hesitantly.

I nod my head feverishly, and am handed both by the woman with the blue hair – who at least has a decent reason to feel pity for me now.

I take them both with an uneasy smile and look back to the crowd, who are – whether they realise it or not – blocking my way out.

'Glease gud you all leg me garsed?' I ask pitifully, massaging my aching jaw as I do so.

They all stare back at me, not comprehending a word of what I've just said.

Cue Winery Smalls again, who has obviously decided she's going to act as my universal translator. 'I think he may need us to do something for him!' she says, leaning forward. 'Would you like us to do something for you, Mr Bellows?' she asks me in a clear, slow voice, as if I'm foreign and looking for the nearest railway station.

Good grief.

''Es. I want do leave, gut you are glocking my way. Can you all glease move?!'

Winery's eyes go wide with comprehension. 'I think he's telling us he wants us to move so he can leave!' she cries triumphantly.

''Es! Glease move!'

And with that, the crowd does begin to part, right down the middle – mainly at the behest of Winery Smalls, who is walking backwards with both arms out to the side, and flapping her hands like a woman possessed.

I walk forward through the gap, the eyes of Fluidity on me as I do so. It's like they've discovered some strange and alien species, and are all wondering what bizarre behaviour it's going to exhibit next.

And also what smells it's going to make.

Finally, I am able to get by Winery Smalls and head for the exit.

'Gum gack and see us again, Mr Gellows!' she calls after me, with her teeth clenched together, as if she's trying to talk to me in my own alien language.

'Dank you,' I reply – for some fucking reason that will never become clear to me for as long as I live.

I then reach the main door to Fluidity's office, hurrying through it as fast as my still-shaky legs can carry me.

When the elevator doors close, I lean heavily against one wall and rub a hand across my sore eyes.

I should be absolutely heartbroken that the presentation went so badly.

I should be angry that Zap Graphics has ripped off my work.

But I'm neither of those things, because all I can do is worry that there might be something seriously wrong with me.

I've never experienced anything like this locked jaw before, and I've never had to take a painful emergency shit in public either. Add both of these to the fact that I've been getting that sharp ache in my neck and shoulders . . . and I haven't been sleeping well either.

What does it all mean?

I know I've got the stress of work to deal with, but that surely can't account for all of this? I've done plenty of presentations for potential clients before, and not once have I nearly shit my pants. Neither have I been robbed of the ability to talk like a normal human being.

No. Something is clearly very, very wrong with me.

'Gludy hell,' I say, under my breath, as the elevator continues its descent.

Without even thinking about it, I pull out my phone and bring up the HowUPooing app. I figure I'd better chronicle the emergency download I've just had to make at Fluidity's offices.

I select 'DIARRHOEA' and 'PAINFUL BOWEL MOVEMENT' from the app's generous selection of choices, and am dismayed when the phone bongs at me ominously, and a message in red pops up on the screen that reads 'These symptoms may indicate a serious health issue. Please consider seeing a doctor.'

Well . . . that says it all, doesn't it?

If the poo app thinks I should see a healthcare professional, then I'd bloody well better do what it says.

After all, if I trust apps to tell me what to eat, where to go and who to date, why wouldn't I trust them when it comes to something like my health?

So that's what I'm going to do. See a doctor.

I'm also going to do something about Zap *bloody* Graphics. None of this would have happened today if he hadn't ripped off my Fluidity designs!

Oh yes. Andy Bellows shall have his revenge. Of that there is no doubt. I will stalk Mr Zap Graphics Andy for a while, taking careful note of how he operates – and then, when I know everything I need to know about him, I will strike!

Aha!

After all, as the famous saying goes:

Revenge is a dish dat is gest served gold . . .

Chapter Two

Dr Google

. . . except for the fact that Zap Graphics did not rip me off in the *slightest*, and those idiots over at Fluidity are all comprehensively *mad*.

The second I got home, I fired up my laptop and went straight to the Zap Graphics website, where I saw that he had uploaded a few of the designs he'd presented to Fluidity on his portfolio page. It's something we all tend to do, as the Internet is the greatest shop window us graphic designers have.

And for the love of crap, would you look at them?

OK, there are a few similarities in colour and methodology, but his designs are hardly 'exactly the same' as mine. After all, we were both pitching our ideas for a campaign at an ultra-trendy fashion house . . . *of course* our concepts were going to cross over, to a certain extent.

And, if I'm being honest, Zap Graphics Andy is very talented. In many ways, I prefer his ideas to my own.

Grrrr.

That's as well as may be, but I would still have had a chance at the contract if bloody Winery Smalls and sodding Pikky hadn't made out that me and Zap had come up with virtually identical designs!

I would have never got as angry as I did, and probably wouldn't have locked up my jaw!

Which is still locked up, by the way. As I sit there looking at the Zap Graphics website with mounting frustration, I can feel the muscles in my jaw tightening involuntarily, making the situation even worse.

So, before I end up fusing my teeth together completely, I click away from Zap's website, and instead go on to Google to see if it can tell me what all of my symptoms mean.

I find a reputable-looking site called Symptopia.com – which purports to be able to diagnose any illness you might have, using its extensive database and patented algorithms. That sounds pretty good to me.

I type the following into the site's search engine:

Lockjaw
Sharp stabbing pain in head
Diarrhoea
Irritable bowel syndrome
Neck pain
Shoulder pain
Interrupted sleep.

And press the enter key.

The website thinks about things for a few seconds, before spewing out a list of ailments that I could be suffering from.

There's about two dozen of the bloody things – but I'm afraid the only ones I pay any attention to are the ones that feature the dreaded C word . . . of which there are no fewer than *seven*.

Yes, the extensive database and patented algorithms are telling me that there's a chance I have cancer, in one of seven different, increasingly terrible ways.

Seven separate ways that my own body could be rebelling against me on a cellular level.

Panic rises in my throat.

I hadn't even considered that I could have something *that* wrong with me. I was thinking it might be some kind of muscular disease, or maybe a problem with my brain chemistry. Those things sound bad enough, but when considered alongside the C word, they obviously pale in comparison.

It's only one website. Try a different one.

Yes. That's right. It *is* only one website, and its algorithms may be patented, but that doesn't mean they're not also a load of old shit.

I move on to another symptom-checking site, this one called CheckSym.com.

I type in the same symptoms . . . and get back virtually the same answers – only this time, it looks like I could have cancer *nine* different ways, instead of seven.

So, I try a *third* website, and then a *fourth*.

But each one spits out the same potential death sentences as quickly as the first. Although website number four only suggests I could die from six types of cancer, which is something of an improvement . . . I guess?

So I abandon that strategy, and instead type my symptoms straight into Google, to see if that comes up with something more constructive, and slightly less life-threatening.

Nope.

If anything, it's even *worse*.

Instead of just telling me I could have one of half a dozen cancers, Dr Google lets me know that I could be suffering from hundreds of them, each one more terrifying and harder to pronounce than the last. Something called a 'cerebrodendroglioma' sounds particularly horrifying.

The panic in my chest rises even more, and I can feel my jaw tightening to such an extent that the sharp, stabbing pains in my head are coming faster and faster.

Oh God. Oh God. Oh GOD!

. . . Now then.

There is a logical part of my brain that knows I'm overreacting.

I have been surfing the World Wide Web long enough to know that trying to diagnose yourself using the Internet is a ridiculous waste of time. Especially when you have so many symptoms.

Pump enough symptoms (*any* symptoms) into any checker or search engine, and the chance of it informing you that you have a terminal disease is nearly 100 per cent.

You could tell the damn thing that you have a ringing in your ears, a mild toothache, a small ache in one knee, a fear of chickens and a slight sense of disappointment about your place in the world – and it'd probably tell you that you have three minutes left to live.

Intellectually and logically, I know that sitting here at my laptop trying to self-diagnose is a bloody fool's game – but I'm not thinking intellectually and logically right now, I'm thinking with my gut.

Another twenty minutes goes by of me feverishly hunting for any website that will tell me that I'm going to be fine, and that there's nothing really wrong with me – but such a thing does not exist. It's all doom, gloom . . . and please make funeral arrangements as fast as you can.

The panic is now clawing at my very soul.

I need some kind of reassurance. Some kind of sage advice from other people that will help me climb off this ledge of fear I've placed myself on.

I know . . .

To the forums!

If ever I am unsure of something, and I'm not convinced that Google knows the answers, I turn to my friends on the various forums that I belong to for advice. They rarely let me down, whatever the subject matter.

I belong to forums that cover every single facet of modern life. If I have a DIY issue, I go straight to HandymanForums.com. If I need advice on something electronic or technological, I pop over to DigitalSpace.com.

If I want to book a holiday and can't decide between the three four-star-rated hotels I've found, then the people on the TripAdvisor forums are right there and waiting.

And, if I have a health issue, I go to HealthSpace.com to get advice. It's there that I discovered how to syringe the earwax out of my ears at home, meaning I could hear properly for the first time in years.

With this in mind, I jump into the forum's general advice section, and compose a suitable post about my latest potentially life-threatening problem.

The replies I get over the next couple of hours range from heartfelt to piss-taking of the highest order. This is to be expected. You can be guaranteed that whatever the topic you talk about on the Internet, you will receive replies that vary from compassionate to stone cold. It is the way of things. It's just important not to take either to heart, and to sift out the actual practical advice from the sarcasm or overblown sentimentality.

And the practical advice I'm getting – whether it be in the gushing response from Trixie1986 or the 'hilarious' reply I received from MrBigTrousers telling me I've probably got Ebola – is that I need to get off the bloody Internet and go to see a doctor.

I chew a fingernail as I read down through the replies, all saying more or less the same thing.

I'm not happy about it, not happy at all.

I know that I have to go and see a proper doctor, and that Dr Google is not the way forward, but I was really hoping somebody on here might at least give me a hint of what I have wrong with me. You know, something along the lines of: *Oh yeah! I had all of those symptoms a couple of years ago! Turns out I had Bob Bobbins syndrome. The doctor put me on antibiotics for a month and it cleared up, no problem!*

That would have stopped me feeling quite so panicky. Nobody wants to suffer from Bob Bobbins syndrome, but if you can solve it with the right pills, then it's not really much of an issue.

The key thing is, at least I would have known that I didn't have anything *that* serious. At least I wouldn't still be thinking I was about to drop dead at any moment.

But nobody has told me I have Bob Bobbins syndrome, and in fact, nobody has really tried to guess what I might have wrong with me *at all*. This cannot be good.

If nobody on this forum wants to venture a guess, then it means it's probably something rare and awful. Nob Nobbins syndrome, for instance – which kills you in a week, but not before your eyeballs start bleeding and your bum falls off.

I compose a short thank you to those who have responded to me on HealthSpace, and surf on over to the newly created digital appointment platform that my doctor's surgery instituted a few months ago. Much fuss was made of this wonderful, new, convenient way to book a doctor's appointment. The local Facebook page has an entire thread dedicated to it.

It's been *terrible*, needless to say.

Public service websites are invariably terrible in the UK. It's just the way things are.

I have a feeling that the day you can seamlessly communicate with any government or public service organisation of your choice via the Internet, will be the day before artificial intelligence finally takes over and murders everyone.

I cross my fingers and attempt to book an emergency appointment with my doctor for tomorrow morning. When the entire web page freezes and boots me out of the submission form, I sigh deeply and reload it to have another go.

This time it tells me that the next available emergency appointment I can book will be on Thursday, 19 September 2097.

I fear that this may be a *tad* too late to help me, so I reload the page again, and have one more attempt.

Hallelujah!

This time around I successfully manage to book the appointment, not for the distant future after the machines have taken over the planet, but for Thursday morning at 8.30 – a mere two days away. This still doesn't really constitute an *emergency* appointment, but I'm not going to look a gift horse in the mouth here. There's every chance that if I reload the submission form and try again, I might not get another appointment until four days after the earth has been consumed by the sun going supernova.

Thursday will just have to do.

And I will just have to cope until then.

This shouldn't be too hard. As long as I can stop myself from obsessively looking up my symptoms on the Internet, I should be fine.

◆ ◆ ◆

By the time Thursday morning rolls around, I am a complete wreck.

In the past two nights I think I've had about three hours of decent sleep. The rest of my time in bed has been spent tossing and turning. Snoregasbord tells me that I've been less restful in my bed than a vampire with a clove of garlic shoved up his arse.

I've also come to the clear and precise conclusion that I have a disease called Sibley-Torrington dismorphenia.

Yep. That's what I've got.

That's the only conclusion I can possibly draw, having narrowed it down from every available option during the solid ten hours of research I've done in the past two days.

Sibley-Torrington dismorphenia is not a type of cancer, you'll be delighted to know. Nor is it fatal, which is even better.

No, Sibley-Torrington dismorphenia is a disease that only three people have ever experienced. All of them are still alive, and suffering in constant agony somewhere clean and clinical, and out of sight of the public.

And it's definitely what I've got too. I am the fourth person.

All of my symptoms fit the early stages of what I'm going to refer to now as STD, which is a lot easier to say, even if it does sound like I've come down with a dose of the clap.

In stage two of STD, you develop vast and uncomfortable rashes across 90 per cent of your body. I can already feel a slight itch under one armpit, so it's started already for me.

Stage three involves abscesses forming across your body that erupt with a noxious-smelling pus after two or three weeks, so there's that to look forward to.

And then in stage four of STD, your nerve endings start to fire constantly and randomly, causing wracking pain to shoot through your body on a daily basis, which can only be kept at bay by the hardest of hard painkilling drugs.

The three people who suffer from STD have all tried to commit suicide at one point or another. It truly is a delightful disease to have, and I'm very much looking forward to the doctor attempting to break the bad news to me in a way that doesn't make it seem like my life is going to be a constant and unremitting hell – until I eventually feel the sweet embrace of death.

Mind you, if there's anyone in this world who can break that kind of bad news in a way that doesn't make you want to jump out of the nearest plate-glass window, it's Dr Hu.

Yes. That's his real name. Let's try to all move past it as quickly as possible, shall we?

Dr Hu has been my GP for the past three years, since he moved to my local practice – and the country – from his native Hong Kong.

He's a lovely man. Softly spoken and unshakeably calm, he sounds like the wisest of wise old Chinese gurus – even though he's forty-three and hasn't even started to go grey yet.

Unfortunate coincidental name aside (which I'm not going to highlight again, so stop thinking there's any gags about phone boxes or screwdrivers homing into view over the horizon), Dr Hu is everything you'd want in a physician.

If I'm going to be told that I have STD, then this is the man I want to hear it from.

And just look how calm he is! Even after giving me a thorough examination and taking copious notes about all of my symptoms.

The poor man must be dying inside at the prospect of having to break the bad news to me, but he's managing to keep it all internalised, bless him, so as not to disturb me too much.

What a lovely man.

Dr Hu sits tapping his pen on the desk for a few minutes, looking over those notes with a thoughtful look on his face.

Eventually, he speaks.

'Well, Andrew. Those are quite the collection of nasty things you've managed to pick up, aren't they?'

'Yes, Doctor.'

'And you were right to come and visit me today. The sudden need for the toilet and the issues with your jaw could be a cause for concern.'

'Yes, Doctor.'

'But I'd say that they are all part of the same overall problem.'

'Yes, Doctor.'

Here it comes.

'I think I can confidently tell you what you've got.'

'OK, Doctor.'

'In my professional opinion . . .'

Oh God, he's leaning forward and smiling. It must be terrible, terrible news.

I'll have to draw up a will before I start spurting pus everywhere.

How do you draw up a will, anyway? Is there an app for it?

My heart sinks into my stomach as Dr Hu looks at me closely, trying his hardest to not come across as the angel of death he surely is.

'Andy?'

'Yes, Dr Hu?'

'There's nothing physically wrong with you.'

. . .

. . . . . .

What did he just say?

'What did you just say?'

'I said, there's not really anything physically wrong with you. Not beyond the IBS anyway, which we know you've had for years.'

I go slack-jawed.

That's *impossible*!

That's *ridiculous*!

'But, the pooing . . .' I reply in a small voice.

'Yes, I know,' Dr Hu says, nodding his head sagely.

'And the locked jaw . . .' I add, one hand going to the side of my face. The jaw unlocked itself after the disaster at Fluidity, but it's been painful ever since.

'I know, Andy, I know,' Dr Hu replies, still smiling slightly and keeping that warm, comforting expression on his face.

Damn him and his warm, comforting face!

Damn him and his sage words!

I've always thought Dr Hu was a brilliant physician, but he's clearly just a crackpot with no idea of what he's doing!

How can there be nothing medically wrong with me? There was all of the poo! And all of the pain! And all of the gottle of geering!

I have Sibley-Torrington dismorphenia, *damn it*! I can feel the abscesses starting to rise on my chest even as we speak!

Dr Hu holds out a hand, as if to ward off the temper tantrum I'm about to fall into. 'Now, I'm not saying there's nothing wrong with you, Andy, please don't misunderstand me.'

My eyes narrow in confusion. 'You're not?'

'No. It's plain that you have multiple symptoms.'

'Then what are you trying to say?'

'That the issue is not with your body, but with your *head* . . . and more specifically, how your head is being affected by your *lifestyle*.'

'What exactly do you mean?' I ask, my tone extremely suspicious.

Dr Hu leans back in his chair. 'You're certainly not the first person to come into my office with these symptoms – although none of the others had quite as many as you, it has to be said.'

That's the STD ruled out then. Maybe that itch under my arm is just where I've changed deodorant.

'In my professional opinion, Andy,' Dr Hu continues, 'you're suffering from a very twenty-first-century condition.'

'And what's that?'

'Too much technology, Andy! Too much time spent on that phone of yours.'

He points down to where my iPhone is clutched in one sweaty hand.

How did that get there? I don't remember picking it up – or opening the App Store. But there it is, on the screen, waiting for me to search for that will-writing app.

'All of your symptoms can be traced to the fact you spend so much time on the Internet,' Dr Hu tells me, not without some sympathy in his voice. 'I don't think I've ever seen you without that phone in your hand. And you talked about googling your symptoms before coming to see me, which tells me you look to the web for answers probably a bit too much.'

'I do?'

'Yes. I'd say so. How long do you think you spend online a day?'

'What? In total?'

'Yes, Andy. How long?' He smiles calmly. 'And do try to be honest. How many hours of the day?'

I sit there for a moment, trying hard to think about how much time I do actually spend with my technology. I feel an uncomfortable flush of embarrassment start to colour my cheeks, as I realise that it's probably a better idea to ask how many hours I *don't* spend online.

'Quite a lot,' I manage to squeak out.

Dr Hu nods. 'Thought so. And that's the problem. All of that time spent playing with technology is not good for you, mentally or physically. Your neck and shoulders hurt because you're looking down at your phone or tablet too much. Your inability to sleep comes from too much time with that bright, white light going into your eyes. And flitting from one app to another just creates more and more stress in your brain, which translates into the rest of your body.'

Good grief.

He *can't* be right, can he?

That can't be the root cause of why I'm feeling so terrible.

I must have some kind of disease. There's just no way I could have been brought this low, just because I like my tech? Just because I spend a lot of time on the *Internet*?

That's *improved* my life . . . not made it *worse*.

Without it, everything would be so much more of a hassle. Getting work would be harder. Shopping would be harder. Finding a date would be harder.

Everything would be harder!

Being tech-savvy and an experienced web user has made my life *better*. In every respect.

And yet . . .

My neck and shoulders do hurt more when I've been on the iPad for a long time.

And I do find it harder to get to sleep if I've been on my phone before I turn out the light.

But none of that explains the emergency pooing! Or the bloody lockjaw!

I say as much to Dr Hu.

'Well, that's not necessarily true, Andy,' he replies, shaking his head. 'That stress I talked about? It can cause some huge physiological changes in the human body, especially when it's allowed to build up. Doing your presentation was a stressful thing anyway, so add that on top of the naturally high levels of stress you experience because of your tech-heavy lifestyle, and it's no wonder your body had such a violent reaction. The same goes for the lockjaw. I bet if you thought about it, you'd realise just how much you clench your jaw when you're online –playing video games, or using things like Twitter . . . which is a very stressful, negative place, in my experience.'

Bloody hell.

Bloody, *bloody* hell. He might be right.

I do end up clenching my jaw a lot when I'm playing games like *Call of Duty*. Usually when some little bastard has just killed me from the same hiding place eight times in a row. And I do end up getting into arguments on Twitter quite a lot. About politics. Sometimes sports. Occasionally TV shows. Every now and again the weather.

Oh hell, I'm *always* arguing on Twitter.

The default emotional state for engagement on Twitter is 'livid about something – anything – doesn't really matter what'.

Then there's Facebook. That's not exactly a place of calm and happy reflection, either. If anything it allows you to argue even more with people, as there isn't a 280-character limit.

But Facebook is where I conduct so much of my social life! It's where I arrange to meet up with people. Where I speak to the people I'm close to emotionally but far away from physically. How else am I supposed to find out what's been happening with Mum's hip? She and Dad moved to the Highlands four years ago, and it's not the work of a moment to get up there.

Facebook has been a *godsend* for communicating with them. As has FaceTime. It's much nicer than just making a phone call. You can't beat a bit of face-to-face interaction, after all.

But then, I think about how upset it makes me that I can't be there with Mum when she's suffering with the pain her hip gives her. That tends to stress me out quite a lot.

'Aah . . . you've got that look about you, Andy,' Dr Hu says.

I shake my head to bring myself back to the present. 'What look?'

'The look of someone realising something rather profound. I tend to see it quite a lot when people present with your symptoms.'

'So you really get loads of people in to see you with the same complaints?'

'Oh my, yes. That's why I was able to diagnose you so quickly. I've been a GP for thirteen years, and in the past five or so I've seen this type of thing get worse and worse. It's reaching almost epidemic proportions.'

'Crikey.'

Dr Hu nods. 'Crikey, indeed.'

'So, what exactly do I do about it?'

I have a feeling I probably know the answer he's about to give, and I'm pretty sure it's not going to involve a new and exciting phone app.

'You need a digital detox, Andy. A period of time away from all of those screens . . . and without being online.'

Jesus.

Can you see how sweaty my palms have instantly gone?

You wouldn't want to vigorously shake hands with me at the moment. There's every chance your hand would slide cleanly out of mine, and you'd whack yourself in the crotch.

'A digital detox?'

'Exactly. By doing one, you should notice an improvement in your symptoms. If you don't, then we'll obviously have to get you back in here to run some tests, but I'm confident that you'll see things get better.'

'No more lockjaw?'

'Highly likely.'

'No needing an emergency shit in public?'

'Quite probably.'

'No more contrary bowels?'

'There's every chance.'

Well, all of that does sound quite appealing, I have to say.

What doesn't sound appealing at all is what I'll have to do to get rid of all those problems.

How on earth can I possibly cope without my technology?

'I'm not sure I can do it,' I tell Dr Hu, with a bare-faced honesty I'm quite proud of.

I wouldn't say I'm cursed with a massive ego, but it's never nice to admit when you don't think you're capable of something. The fact that I can shows just how scared I am, and in need of counsel.

'I think you can, Andy. It'll be a lot easier than you think. Here, take this.'

Dr Hu opens a drawer in his desk and produces a pamphlet, which he holds out for me to take.

My face contorts. I have a natural aversion to pamphlets, ever since I contracted the worst flu bug I've ever had from a pamphlet handed to me by an unsavoury character outside Tesco.

The pamphlet was for 20 per cent off tacos and fajitas at the Mexican restaurant around the corner, and I'd always wanted to try more Mexican food, so I took the damn thing, thinking it might come in useful.

Now, every time I so much as contemplate the idea of a burrito, I think back on that unsavoury character and the three weeks I spent dying in bed, and elect to eat a cheese sandwich instead.

Of course, Dr Hu is not unsavoury in the slightest, but that doesn't mean I don't still have an aversion to taking the pamphlet. It'll take up valuable room in my pocket.

'Er, can you email it to me?' I ask him, staring down at the pamphlet with barely disguised loathing.

Who has stuff on *paper* in this day and age, anyway?

Dr Hu gives me a look that would surely scare off any Daleks who happen to be in the vicinity.

(OK, sorry. I know I promised, but it's just too easy a gag to make.)

'*Take it*, Andy. Read it thoroughly. It will do you no end of good, I'm sure of it,' he tells me.

I swallow hard. 'OK,' I reply, reluctantly taking the pamphlet from his hand and depositing it straight into my jeans pocket – where it instantly takes up valuable space.

'Why don't we agree to see each other again in about a month?' Dr Hu says. 'That should give you enough time to see if the detox is helping.'

'Yeah, OK. That sounds good.'

'Excellent.'

Dr Hu rises from his seat and holds out a hand, indicating that he's happy to conclude the appointment. I also rise. I'm not quite so happy, as my GP has just dropped a bombshell into the middle of my life, but I affect a pleasant smile anyway, and take his hand.

He wishes me well and shows me to the door.

After arranging a follow-up appointment with the receptionist, I make my way out of the building and into the bright light of day. Once there, I start the twenty-minute walk back to my flat in a very thoughtful state of mind.

I don't doubt that Dr Hu has a point, but can I really do what he's asked? Can I really do this digital-detox thing?

I yank the pamphlet out of my pocket and actually have a go at reading it as I amble along the pavement. As I do, my face falls and my walking pace slows to a near halt.

Oh, good grief. This is so much more awful that I even thought it could be.

I know I could stand to spend less time looking at Twitter and playing *Fortnite*, but this horrible little leaflet is basically suggesting that I give up *my entire life*.

'Digital Detoxing and You' might as well be called 'Say Goodbye to Everything That Makes Life Have Any Meaning Whatsoever, You Sad Little Twat'.

OK, that wouldn't have fitted on the narrow front cover, but it would have been a damn sight more accurate.

If I truly do have to follow all of the advice given here, I think I'm going to go crazy.

The digital detox didn't sound like an easy proposition when Dr Hu suggested it, but now I can see the cold hard facts laid out for me – on bloody *paper* – it's a million times *worse*.

'Are you all right, young man?'

I gaze down to see a small, elderly woman looking up at me with some concern.

'Yes, fine thanks.'

'Ah. Only you're staring into the clouds and weeping slightly. I thought there might be something wrong?'

'Oh, there is,' I tell her, unconsciously crumpling the hideous pamphlet as I do so.

The woman produces a smartphone from one pocket of her voluminous beige coat. 'Do you need me to call anyone for you?'

I suppress a groan. Even pensioners have smartphones these days.

I am seriously contemplating being less technologically capable than a little old lady.

As if on cue, a stabbing, sharp pain shoots through my temple again – reminding me what this is all about.

Jesus Christ.

It's either stabbing pain, or a return to the Dark Ages.

I'm not so sure which is worse, to be honest with you . . .

DIGITAL DETOXING AND YOU!

A Guide to Living with the Best Version of Yourself!

Thank you for taking the time to read this informative guide about how to make your life a calmer, better place – without the need for the digital world!

In today's society, we are bombarded by a constant stream of information, and that isn't good for our BRAINS!

If you spend too much time on the Internet – using social media, playing games or just mindlessly surfing websites, you could be doing real damage to your MIND and BODY!

You've been given this information guide to show you what you should do if you want to make a digital detox part of your life – and trust us, it will be worth it! The results are AMAZING!

There are some simple rules to follow:

No unnecessary use of the Internet

The Internet is a part of our lives that isn't going away, but you should only use it when you have to – for work or emergencies. Answer those work emails, but stay away at all other times!

No use of social media

At all! We have become far too reliant on social media sites like Twitter, Facebook and Instagram. Instead of using them, communicate with people by picking up a phone or arranging to meet with them. It will be completely WORTH IT!

No online gaming

In fact, try not to play video games at all. Instead, go outside and play with a ball, or go for a lovely, long walk. Try activities that get you up and about, instead of glued to a screen with a controller in your hand!

Avoid temptation

The easiest way to avoid the temptation of going back to the digital world is to make sure you don't have anything around you that can access it. Swap your smartphone for a landline. Store your tablet away, and pick up a book instead. Keep your PC at home somewhere out of sight.

Remember to enjoy your new-found freedom!

This is the most important thing! You're starting a new, calmer, happier life by doing this digital detox. It's a chance for you to reconnect with the people you love, and the world around you. Use the time you would have spent online on new, beneficial hobbies. Try meditation or yoga, or take up a sport, or try a bit of writing. The world is your oyster! ENJOY IT!

How Long Should You Detox?

We recommend a period of at least two months. Yes, just sixty days can show you how much better off you can be! So, give it a go! It will change your life, we absolutely PROMISE!

Chapter Three

The Detoxification of Andy Bellows

It's quite clear to me that 'Digital Detoxing and You!' was written by a raving psychopath.

No one with a grip on their sanity would structure sentences like that, or use quite so many exclamation marks.

If you met someone who talked the way that damn thing is written, you'd be backing away slowly, and speed-dialling 999.

If doing a digital detox turns you into the kind of person who thinks writing that many random words in capital letters is perfectly OK, then I don't want to be any part of it.

But.

And it's a big BUT – most certainly written in capital letters, and probably in a bold font.

I *have* to do something. I *have* to make some changes.

I woke up at 3 a.m. last night, and stayed awake for two hours. Snoregasbord said I only got about an hour's deep sleep.

This morning, I am as constipated as everybody's favourite plasticine-eating dog, and there's a very tight feeling in my jaw that I don't like one little bit.

I've taken three Anadin Extra to try to stave off those sharp, stabbing temple pains, and I'm hoping they'll also take care of the ache in my neck that came on almost the instant I picked up my iPad.

I've spent the morning googling digital detoxes to see if anyone can give me any advice that can help me.

The Internet is full of conflicting reports on their effectiveness. Some people swear by them, some people think they are the work of the devil.

This is no surprise.

I've already proved that one of the laws of the Internet is if you punch a load of symptoms into a search engine, it gets you diagnosed with terminal cancer every single time. Another law is that if you seek an opinion on a subject matter – any subject you like – you will get as much fulsome support for it as you do harsh criticism.

The law holds true even if we're talking about the greatest evils ever visited upon mankind. You can find people who will actively defend Hitler, the Ebola virus and Hanson – believe it or not.

Needless to say, digital detoxing is regarded as being the best thing ever, or the biggest waste of time on the planet, depending on who you ask.

In disgust, I throw the iPad down and cross my arms over my chest in a grump of the highest order. None of that helped one bit. I'm back to having to make a decision on my own.

. . .

I'm going to have to bloody do it, aren't I?

I'm going to have to give this stupid digital-detox thing a go.

As I sit here, I can hear my bowels rumbling in a manner that means I'm going to have to remain close to a toilet for the entire day, and the Anadin Extra really aren't strong enough to counter-attack that stupid stabbing pain I'm getting in my head, thanks to all the jaw-clenching.

Sixty days.

It can't be that bad, can it?

I'm not being asked to give everything up forever. Just for a couple of months.

Two months really isn't all that long a period of time. I should be able to cope, surely?

. . .

Bollocks.

Let's give it a go.

It takes me about twenty minutes to find my old landline phone, which is in a box at the top of the cupboard in the spare bedroom. I haven't used the thing in yonks, but it still works – the dial tone still sounds loud and strong as I put my ear to the receiver, having plugged the phone back into the phone socket on the kitchen wall for the first time in about six years.

The dial tone sounds strange and alien to me, but there's also something ever so slightly comforting about it, for some reason. I think it probably has something to do with the nostalgia of it all. The memories of years gone by, when things seemed so much simpler.

I remember the time before the Internet, and this dial tone feels strangely symbolic of it.

Of course, I'm going to have to update my work website and all of my contacts with the landline number, because I haven't given it out publicly for a very long time – but the evil pamphlet says I'm still allowed to use emails purely for work purposes, so it shouldn't be all that difficult.

Having reconnected the ancient device, I then find a big cardboard box, into which I place my iPhone, iPad, PlayStation, Alexa and Kindle.

I can't fit my TV in there, as it's got a 55-inch screen, but I can unplug the Ethernet cable, wipe all of the apps and turn off the Wi-Fi, so it can't go online any more.

The iMac has to stay out for obvious reasons – I can scarcely run a graphic design business without my computer – but that is safely tucked away in one corner of the spare bedroom, and I can shut the door on it when I need to.

I sellotape the cardboard box up, pop it on top of the cupboard where I found the old phone, and take a few deep breaths.

Well, there we go, then.

Like a cigarette smoker who has just thrown his last packet away, I have divested myself of my addictions as much as I possibly can. Now all that remains is to go online for one final time and let everyone know that I'm doing a two-month-long digital detox.

It doesn't take me that much time to compose a suitable post, which I can copy and paste across all of my social media accounts and public forums. The only one that gives me any difficulty is Instagram, because I have to accompany the message with a suitable picture. What kind of picture can you use to denote the fact that you're taking a break from all of this wonderful online jiggery-pokery in order to improve your health?

I elect for an image of a small puppy being told off for peeing on the carpet. I can't tell you why, but it feels appropriate.

The response I get from my small accumulation of online followers is largely to be expected. Most are quite supportive, some are confused, a few are highly amused, and a minority are actually angry at me for having the temerity to blame the online world for any of my problems.

I'm willing to bet they are the kinds of people who could probably do with a detox themselves.

Good old Jerry Pimbleton sounds quite disappointed that he won't be able to cross verbal swords with me about the local building works for the foreseeable future. Apparently, the company that are throwing up the new houses on the site of the old dairy farm have put up a sign saying that construction begins soon – and Jerry is clearly not happy about it.

Well, he'll just have to vent to someone else, as I'm not going to be around.

I have to confess, I do feel a small sense of relief about this. The ongoing argument with Jerry is meaningless to me in the grand scheme of things, and it was something I'd probably begun to invest too much of myself in. I don't really care that much about whether they build on the land or not, if I'm honest.

Wow.

OK. That's interesting. Maybe this enforced period offline will come with some advantages, after all . . .

I spend a fairly constructive final hour on the Internet, replying to the goodwill messages I receive about my attempt to do the detox. It's only polite, and they really are a good bunch, when you get right down to it. I may not know many of their real names, and have no idea what a lot of them look like, but they've been a good circle of friends to me over the past few years. I shall miss them while I'm away.

With my replies completed and my goodbyes said, I shut down the iMac and spend a few seconds staring at the blank screen.

'Right then. That's that,' I say into the void.

The black, horrible void . . .

No. Come on, Andrew. Don't be like that. This is a good *thing. This is a* positive *thing. This is a thing that you shall do, and be proud of when you have finished.*

'Yes. I shall be proud,' I say, still looking at the black screen.

Get up out of this chair and go and do something constructive.

I get up out of the chair and go to find something constructive to do.

Like tidy my kitchen cupboards.

Yes! That is the kind of very constructive thing I can do, now that I have the free time to do so.

That takes fifteen minutes.

So then I decide to have a nice vacuum.

That takes a further twenty minutes.

What else?

I spend the rest of the afternoon giving my flat the kind of deep clean that it will probably never recover from.

By the time the shower grout has been divested of all its mould growth, I have reached teatime, and am feeling quite good about myself.

I haven't once thought about going online. It's a little hard to when you're up to your elbows in bleach.

With the flat cleaner than the cleanest of the newest of new pins, I feel a rumble in my stomach as I behold the new world order that I have wrought upon my living space.

It looks splendid.

And it's clearly time to eat something.

The problem is, I don't want to ruin the kitchen. It's not been this clean since the day the building work was finished, and I'd like it to stay that way for a little while longer.

I'll just pop on Deliveroo and order myself a Chines—

My hand is halfway to my pocket before I remember.

Shit.

There will be no ordering of Chinese food for me. Unless I decide to – *aaarrggghh* – pick up the phone and give them a call.

No. I can't do that. I'll just have to order a pizza instead.

But I don't know the number for the pizza place.

Come to think of it, I don't know the number for the Chinese restaurant either.

I'll have to go out and actually *look* for food.

Like some kind of *Neanderthal*.

Bugger.

Still, at least that will kill some more time, won't it? Searching for appropriate fast food without any online help should take a good half an hour or so.

'Yes. That is what I will do,' I say, into the void once more.

I have never spoken to myself this much in my entire life. Not out loud, anyway. I hope this isn't indicative of things to come.

I grab my car keys and walk out of my pristine flat, on the hunt for some tasty treats.

It's three hours later.

I am *starving*.

It's not that I've been unable to find any takeaways (although they all appear to be a lot further from my front door than I'd thought), it's just that I have no idea which one I should order from.

How the hell are you supposed to know whether you're getting good food or not, if you don't have an app to tell you what the reviews for it are?

I have been in an agony of indecision as I drive between the local Chinese, Thai, Indian, pizza and kebab restaurants, just trying to make my stupid mind up.

God knows how much petrol I've used.

The various staff at the takeaways have become very used to seeing my stricken face as I stare at their menus, unable to do so much as decide on what cuisine I want, let alone what specific meal I want to order.

In the end – and to avoid an incipient nervous breakdown – I buy a chicken and bacon sandwich from the garage, after I've filled up the tank. It looks limp and very boring, but it was either that or go back to A Taste of Siam and spend another twenty minutes staring at the girl behind the counter with a confused look on both our faces.

At home, I devour the sandwich.

I then make myself a larger and more filling bacon and egg sandwich in the kitchen – ruining my excellent cleaning job completely.

When bedtime more or less rolls around, I am stuffed with bread and feeling dreadfully anxious.

It's at this time of night I usually sit down with my iPad and surf, and the absence of it is making my palms a bit sweaty. I try to watch some TV, but there's nothing on I fancy watching, and the news is just too miserable, so I turn the box off and stare once more into the void.

That gets me absolutely nowhere, so I figure I might as well go to bed.

According to Dr Hu, I should sleep much better, having not spent most of the evening with the iPad surgically attached to my hand.

◆ ◆ ◆

He's wrong, of course.

It takes me bloody *ages* to get to sleep.

Mainly because I have a small but permanent niggle at the back of my head that I've gone to bed without having done something vitally important . . .

If you can call checking all of your social media accounts 'vitally important', that is.

But that's been my routine for the past several years, and not doing it makes me feel decidedly apprehensive and out of sorts.

So much so that it's gone two in the morning before I do finally get off to sleep.

It's only a quarter past six when I wake up, with that feeling of apprehension now having ballooned into something approaching a real sense of dread.

The dreams didn't help.

The first involved me standing naked in the middle of the Apple Store. The really big one on Regent Street. I'm holding my penis for dear life in the dream, as several Apple Geniuses – all holding scissors – try to tell me I'd be better off without it.

'But I want my penis!' I shout at them. 'I *need* my penis!'

These pleas fall on deaf ears, though, and they start to pursue me around the shop. They're just about to pin me down by the overpriced phone cases when I am woken by the urge to urinate. I do so with my heart beating out of my chest, and a grip on my penis that is just this side of too tight.

The second dream, if anything, is even *worse*.

In this one, I am standing on the pavement of a busy street. The people rush past me like a fast-flowing river, with me like a rock cast into its chaotic stream.

Behind me, I can feel . . . *something*.

A presence so vast and overwhelming, it terrifies me to my very core.

I try to move. I try to get away from the thing. But I am frozen to the spot.

So I call out to the people passing me by, screaming at them as loud as I can that I need help – that I need saving. But none of them can hear me. They just continue to flow past, completely ignoring my pitiful cries.

Just as I feel something touch me on the shoulder, I awake in a cold sweat.

'Oh, for the love of God!' I cry out loud into the void, as I sit bolt upright in bed, breathing hard.

I've never had dreams as bad as that before. Not having a clue what they mean, I reach over to grab my iPhone so I can look them up online—

'Oh, fuck it!' I cry in frustration.

With this hideous start to the day over and done with, I climb out of bed and try to get moving.

This is extremely hard, as I'm sleep-deprived and a bundle of tight nerves due to my inability to satiate my desire to have a look on Twitter.

I just have to drink a cup of coffee, settle down into some work, and get through what is already turning out to be a highly miserable day.

Did I say miserable?

I meant *soul-destroying*.

It's throughout the next few hours that I really come to appreciate the depths of my reliance on the digital world.

I feel antsy all day.

I've never felt *antsy* before in my entire life. It's an extremely unpleasant feeling.

I also feel *twitchy*.

There's a good chance 'antsy' and 'twitchy' mean exactly the same thing, but I'm not allowed to go on Google to check, so you'll just have to put up with the mistake – if I've actually made one.

I'm so twitchy that I'm finding it hard to concentrate on work.

I'm in the middle of putting together another presentation of my graphical prowess – this time for a pie shop, rather than a hot and trendy clothing brand. OK, pies aren't exciting in the slightest, and the job won't pay a great deal even if I do get it, but at least it's an easy project. There's only really so much you can do with a pie, graphically speaking. Because it's a *pie*.

I say it's easy . . . but I'm still having a huge problem with it today, such is my discombobulated state of mind.

This must be what smokers feel like when they quit. Or heavy drinkers.

Bloody hell.

Can I really be *that* bad?

Can I really have developed such an addiction to the online space that being off it for even just a few hours makes me crazy?

The answer to that is clearly yes, when I discover that the pie I've been drawing for the past hour on my graphics tablet looks more like a dog turd. A big, brown dog turd with steam rising off it.

'Aaargh!' I exclaim in frustrated disgust, throwing my stylus down and rubbing my face with both hands.

I need to get out of the house and go for a walk. That'll calm me down a bit.

And, for an hour or so, it actually does.

I am able to take a few deep breaths as I walk along the pretty canal path that's only a five-minute drive from my flat.

I'm not even that bothered when I spot a large, abandoned dog turd that looks just like my latest attempt to draw a pie.

However, I become *extremely* bothered when I spot a black cloud overhead. I'm bothered because I hate getting wet when I'm out and about, and usually take every measure available to me to avoid it happening.

This, of course, usually includes looking at the four separate weather apps I have on my phone, to check whether I need to get undercover or not in the near future.

But now I have no way of knowing if that black cloud is going to bugger off, or dump its contents on me in no uncertain terms.

Given the day I'm having, it's no surprise that it chooses the latter of the two options, and my pleasant, relaxing walk is destroyed when I have to sprint a good half-mile back to the car in the pouring bloody rain.

I cut what you could only describe as a highly miserable figure, as I sit clutching my steering wheel and gently dripping all over the interior of my Volvo.

Does rainwater stain car upholstery?

Who knows!

Certainly not *me*!

Not without the bloody Internet to check!

The drive back to the flat is conducted with sulphurous swearing going on under my breath. The dread from this morning and the frustrations from work have now bonded in an unholy union of barely contained apoplectic rage.

I screech the car to a halt in my parking space. I slam the car door so loudly it makes a nearby cat run for cover. I stamp up the stairs to my flat, drizzling the tiles with rainwater as I go.

Back inside, I decide to make myself an angry cup of coffee. This is much like a normal cup of coffee, only it contains twice the amount of coffee, three times the amount of sugar and a quarter of the amount of milk.

Imagine – just try to imagine – the absolute *fury* that consumes my being when I realise I'm out of instant coffee.

'Fuck!' I scream.

And I can't use Amazon *bastard* Prime *bastard* Now to order any more, like I usually do. Yesterday, I could have had a fresh jar of the good stuff delivered to my door within the hour, along with whatever other goodies I felt like impulse-buying at the same time.

But oh no.

Now I have to go back out of the bastard flat, get back in my bastard car and drive to the bastard shops to buy bastard coffee.

It appears being denied my right to the World Wide Web has turned me into a right potty mouth.

Bollocks.

There's nothing else fucking for it – I'm going to have to go back out in the rain, just to pick up some Nescafé.

I storm over to the front door and fling it open with an audible grunt.

This absolutely terrifies my best friend, Fergus, who was just about to knock on the door.

'Fuck me!' he screams, and stumbles backwards.

'Fergus?!' I exclaim, in shock and anger.

The last thing I need right now is to have to talk to anyone. Anyone except the cashier at Tesco when I pick up my coffee, that is.

'You scared me half to bloody death!' he cries, hand clutched to his chest.

'Sorry,' I reply, through gritted teeth.

Oh great, that's bound to set off the lockjaw again, isn't it?

'What the hell's the matter? You look like you're about to chew your way through the brickwork.'

Fergus, as you will soon discover, has something of a way with words. It's what makes him a good journalist, and a fascinating conversation companion.

Usually I love to spend a good few hours talking to him about whatever the salient topic of the day is. Fergus is just about the only person I actually converse with offline, I think.

Not today, though. I don't want to talk to him today.

Today I am a one-man wrecking crew, and not to be trifled with.

'Sorry,' I repeat. 'I'm not in the best of moods.'

'Best of moods?' he replies, incredulous. 'I've seen happier-looking cows going to slaughter. What the hell's going on? What's got your goat?'

I shake my head. 'It'd take too long to explain.'

'Does it have anything to do with why you missed the party last night?'

My heart drops like a stone as I realise what I've done. 'Oh God! I'm so sorry, mate! I . . . I . . . I . . . I . . .'

'Have become an unconvincing pirate impressionist?'

'No! I . . . I'm just . . . not doing all that great at the moment, Ferg . . . and I just . . . forgot, mate. I'm really sorry!'

'Yes, I thought you probably would be. Not like you to miss a social event. It was on Facebook.'

I feel my jaw tightening again. 'Yes. That's part of the fucking problem.'

'Maybe I should have ordered you a chauffeur-driven limousine as well, but I figured you could have arranged your own transport, being a fully grown adult and all that.'

'I really am super sorry, Ferg.'

'Yes, you've said that.' Fergus gives me a concerned, curious look. 'I only popped round to check you hadn't died and been eaten by cats . . . but now I see what state you're obviously in, I think I should take you for a nice cup of coffee somewhere, so you can explain to me just why you missed your best friend's glorious promotional celebrations.'

I consider this for a moment.

On the one hand, I'm still pretty damn enraged, and unwanting of human companionship.

On the other, I do want coffee. And I do feel bad about missing Fergus's party.

I nod my head. 'Right. OK then. Coffee it is.'

'Good.' Fergus cocks his head. 'Why are you so wet? Did you get caught out in the rain?'

'Yes.'

Fergus chuckles. 'That's not like you. You're usually right on the ball with the weather. Did your phone run out of battery?'

It takes me a superhuman amount of effort not to collapse on the floor in a screaming, childish tantrum at this point. I'd better get out of the flat and get some coffee down my neck as quickly as possible.

Fergus Brailsworth is a man possessed of both a fabulous name and a very creative turn of phrase. We've been friends for the past four years, ever since we met while I was freelancing at the local paper he works for.

The *Daily Local News* is possibly the most boringly named newspaper in human history – and is something of a relic of a bygone age.

It only continues to exist because we have a healthy contingent of the older generation in our neck of the woods, who still enjoy having the paper delivered to them every day. Also, Fergus's uncle Barrington Brailsworth (yes, I know – it's incredible, isn't it?) owns the paper, and has more money than he comfortably knows what to do with.

What he does with it is ploughs it consistently into the *Daily Local News* – keeping the paper afloat in an environment where more of them die off every day, and his nephew Fergus in a job.

Not that there's much nepotism going on there. Fergus is immensely talented. Something both he and his uncle are well aware of. Barrington pays Fergus extremely well, to make sure Fergus doesn't leave for greener pastures. In return, Fergus keeps the local news stories rolling in, managing to put an interesting twist on even the dullest of subject matters. He once wrote a two-thousand-word article about a man who had grown a marrow that vaguely resembled Bruce Forsyth. It won awards.

His rampant success has led to Barrington giving Fergus a well-deserved promotion at the paper – hence the party I missed out on, because my life (unlike Fergus's) has become an uncoordinated mess.

I should also point out that Fergus is enormously ginger. He was born with a perfectly acceptable blond head of hair, but you can't be named Fergus without becoming ginger at some stage. It's the fifth law of thermodynamics, and the universe wouldn't function properly without it.

'Flat white?' he asks as I plonk myself down angrily in a chair.

'Yes please,' I tell him, chewing on one fingernail as I do so.

Look!

Look at all the people in here who are using their mobile phones!

The broadband in Costa is always pretty good, and the place is a mecca for those seeking fast, free Wi-Fi and a hot caffeine injection.

Look at them all!

Surfing the Internet. Looking at Twitter. Playing *Candy Crush*.

The lucky, lucky *bastards*!

I have only been offline for twenty hours, and I'm already insanely jealous of everybody else in the world.

'Why are you staring at that bloke with the iPad like you want to do horrible things upon his person?' Fergus asks, brows knitted.

I look up at him sharply.

'He's on the Internet. I can just tell,' I spit.

Fergus looks over at the inoffensive member of the public, before looking back at me. There's a suspicion dawning in his eyes, and I feel like he's about to make an accurate intuitive leap.

'You're angry that he's on the Internet?'

'Yes.'

'And you're . . . not, I see.'

'No. I am not.'

Fergus's eyes narrow. 'There's something fundamental going on here, and I am most keen for you to elucidate further, but I fear I should not ask more until I have placed milky coffee into your hands.'

'Indeed.'

'Hold that thought, then. I shall return promptly.'

Fergus turns and hurries over to the counter. He knows I have a story to tell, and nothing gets Fergus's dander up more than someone with a story to tell.

Well, that and being able to justifiably use the word 'dander' in an article. He'd be intensely jealous if I showed him that last sentence.

While he's gone, I think about what exactly I'm going to say to him about it. Should I be completely honest? Should I tell Fergus everything? Including the emergency poo and the penis-holding dream?

He's my best friend – and my only friend out here in the real world, if I'm being honest – but do I want to give him all the gory details? Can I trust him to keep them to himself? After all, we're talking about someone whose most natural instincts are to spread any interesting stories they hear as far and as wide as possible.

He'd probably do it on the Internet, a horrible voice in my head tells me.

Yes, he probably bloody would. And all of the people in this Costa would see it if he did, wouldn't they? Because *look at them*, would you? Look how they gaze upon the might of the World Wide Web, accessing information from all corners of the globe. See the looks of happy concentration on their faces as they engage with mankind's greatest creation!

I've clearly lost all sense of perspective at this point. Not being allowed on the web for a whole day has left me with a warped sense of its benefit to society.

While I am quite happy to wax lyrical about the Internet's joys, I am deliberately forgetting about all of its shortcomings. The way it lets truly awful people have more of a voice than they ever should have. The way it turns societies against each other, and drops us all into our own silos, where we never communicate constructively with those we disagree with. Things of that nature.

And then there's Kim Kardashian . . .

She wouldn't have a career without the Internet and social media. Surely that's the web's greatest crime, isn't it?

Right now, though, none of those things are at the forefront of my thinking. Right now, I am like someone who has given up smoking, who only misses the buzz and the taste, and completely disregards the smell and the risk of cancer.

The guy with the iPad is smiling and tapping one finger on the screen. He's happy. I am not. This is the absolute, inescapable fact of the matter.

I feel my jaw start to clench, and don't even bother to try to stop it.

'One flat white,' Fergus announces, placing the cup in front of me. 'Please drink up, and stop looking at that poor chap like you want to remove his tongue with red-hot forceps.'

I glower at Fergus, but do as I'm bid.

The coffee does go some way to calming my inner turmoil. This should be something of an oxymoron, given that caffeine is a stimulant, but my mind is extremely topsy-turvy at the moment so it makes a strange kind of sense . . . if you don't think about it too much.

'Well then,' Fergus says, regarding me solemnly. 'Clearly something has got your goat. I'd go so far as to say it looks like your goat has been stolen, was sent to the nearest abattoir and is now hanging in a butcher's window somewhere. Spill, Mr Bellows. I need to know why you missed my lovely party, and why you have a face like the arse end of the same dead goat, before we go any further.' The slightly wry smile drops off his face. 'Look, in all seriousness, I was gutted you didn't turn up, mate. It's not like you. What the hell's going on?'

I sigh.

Might as well get this over and done with. Fergus won't be happy until I've told him the whole story. And I have decided not to skip anything. He'd only wheedle it out of me anyway. That's the way he is.

The article about the Bruce Forsyth marrow won as many awards as it did because it was really a very in-depth story about the man behind the marrow – a gentleman with a sad and tumultuous past, involving an unfaithful wife, a stolen inheritance and connections to the Italian mafia.

That's what Fergus does. He opens people up like he's a psychological can opener. Gets them to spill their guts all over the place. The reason he's such a good journalist is that he knows that the real story is always about the person – never the marrow.

I consume two flat whites during the course of my sorry tale. By the time I'm finished, I have dropped into a far calmer state of mind, thanks to the combination of the finest Colombian coffee beans and sweet, silky cow's milk.

'And that's why I wasn't at the party. I've been consumed by my health problems, and the bloody digital detox. I never saw any of the reminders you sent, because I haven't been online. Again . . . I'm sorry I wasn't there.'

Fergus sips the last of his own coffee as he regards me over the rim of the cup.

'Well? Aren't you going to say anything?' I ask, curious at his silence.

'I will. I'm just evaluating.'

I roll my eyes. 'Of course you are.'

'To be honest with you, I'd say a digital detox is just what you need.'

'You think so?'

'Indeed. It's clear from your general demeanour today that being offline is the source of much psychological distress.'

'You can say that again.'

'Which rather indicates that it's become something you're altogether too reliant on.' He pauses for a second in thought, before continuing. 'Mind you, I could have told you that much anyway. I've known you long enough to know how addicted you are to it.'

'Really?'

'Oh my, yes. Frankly, I'm still trying to get used to the idea of seeing you without a phone in your hand. You've made more eye contact with me today than you have during our entire friendship. There have been times in the past I've felt like I've been holding a conversation with Siri more than Andy Bellows.'

'Oh, fuck off,' I reply hoarsely. Realising you have an issue is one thing; finding out that other people have been aware of it long before you were is quite another.

'Not a chance,' Fergus replies with a smile. 'I want to see how this all turns out.'

I sit back with my arms folded. 'Well, you're not going to, because I'm not going through with it.'

'You're not?'

'Nope. Fuck it. As soon as we leave here, I'm going home and getting everything out of the box again.'

I arrived at this decision about halfway through telling Fergus about what's been happening to me over the past few days.

I don't care how much my jaw hurts, or how tight my neck feels; I cannot and will not go through the next sixty days in the kind of foul mood I am currently in. That horrid feeling of *discon-nection* is just too much.

I will try my level best not to go online as much, but there's no way I'm cutting it out of my life completely. I just can't do it. I don't want to spend the next two months angry, frustrated, antsy and twitchy.

'Antsy and twitchy mean the same thing,' Fergus tells me.

'Oh, bugger off.'

'So, that's it then? You're just going to give up?'

'Yes! Yes I am.'

'Why?'

I shake my head and look at him in disgust. 'What do you mean, *why*? I told you why! It's too hard!'

'Why's that?'

'Because . . . because . . .' I look around at the people on their phones. 'Because I can't do what they're doing!'

Fergus also looks at them. 'And what are they doing?'

'Having fun!'

He raises one eyebrow. 'They don't look like they're having that much fun to me. Those two girls in the corner could be talking to one another, but instead they're hunched over their phones. That old boy in the other corner is clearly having problems trying to get his stupid phone to work in the first place, and matey-boy on the iPad there might be smiling, but there's a haunted look in his eyes that speaks volumes.'

I grunt. 'Stop being melodramatic.'

Fergus chuckles. 'You nearly bashed your front door off its hinges because you can't go on Twitter, and *I'm* the one being melodramatic?'

'It's not just that!'

'Of course it's *just that*. You yourself said you can still use the Internet for work. It's still there for everything that's *necessary* in your life. So, what's your bloody problem? You don't *need* the Internet. You don't *need* social media. You got on fine without it before it existed, so why can't you cope without it now . . . especially just for sixty days?'

'I . . . I don't know!' I snap, clenching my fists.

'No, my friend. You don't. And you never will unless you go through with it, will you?'

'I guess . . . I guess not.'

What the *hell* is going on here?

I was adamant that I wasn't going to carry on with this stupid detox, but here I am agreeing with Fergus.

It's because the bastard is making a very good point.

Am I really so weak-willed that I can't go even a day without my phone in my hand? Without checking what the latest hashtags are? Am I that pathetic?

You see? He's like a bloody can opener.

And I'm about to spill my guts.

'I know I probably need to do this, Fergus. It just feels . . . feels so difficult. Almost impossible. Yes, I know I'm addicted, but I don't know if I have the strength to go without it all.'

'Right. So, you're not worried so much about not being on Facebook. You're just worried you'll fail.'

I blink a couple of times. 'Yes. That's it. I don't want to fail.'

'So it's easier to not try?'

I blink again.

How is this man not a psychologist?

'Yes. That's right.'

'You'll live with the pain and discomfort, just because you can cope with them better than the idea that you failed at something.'

'Oh, all right. Give it a bloody rest. I feel like I should be laid out on a couch.' I stare at him. 'How does a ginger twat like you know so much about this kind of thing?'

'Because this ginger twat used to drink two bottles of red wine a night.'

'Is that why you're so ginger?'

'Yes.'

I laugh and rub my face. 'Oh, God almighty. What am I going to do?'

'Sixty days without technology. That's what you're going to do.' Fergus also smiles. 'And this ginger twat is going to help you do it.'

'Really? How?'

'I'm going to write a story about you for the paper.'

'No you're bloody not.'

'Yes I bloody am.'

'*No*, Fergus. You really bloody are *not*. I do not have an amusingly shaped marrow anywhere about my person.'

Fergus steeples his fingers in front of him, sinking down into the Costa chair a little more. 'Tell me, Andy. Do you think you have the willpower to last sixty days? Be honest.'

I stare into my empty coffee cup, giving this some thought.

'No,' I say, being as truthful as I can. 'I don't think I do. I *want* to. But I don't think so.'

Fergus nods. 'But we can agree that the sixty-day detox is something you need to complete?'

'Yes. I guess that's true. No matter how much I hate the idea.'

'Good. So what you need is *incentive*.'

'Incentive?'

'Yes. You need something to keep you on the straight and narrow. Trust me. I know what I'm talking about. I'd never have stopped drinking were it not for my uncle threatening to fire me.'

'I never knew that.'

'No. It's not the type of thing I like to talk about. Were it not for him, there would be no Bruce Forsyth marrow.'

'Well, technically the marrow would still exist, unless your journalistic powers extend as far as telepathically growing vegetables that resemble light entertainers.'

'Stop changing the subject, Andy.'

'Do I have to?'

'Yes.'

I look towards the heavens in exasperation. Fergus clearly isn't going to drop this, is he? 'Who the hell wants to read a bloody newspaper article about *me*?'

'You're kidding, right? This is a great human-interest story.' Fergus looks instantly more animated. 'I can picture it now. A searing indictment of one man's struggle to live an analogue life in a digital world!'

'I'm only doing it for a couple of months.'

Fergus waves his hand at me. 'Semantics. It's a good story, Andy. Trust me.'

'And how exactly is it supposed to stop me from backsliding?'

'Well . . . if I write a story about you for your wonderful *Daily Local News*, then our readers will know about it, won't they?'

'So?'

Fergus smiles in a knowing fashion. 'You wouldn't want to make a liar of your old friend Fergus, would you? If I highlight your detox and you fail before it's over, you'll make us both look bad. You wouldn't want that, now, would you, Andy?' Fergus affects a pitiable look that makes my hair itch. 'After all, you missed my lovely party, which I am endlessly hurt about, obviously. You wouldn't want to also ruin my reputation as a journalist, would you?'

I suck air in through my teeth. 'No . . . I guess not.'

'Well, there you go. That's all the motivation you need, isn't it? Surely the hideous idea of everyone knowing you're a failure will stop you from falling off the analogue wagon?'

'*Everyone?*'

Fergus contrives to look slightly offended. 'Our readership is growing, thank you very much. Both in physical format and online.

Barrington is very happy with the way things are going – that's why he promoted me, and that's why I threw a party you didn't turn up to.'

I ignore that. Fergus will beat me over the head with it as much as possible, and I don't want to give him any added ammunition. 'Well, Barrington won't be happy if he finds out you're writing stories about your mates.'

'Oh, pish. Stop trying to make excuses. It's a good idea, and you know it.'

I go wide-eyed. 'Do I now?'

'Of course. Think of the exposure it'll give your work.'

This makes my ears prick up. 'I'm sorry, *what?*'

Fergus holds out his hands. 'I can scarcely do a human-interest story about a local graphic designer without featuring some of his wonderful artwork, can I?'

By now, you are hopefully starting to see what makes Fergus good at his job. Someone in his line of work has to be very per-suasive – and dangling that particular carrot in front of me is just about the most persuasive thing he could have done.

'You'd feature my work?'

'Of course!' He snaps his fingers. 'Hey! Maybe you could do a nice little illustration for the story itself!'

'What?'

'Yeah, you know . . . I give you the title, and you do me a pic-ture for it.' Fergus brings his hands together and laces his fingers. 'Pulls everything together nicely, that does. I just have to think of a good title for the story.'

'"One Man and His Descent into Madness"?' I suggest. This earns me a dark look, so I have another go. '"Detox Dickhead"?'

'Do be quiet, I'm thinking,' Fergus admonishes, and looks upwards in thought. 'It has to be a punchy title . . . Something memorable . . .'

I roll my eyes as I watch him go off into his own little world.

His idea sounds quite, quite crazy to me. He may be a very good journo, but I struggle to see how he can make a story about my detox that interesting. I have a few talents, but being interesting is not one of them.

I'm never the guy who's the centre of attention at parties (thank God).

I have carved out my own little niche, and I'm more than happy to be one of the people on the periphery. All I want is a nice, quiet life – where I can use social media and play online first-person shooters in peace. Sadly, my body has decided I can't do that, and it looks like Fergus is determined to thrust me into the spotlight, whether I like it or not.

Mind you, I can't pretend that seeing my graphics work splashed across the pages of the paper doesn't give me something of a thrill. It certainly can't hurt my chances of getting future commissions. And I could do with all the help I can get after what happened at Fluidity.

OK, then. I'll let Fergus do his silly little story about me.

I doubt it'll get all that much attention, but if it does give me the impetus to keep going with the detox – as well as potentially helping my business – then what have I got to lose?

I don't think he's going to come up with a better title for the story than 'Detox Dickhead', though. Who doesn't enjoy a nice bit of sweary alliteration?

Fergus snaps his fingers again. 'Ha! I've got it!'

'Have you now.'

'Yes! We'll call the article . . .' Fergus sits up straight and holds his arms out, fingers splayed dramatically. '"Logging Off"!'

I scratch my chin thoughtfully for a second.

Actually . . .

You know what?

That's not half bad.

LOGGING OFF!

Story by Fergus Brailsworth

Artwork by Andrew Bellows

LOCAL MAN SWAPS THE DIGITAL FAST LANE FOR A LIFE LESS HECTIC!

Modern technology can be such a pain in the neck, can't it?

Literally, for a lot of people!

We live in a world where the Internet and the online world rule our lives, and doctors across the country are increasingly diagnosing patients with a whole variety of problems related to all that time we spend on our tablets and phones.

'Many people have chronic conditions these days,' says local GP Dr Christopher Hu, 'and there are many studies to show these can be linked to spending too much time hunched over a screen. I can't tell you the number of patients I have coming to my office who have muscle aches and pains, headaches, stomach issues, eyesight problems. It's an epidemic.'

An epidemic that has caused one local man to take a stand!

Andy Bellows, 36, has been suffering for months with the kinds of health problems that Dr Hu highlights, and has decided to quit the Internet and technology, to see if that can help him.

'I figured it was worth a shot,' says Andy, who works as a freelance graphic designer. You can see some examples of his design work alongside this story. 'I probably spend too much of my time on things like Twitter and Facebook, so doing a digital detox seemed like a sensible move. It's a sixty-day programme I'm on. In that time, I have to avoid going online as much as possible, to see if that puts me in a better place, emotionally and physically.'

The rules of Andy's digital detox are quite simple.

He is not allowed to use his phone, tablet, PC or any other item of technology to access the online world, unless he absolutely needs to do it for work.

For an entire two months, instead of spending his time on social media and video games, Andy will try to fill his life with more meaningful pursuits.

'It's a good excuse to do a lot of things I otherwise wouldn't,' he says, when I ask what he's going to do to fill his time. 'I could certainly do with more exercise. And I have some books I'd like to read that I've never gotten around to. Who knows? Maybe I'll even find a new hobby to try!'

And maybe he will . . .

Andy seems like a determined man, and I have no doubt that he'll be able to make it through those sixty days with no problem whatsoever – and come out the other side happier, healthier and feeling great!

So, if you see Andy around, do say hello and let him know you're supporting his digital detox. 'I'm happy to speak to anyone about it,' Andy tells me. 'Maybe if it helps me, it could help other people too.'

This reporter is sure it could.

We'll catch up with Andy again at a later date, to see how the detox has gone for him. In the meantime, I'm sure we'd all like to wish him very well as he embarks on a life unattached from the screen, and hopefully one a lot less hectic!

To see more of Andy's work, visit his website at www.bellowsgraphics.co.uk.

Chapter Four

Instagram Influenza

Let me tell you of my week.

A week in which I have become a minor celebrity via the local paper, because I have an interfering best friend who has my best interests at heart.

I was recognised over the plums yesterday.

There I am, carefully inspecting each and every plum for the correct level of ripeness (not too firm, not too soft, if you're interested. Give it twenty-four to forty-eight hours and it'll be the perfect amount of juicy) when a man in a pink polo shirt asks me if I'm the detox bloke.

'Yes. I guess I am,' I reply hesitantly, as I place a couple of likely looking plums into my Tesco trolley.

'Yeah. Fought so. I saw you in the paper.' He gives me a searching look. 'So, are you all fucked up and that, then?'

'Pardon?'

He points a finger. 'Story said you was fucked up because you like Twitter.'

Which is, if nothing else, a fairly accurate summation of my current situation.

'Um . . . yes. I suppose so.'

'I hates Twitter,' my new friend says to me. 'My wife Shez is on it all the time, and keeps making me eat cabbage.'

And with that, Mr Pink Polo Shirt walks away from me, leaving me in a state of complete befuddlement.

Part of me wants to follow him to ask why his wife going on Twitter means he has to consume cabbage. There is a tale to be told there, of that I have no doubt.

But I'm not Fergus, so I'm not one to chase a story. Instead, I shrug my shoulders, pick a third plum to add to the other two and continue about my shopping, hoping and praying nobody else recognises me and wants to tell me how Instagram has made them eat more Brussels sprouts.

Speaking of Fergus, he is apparently not a man above embellishing a story to suit his purposes. Those quotes he ascribed to me were completely made up. I never said anything of the sort.

'You sound miserable about the whole thing, Andy,' he admonished me. 'I'll just include a few words that sound like you don't think it's the end of the bloody world.'

I never said anything about being happy to speak to other people about the detox. That was just Fergus's way of making me stick to the bloody thing. What the hell do I say to someone if they want to know more about how the damn thing is going, and I have to tell them I'm thinking of quitting?

I am not a convincing liar.

I once tried to tell my mother that my school shoes had been eaten by a rabid dog, which from my description of it was the size of a small horse, and appeared to have leapt from the very bowels of Hades itself – just to nick my shiny black size sevens.

She didn't believe a word of it, of course, and I eventually (in about thirty seconds) broke down and admitted I'd left them on the bus on the way back from the leisure centre. It was all very humiliating.

Fergus has now made me a target of the public's attention, and he knows I hate to be embarrassed. So I have no choice but to stick to the detox, otherwise I'll have to lie to complete strangers about how Cerberus the Hellhound made me log on to eBay to check if anyone had a pair of school shoes for sale it could munch on.

The story in the paper is having its desired effect – for better or worse. I haven't been tempted to go online for a whole week now.

. . . Well, all right, I have been *tempted*. Very, very tempted.

But I haven't actually *done it*. I've been a very good boy.

A very good boy who feels like he's living a surreal life.

That's what happens when such a massive change is enforced upon you.

The second and third days were nearly as bad as the first. I was almost climbing the walls with frustration . . . and that antsy feeling I mentioned before.

I threw myself into work as much as I possibly could. I sat at my desk for ten hours straight both days, I think, just trying to lose myself in something practical, rather than continuing to stare into the void of a social-media-free existence.

Fergus's story led to two new potential clients, so the bastard was right about that as well. I haven't been this busy in months. My days have been pretty full, thankfully.

The evenings aren't good, though.

Would you believe that a couple of times I ended up pacing up and down in my small living room for over an hour, my brain afire with thoughts of all the things I was missing out on?

What was trending?

Who was talking on Facebook?

Who was playing *Death Curse Intransigent*?

What kind of onesie was Robert Downey Jr. wearing?

What piece of sage wisdom had Lucas La Forte come out with today, as he sat astride his Ducati motorcycle?

What the hell was going on in the world?!

I eventually had to force myself to sit down and read a book, just to fill up the time. There was nothing I wanted to watch on TV, so a big, thick doorstop of a novel felt like the right thing to have a go at.

I have never read *The Lord of the Rings*, so I figured this was a good time to have a crack at it. I've seen the films, of course – there's a lovely Blu-ray box set of the extended editions on my bookcase – but never had the inclination to sit down with Tolkien's actual novel.

Not until now.

That got me through the evening . . . just about.

The following night was easier, though, and I actually started to enjoy reading all about Frodo and his ring – despite the fact that Tolkien writes with a stick up his arse. Once you get into the rhythm and style of his prose, though, you start to forgive his rather Victorian language and generally quite prissy writing demeanour.

So that's how I spent the rest of the week.

In a bubble of work and Tolkien.

And that got me to the point where the initial shock and horror of leaving the online community had faded somewhat, and I was actually able to appreciate the novelty of it all.

Of living a day-to-day existence without that phone in my hand. Without that constant connection to a sea of information that never ends, never stops, and sometimes never actually goes anywhere.

I still felt disconnected from the world, but I started to realise that this wasn't an entirely *bad thing*.

I've been sleeping like a fucking log.

Frodo, Sam and Gollum had only just arrived at the steps of Cirith Ungol last night when I conked out.

I woke up this morning with the book open in front of me, bleary-eyed and amazed that I hadn't stirred for a good nine hours.

I can't remember the last time I slept for nine straight hours. It felt alien and wonderful in equal measure.

So, it appears that, after a week, I am starting to adjust to a life less digital. I'm still missing my online interactions, and the sense of being connected to the wider world – but I'm also realising that you can replace those things with other pursuits . . . if you really have to.

And I have to. I really, really do.

Today, that pursuit is all about the light bulbs.

More specifically, two new light bulbs I need for my bathroom. This requires a visit to B&Q.

Because while I call the sodding things 'light bulbs', they are in fact these weird, hard-to-find spotlight LED things that cost a small fortune, are (for some unknown reason) hexagonal in shape and can only be found in B&Q – provided they've received some stock in, which only seems to happen once in a blue moon.

The bulbs were almost impossible to find online in days gone by. Most people are sensible enough to have normal, round bulbs in their house, but I have hexagonal ones. This probably says something about my place in the universe – but I'm not philosophical enough to decide how.

Given how hard it is to buy the damn things, I have spent the last couple of months peeing in semi-darkness. This is not good for your personal hygiene, or your eyesight. Today, I have resolved to track down a couple of new spotlights, so that I may illuminate my urination in the way that God intended.

There's every chance that if I still had my nose buried in an electronic screen for most of the day, I would not get around to this important errand, and would continue to narrowly avoid splashing on the bathroom tiles for the foreseeable future – but just look at this, would you? I'm *solving a problem*. I'm *fixing an issue*. I'm pro-actively *making my life better*.

Go me!

It might seem incredible to you that running such a bog-standard errand would feel like such a major achievement, but then I doubt you've spent the last few years of your life letting a bunch of ones and zeros pretty much sort out every errand for you.

It bizarrely feels like I'm finally being a proper grown-up, after letting my parents do all the work for me for so long. I'm a big boy now – able to pop down to the shops and pick up a few essentials, without the help of Mummy One and Daddy Zero.

Good lord.

I rang ahead to check that B&Q had the silly hexagonal bulbs in stock, so it only took me a couple of minutes to find them on the shelf, pay for them and exit the large out-of-town store, feeling good about myself.

I will be peeing in glorious 80-watt brightness this evening, folks!

I have a short walk to the car, as the B&Q car park was full so I had to pop the Volvo in the next car park over, outside Currys.

As I meander my way back, my brain once again starts to think about all of that lovely online stuff I'm missing out on.

I'm going to have to try to do something about that. There's not a lot of point in going offline in the real world if I'm just going to continue living online in my imagination.

Maybe I could try some aversion therapy? Pop a rubber band around my wrist and snap it against my skin every time I think about Instagram? Stick a pin in my leg whenever I start wondering about what my friends are up to on Facebook? Rub some chilli powder in my eye if I begin to—

I stop dead in my tracks.

I blink a couple of times.

I go slack-jawed.

Oh my God, I'm *hallucinating*.

This digital detox is playing such havoc with my brain that it's started to malfunction and show me things that quite clearly cannot be there.

I've been walking along thinking about all the things I'm missing online, and my stupid psyche has decided to conjure up an image of one of them right in front of me, standing at a bus stop.

Because, friends and neighbours, that man slouched against the side of the bus stop shelter is most assuredly Lucas La Forte – or my name isn't Andrew Bellows.

But this is impossible, of course.

Why on earth would an incredibly popular star of Instagram be standing at a bus stop between B&Q and Currys on a Saturday afternoon?

No.

My mind has clearly cracked, and all of that lovely online stuff I am not allowed access to in reality any more has started to manifest as a horrible, hallucinatory fantasy – right where you would normally catch the number 37.

The hallucinatory Instagram star looks every inch the man I've been following on the social media site for these past few months. That silvery grey Armani suit is as sharp as it is undoubtedly expensive. The haircut is as perfect as ever. The stubble on his chin is just the right length to appear manly, but not too scruffy. The shoes are sleek, black and probably made from the comfiest of Italian leather.

This is not a man dressed to be standing at a bus stop, waiting for the number 37.

I am definitely hallucinating.

'Can I help you?' Lucas La Forte says to me, noticing that I'm staring at him.

Oh, marvellous. The hallucination is auditory as well as visual.

Do I play along? Or simply ignore his imaginary self and walk on?

'I said, can I help you?' The rich baritone voice sounds exactly like you'd imagine it would.

'Er, I'm not sure,' I reply, hating myself. I'm positive there must be something in a medical manual somewhere that says if you experience a hallucination, it isn't a good idea to start interacting with the bugger. It could lead to all sorts of problems – up to and including walking right off the edge of a cliff you thought had a bridge going over it.

'Well, you're kind of staring at me,' Lucas says. 'Are you a fan?'

'I'm sorry?'

'A fan of mine? Do you follow me on Insta?'

Oh my God, he's *real*.

Panic stations!

I don't do well meeting celebrities.

Never have.

I once met Sinéad O'Connor at a concert. In my sheer embarrassment and star-struckedness, I accidentally called her Skinhead O'Connor. She wasn't impressed. Nothing might well compare to you, but that night I convincingly compared to an utter cock.

'Er, ah, eh, um,' I respond, going bright red. Lucas La Forte isn't what you'd call a 'proper' celebrity, like Robert Downey Jr. or Ryan Reynolds, but he does have nearly one hundred thousand followers on Instagram, which most definitely places him in the category of *social media* celebrity.

And I know my social media celebrities.

This is one of them. Standing in front of me.

At a . . . at a *bus stop*?

'You OK, pal?' Lucas asks, probably worried that I might be about to have a heart attack.

'Yes! I'm fine, thanks. And I do follow you, yes, Mr La Forte.'

Lucas La Forte stands up straight. 'Please . . . call me Lucas!'

'OK . . . *Lucas.*' I point at the bus stop behind him. 'Why . . . why are you *here*?' The incredulity in my voice is unmistakeable. This is a man who I am used to seeing either sitting in a very expensive sports car, sitting on an equally expensive motorbike, sitting in an exquisite leather armchair on his penthouse terrace or sitting on a luxury yacht.

Basically there's a lot of sitting involved with Lucas – generally in places I'd be thrown out of, or off of, at the earliest opportunity. Seeing him *standing* at a *bus stop* is incongruous, to say the least.

Lucas looks a little alarmed for a second, but instantly covers it up again with a self-assured smile. 'Bit of trouble with the Porsche,' he tells me. 'Damn titanium connecting rod threw a wobbler while I was doing a hundred. You know how it goes.'

No, Mr La Forte. I do not know *how it goes*. I drive a 2004 Volvo. I wouldn't know what a titanium connecting rod was if you poked one up my bottom.

'Ah, yes. I . . . bet that was . . . annoying,' I reply, trying to sound like I think I should remain part of this conversation involving Porsches and titanium connecting rods, but knowing that I probably shouldn't.

'Damn right, pal!'

'Couldn't you get a taxi?' I ask, still flummoxed as to why this ultra-successful man would be at a bus stop.

'What? And miss the chance to travel like an honest man for once?' Lucas says, and laughs. 'In life, when an opportunity to see how others live arrives, you should grasp it with both hands. It will broaden your horizons and make you a better person.'

Jesus Christ. He talks like he Instagrams. I'm pretty sure he wrote that little epithet on a post that accompanied a picture of him sitting on a luxury powerboat in the Med.

'Ah well, that explains it then,' I say, still not 100 per cent convinced. Something feels a little . . . *off*, here.

But this is my chance to get to know someone from my online life a little better – right here in the offline world.

I'm going to take Lucas's advice to heart and grasp an opportunity to see how others live, in both of my sweaty little hands. 'I could give you a lift, if you'd like?'

Lucas appears to weigh this up for a moment, before nodding his head. 'Thank you. I always say that when the hand of friendship is reached out, you should take it without hesitation.'

'Yes. I'm sure. That sounds . . . like good advice,' I tell him. 'My car's parked over there, outside Currys. Happy to take you to wherever you need to go. Back to your penthouse at Southern Quay, if that's the way you're headed?'

Lucas's face darkens briefly.

Oh, shit. I've obviously overstepped here. Now I look like some kind of weird stalker – knowing where he lives, and everything.

But he plasters it all over Instagram! Everybody who follows him knows where he lives!

'Ah . . . no. Not there, thank you,' he says, suddenly looking very awkward.

Oh, well done, Bellows! You've made a right fool of yourself!

'You could . . . you could take me to my mother's house though,' he suggests. 'I like to pop in on her when I can.'

'Oh . . . OK.' This is slightly disappointing. I wanted to see that penthouse in the flesh.

'She's a wonderful woman,' Lucas continues. 'And as I always say – cherish the moments you have with those you love. They will not be around forever, so grasp those times with both hands.'

'Yes. I'm sure . . . sure that's correct.'

Lucas nods, smiles and starts to walk off in the direction of my car.

That Armani suit really is quite exquisite. He must work out like a bastard to fit into it so well.

I'm still feeling somewhat star-struck as I pull out of the Currys car park with the Instagram influencer sitting next to me, looking entirely out of place on the threadbare Volvo passenger seat. But there's something I'm definitely not too sure about going on here . . .

I guess I'd built a picture up in my mind of what Lucas La Forte was like, based on his Instagram feed, but the reality is not quite matching up to expectations. Maybe it's just the strange circumstances under which we've met. If I'd bumped into him at a party in the Seychelles, I'd probably feel a lot differently, but as it stands, there's a small part of me that's feeling a little disappointed by the encounter so far. Perhaps it's the way he insists on coming out with those trite little aphorisms. They seem very wise and interesting in a social media post, but rather silly when spoken out loud.

I am still very pleased to have him sitting in the car with me, though. Lucas La Forte represents a part of my life I no longer have access to, and having him here in the real world with me makes me feel strangely comforted. He's a constant reminder that all that stuff is still there . . . whether I can see it or not at the moment.

'It's great to meet you, you know,' I confide to Lucas as we drive along. 'I'm actually currently on a digital detox, so can't go on Instagram to see what you're up to, so it's nice that I've been able to do it in real life!'

'A digital detox?' Lucas asks, obviously unaware of the term.

'Yeah. You know . . . when you come off the Internet completely for a while?'

He looks horrified. 'Why would you want to do *that*?!'

'Because I've been having a few health problems,' I tell him, a bit awkwardly. 'The doctor told me it would be good for me.'

Lucas nods sagely. 'Ah. That's interesting. When someone wise tells you to take a course of action for your own benefit, you would do well to grasp it with both hands.'

Jesus. He likes a lot of hand-grasping, this chap, doesn't he? I hope he has some anti-bacterial gel tucked away in that suit somewhere.

'I haven't been doing it long, but it's really hard.'

'Is it?'

'Yes. I feel like I've had a limb cut off, you know?'

'Really? Sounds horrible. I could never do the same kind of thing. I'd die if I wasn't online.'

'That's what I thought too . . . but I haven't keeled over just yet. I guess . . . I guess I'm starting to see some benefits of not being online so much, as well.'

Lucas vigorously shakes his head. 'No. No. I couldn't do it.'

'Ah well, that's probably because Instagram has made you rich and famous!'

Lucas shifts in his seat. 'Yes. Rich and famous.' He stares out of the windscreen for a moment, looking quite exceptionally uncomfortable, before he visibly relaxes as something occurs to him. 'But, as I always like to say – if you find a job you love, then you must grasp it with both hands and never let go. Then you will never actually have to work another day in your life.'

I'm pretty sure it was Mark Twain who said that one, actually – without the grasping bloody hands part – but we'll let it pass, as this is probably a very strange situation for Lucas, and he's no doubt a bit discombobulated.

Being forced into a journey alongside a freshly minted technological Luddite in his rather tired and rusty Volvo must be *extremely* discombobulating for someone used to the finer things in life.

'Well, I do love my job as a graphic designer, but it's not one I really need the Internet for a lot, unfortunately,' I confide as we turn in to a suburban street at Lucas's direction. 'So I had no excuses when it came to starting the detox. Especially when I was having so many health issues.' I glance at Lucas. 'Would you like to hear about them?'

'Ah . . . OK,' he says, clearly unsure.

I barrel on regardless. 'Well, there's the irritable bowel syndrome, that's the worst. Gives me a lot of anxiety – not knowing how difficult it's going to be to go to the toilet from day to day!'

'Oh, right.' Lucas looks a little grossed out by this.

'Then there's the muscular aches and pains. I feel like an old man some mornings.'

'OK.' Now he's slightly leaning away from me.

'And the headaches! Boy have they been a nightmare. I just get these *bad headaches*, Lucas. Really bad.'

'Do you?' Lucas actually gulps nervously as he says this.

'Yes! And all of it drags you down psychologically, you know? Makes you feel . . . I don't know . . . *less*. Like you're not being the person you should be. You know what I mean, Lucas?'

'Um . . . it sounds . . . difficult.'

And *he* sounds slightly terrified.

'Oh, it is. It really, really is.'

'Mmmmm.'

'But then I think to myself – is feeling better really worth losing such a massive part of my life?'

'OK.'

'Am I giving up too much of who I am? Am I letting go of the things that make me . . . *me*?'

'You, you?'

'Yes. Me . . . *me*.'

'You, you.'

'Me, me. That's it, Lucas.'

'You get headaches, and you don't think you are who you are.' Lucas's eyes have gone rather wide.

'Yes, that's about it.'

Right, what the hell is going on here?

I've only just met this bloke, and yet here I am talking to him like he's a long-lost friend.

No wonder he keeps shifting around in his seat awkwardly and staring out of the window like he wants to smash right out of it to get away from me.

Then it hits me – I'm talking to this complete stranger like I know him well, because part of me thinks I *do* know him well. The part of me that's checked his Instagram feed every morning, noon and night for months. I've read all about Lucas La Forte's thoughts on the world, and seen him in a variety of exciting sitting positions. I've developed a relationship with him – even though I've never actually met the poor guy before today.

But as far as he's concerned, I'm just another one of his hundred thousand followers, and he does not want to hear all about how hard it is for me to have a poo!

Oh for the love of God, Andy. Just clam up, and give the poor man a rest.

'Sorry, Lucas. You don't need to hear all about my problems,' I say, trying to mitigate things somewhat.

'Turn here!' he replies, pointing down a street to our left. 'My mother's house is just along this road.' There's an air of urgency in his voice that suggests I've already gone way too far. He's obviously got me pegged as some kind of crazy fan he needs to get away from, before I start telling him I love him and have baked him a pie with my pubic hair in it.

I'm never going to see that penthouse up close and personal now.

Part of me has probably been harbouring a fantasy that Lucas La Forte and I would become the best of friends. That he would invite me on to his yacht. Maybe let me wear one of his suits.

We could have been Instagram buddies and—

Oh, bugger. No. That wouldn't have happened, would it?

Sigh.

Never mind.

Looks like I'm not getting to be best friends with an Instagram millionaire any time soon.

'Pull up here,' Lucas says, his hand already hovering over the door handle.

I do as I'm bid, and the Volvo has barely come to halt before he's opening the door and sticking one leg out.

'Herbert!' a woman's voice screams. I look past Lucas to see a very angry lady in her sixties come marching down the front garden path of a semi-detached house, making a beeline straight for my car. 'Herbert! You get over here right now!'

'Oh God!' Lucas La Forte cries, and immediately slams the car door again. 'She's not supposed to be home yet!'

The woman, clearly enraged about something, is now right outside my car, brandishing a credit card. She knocks on my passenger-side window with it repeatedly, giving Lucas a look of absolute fury. 'You get out of that car now, Herbert! You get out now and tell me why you've maxed out my bloody credit card . . . *again*!'

WTF?

What's the hell's going on here?

'Who is she, Lucas?!' I ask him, wincing as the woman continues to bash the credit card against the window. I hope she doesn't scratch it. 'Why is she calling you Herbert?'

'It's my mother!' he replies, cowering.

The transformation that Lucas La Forte has undergone is nothing short of miraculous – if God was in the habit of performing miracles that turned self-confident, well-dressed men about town into terrified little boys.

'Your *mother?*'

'Yes!' He gives me a desperate look. 'You have to help me!'

'Help you?'

'Yes!'

'How?'

'Just . . . just play along!'

And with that, Lucas winds the window down and holds up both of his hands protectively. 'Now look, Mum. Please don't be angry!'

Lucas's mother starts to visibly shake with rage, placing both of her hands on her hips in the classic matronly pose of extreme disapproval. 'Don't be angry?! Don't be bloody *angry?*! You did it again, you little monster! The bank called to tell me the card was maxed out again. Five thousand pounds, Herbert! How many stupid suits did that buy you this time?'

'It's not as bad as it seems, Mum, honestly!' He whips his head around. 'Tell her!'

'Pardon me?'

'Tell her it's not that bad!'

I look at the woman and slap on a fake smile. 'It's not that bad?' I venture – not really knowing what the hell I'm saying.

'Who the hell is this, Herbert?' she demands. 'Another one of your wastrel friends?'

'He's a fan of mine!' Lucas (Herbert?) replies.

This earns me a look half full of derision, but disturbingly, also half full of pity. 'Oh . . . another one fooled, I see. There are so many of you these days.'

'Fooled?' I reply, confused.

Lucas doesn't give his mother a chance to respond, because at this point he decides to jump out of the car. I can't tell if this is because he's manning up to the situation, or just because he doesn't want his mother continuing to speak to me . . .

'Let's go inside, Mum. Nobody needs to hear about this!' He throws a look back at me. '*He* doesn't need to hear about this.' Lucas slams the passenger door and bangs on the roof. 'Off you go, mate! Thanks for the lift!'

'Oh . . . OK,' I reply. I have been dismissed in no uncertain terms, and should probably get the hell out of here.

The woman's eyes narrow. 'Oh, I think it might be a good idea if your friend sticks around for a while, Herbert! Maybe if one of your Instachat followers hears all about who you really are, it might make you think twice about carrying on the way you have been!'

'Insta*gram*, Mum,' Lucas corrects, in a whiny voice.

'Quiet!' She points a finger at me through the car window. 'You! What's your name?'

'Andy!'

'Right, Andy . . . my name is Helen Bilch, and I'd very much like for you to come into my house to hear my son explain himself to both of us!'

'OK!' At this point, I don't feel like I can argue. Helen Bilch is currently channelling every angry mother who has ever walked the face of God's green earth, and as such has complete control over my actions.

I'm pretty sure that if you stuck this lady in a room with every male world leader, the planet's problems would all be solved in about half an hour flat – just in time for tea.

I climb out of the car as Helen starts to push her son towards the house. I follow as close behind as I dare, wondering what the hell is in store for me inside.

I should probably just run away, but my curiosity has been set afire by all of this. It's quite clear now that Lucas La Forte is *not* the man I thought he was, and I must . . . *must* . . . know more.

Inside the house, Lucas is frogmarched into the living room by his irate mother, and I follow them in somewhat tentatively.

'Do take a seat, Andy,' Mrs Bilch tells me, and I instantly park myself on a comfy-looking armchair, as Lucas is thrust down on to the matching settee. Mrs Bilch stands over her son with her arms folded and a glower in her eyes so incandescent you could boil an egg with it. Lucas, for his part, looks like a little boy sitting there on that voluminous couch with his shoulders slumped.

'Right then, Herbert. I've tried to get through to your thick skull more times than I care to mention how you have to stop living the way you do, with no success at all. Let's see if having to talk to Andy here can make any difference! Why don't you tell him all about yourself?'

Lucas (do I keep calling him that?) looks down at the beige carpet. 'Don't want to,' he says in a grumpy voice.

Mrs Bilch rolls her eyes. 'Oh yes. This is what happens. He's got his father's gift of the gab – right up until someone confronts him with the truth!' She looks at me. 'Is there anything you'd like to ask Herbert, Andy?'

About seventy million things, actually, but we'll start with the most obvious one:

'Is your name really Herbert?' I ask the man I've known for months as Lucas La Forte.

He remains silent.

'Herbert Bilch! You answer the nice man, or so help me God, I will throw you out of this house!' Mrs Bilch tells him, her voice rising several octaves as she does so.

'Mu-u-um!' he squeals in response.

'*Talk*, Herbert!' she demands again.

This earns me a look of childish loathing from her son, which takes me somewhat aback. It's not my fault he's been placed in this awkward situation, is it?

'Yes, my name is *Herbert*,' he snaps.

'Not Lucas?'

'Hah!' Helen Bilch exclaims.

'No,' Herbert admits.

'And your surname is Bilch? Not La Forte?'

'Pfft!' Mrs Bilch remarks. She has a real talent for derisory, monosyllabic comments, it appears.

'Yes,' Herbert says.

'You made up that name for Instagram?'

Now Herbert sits up, looking a lot more animated. 'Do you blame me? *Herbert Bilch!* My name is Herbert Bilch! Would you follow someone on Instagram called Herbert Bilch?'

'Herbert!' Mrs Bilch snaps. 'Herbert is a perfectly good name!'

Herbert looks disgusted. 'Is it, Mum? *Really?* He throws me a forlorn look. 'I'm thirty-seven, mate. Do you know what it's like being in your thirties and being called Herbert?'

'No.'

'Nearly as bad as going through your twenties being called Herbert!'

'Why are you called Herbert?' I ask Herbert.

. . . Look, I know there have been a lot of Herberts already in this conversation. You may be reaching the point where having to hear the word 'Herbert' again fills you with a certain degree of dread. Please cope with it a little longer. It will be over soon, I promise.

And think about how bad poor old Herbert must feel about being *called* Herbert. Not a day of his life goes by without him having to hear it.

The pain of all these Herberts will be over for us very soon, but for him it's a life sentence . . .

'Herbert Glerbett,' Herbert replies. 'Herbert Glerbett and his bloody sherbet.'

'I'm sorry?' I say, worried that Herbert may have had some kind of mental breakdown right in front of me.

'My dad named me after that poem from the seventies. You know the one.'

I shake my head. 'I truly, truly don't, Herbert.'

Herbert sighs. 'Herbert Glerbett. The poem is about Herbert Glerbett. He likes to eat sherbet.'

'It was his father's favourite,' Mrs Bilch interjects. 'A great lover of poetry, was my Malcolm.'

It's clear from the emotional way she's speaking that Herbert's father is no longer with us. 'I'm sorry for your loss,' I tell her.

'What loss?'

'Your husband's passing.'

'What are you talking about? Malcolm isn't dead, he's in Braintree.'

Herbert sighs again. 'Mum and Dad got divorced. On account of Dad's . . . er . . . hobby.'

Suddenly Mrs Bilch looks as mad as all hell and back again. 'Pretending you are a member of the royal family is not a bloody *hobby*, Herbert!'

'A member of the *royal family*?' I splutter.

Mrs Bilch provides me with a woeful expression. 'Yes. He pretended he was Baron Mobbington of Potherbrooke. Lied his arse off, he did. Mostly to blag free stuff and get into cocktail parties.' She sniffs unhappily. 'Went on for *years* . . . until I eventually threw him out.' She glares at Herbert. 'And now his bloody son is up to the same bloody thing!'

'It's not the same, Mum!' Herbert implores.

'It damn well is, young man! The cars . . . the girls . . . the bloody suits! All of it's a load of old claptrap – just like your father – and you know it!' She stares at me again. 'Malcolm once spent the money for the conservatory on an ermine cloak! And you know what an ermine cloak most certainly is not, Andy?'

'No, what?'

'Machine bloody washable! Damn thing fell apart! Thousands of pounds down the drain, just because my ex-husband had ideas above his station!' She glares at Herbert. 'And the apple hasn't fallen far from the tree, has it?'

I look back at Herbert. 'But I don't understand. What about all the sports cars I've seen you sitting in?'

Herbert looks deeply guilty, like a little boy caught with his hand in a very expensive, possibly ermine-lined, cookie jar. 'My mate's dad runs a posh garage,' he explains. 'All sports cars and bikes. He lets me take pictures with his stock every once in a while.'

'Bloody hell,' I reply, feeling irate for the first time. 'And what about the penthouse flat?'

'Did all those pictures in the same week,' Herbert sniffs. 'Was working for a builder called Fred Babidge. He was doing some renovations on the flat, and had me in as a part-time labourer. He thought it was hilarious – me taking all those pictures – but let me get away with it, as long as I cleaned up the plasterboard and made a decent cup of tea.'

'You took all of those photos in the same week?!'

'Yeah. Took bloody *hours*. I did it after everyone else had gone home.'

I'm flabbergasted.

Although . . . come to think of it . . . when I put my mind to it . . . all of those glamorous shots of Herbert lounging around in the penthouse were very *similar*, weren't they? All taken in the early evening, with the sun going down, and all confined to just the outdoor terrace and a bit of the living room. The suits were the only thing that really changed.

Speaking of which . . .

'What about all of your lovely Armani suits?' I ask Herbert.

'Hah!' exclaims Mrs Bilch again. 'Why do you think my credit card is maxed out? Why do you think we never have any *money*?'

Now Herbert gives me a desperate look. 'I *need* those suits, mate! I *need* them! How can I be Lucas La Forte without them?'

'You're not Lucas La Forte, Herbert!' Mrs Bilch spits. 'You're Herbert Bilch, whether you like it or not!'

'Herbert bloody Glerbett,' Herbert replies sullenly.

'But you've got a hundred thousand followers!' I say in disbelief.

This perks Herbert up a bit. 'Yeah, I know! Great, isn't it?'

I shake my head. 'Not really, Herbert. They – we – all think you're some kind of hot-shot millionaire. We all think you're *Lucas*, not *Herbert*. Living a life of luxury on yachts in the Mediterranean.' My eyes go wide. 'How the hell did you do *those* pictures?'

'Boat show and Photoshop,' he replies.

I'm incredulous. That can't be possible, can it? I'm a *graphic designer*, for crying out loud; I can instantly spot when someone's been messing about in Photoshop!

Except . . . how closely have I really *looked* at the Instagram posts of 'Lucas La Forte'? Have I studied the pictures properly? Taken them in?

Or did I just glance at them with envy, read the trite aphorism of the day and move on to see what Chris Hemsworth was up to with his hammer?

I feel like such a bloody *fool*.

And that makes me quite *angry*, actually. As much with myself as with Herbert Glerbett.

'You've fooled a lot of people, you know,' I tell him. 'Lied to a hundred thousand of us.'

'Twenty,' Herbert states matter-of-factly.

'What?'

'Twenty thousand people. The rest are paid for.'

'You what?!'

'Paid for, mate. You can go online and pay these companies to get you loads of fake followers. It's easy.'

'And expensive!' Mrs Bilch cries, waggling the credit card again.

Oh. My. God.

This is absolutely *unbelievable*.

At the same time, though – given my knowledge of how social media works – it's completely and utterly believable in every single respect.

And *I* can't *believe* I've been taken in so completely by this grotty little Herbert.

For months and months I've been following the exploits of Lucas La Forte, thinking that he was a real person and admiring him from afar – when in reality I've been duped by Herbert Glerbett, and his mum's credit card.

Aaaaargh!

'Why?!' I snap at Herbert.

'Why what?'

'Why *do this*? Why pretend to be someone you're not? Why fake it all?'

Herbert looks at me like I've gone mad. '*Why?*' He gestures around the room. 'I'm in my mid-thirties, I live at home with my mother, have no money, no qualifications and no car. What the hell else am I supposed to do to make myself feel better?'

I visibly start to shake. 'I don't know, Herbert . . . how about *getting a fucking job*?'

'That's exactly what I keep telling him!' Mrs Bilch cries in agreement. 'You see, Herbert? You see what the nice man is saying to you?'

This nice man has had just about enough of this claptrap for one day.

I rise quickly out of the armchair. 'I'm leaving now. I think you two need to talk amongst yourselves, and I need to re-evaluate a few things myself.' I give Herbert the stink eye. 'Chiefly, how much trust I put in people.'

And with that, I turn and stalk out of the lounge, with mother and son staring at me as I go.

Herbert isn't staring by the time I reach the front door, though. He's caught up with me and is looking like I'm about to shoot his dog, possibly on Instagram.

'Please don't tell anyone!' he cries, in real and obvious anguish. 'Don't tell anyone I'm Herbert!'

'Go away, Herbert!' I demand as I stride down the garden path.

'Please don't say anything!'

'Leave me be, Herbert!'

'I'll do anything!'

I come to a standstill on the pavement in front of my car, and give Herbert a hard look. 'Anything?'

'Yes!'

I think for a few seconds.

This could be my chance to salvage something from this awful revelation – and the months I've wasted following this little bastard on social media.

'All right . . . I won't tell anyone that Lucas La Forte is really Herbert Bilch, but in exchange, you're going to change your Instagram feed.'

'I am?'

'Yes! No more shots of you sitting in sports cars . . . and no more bloody "helpful" advice about grasping things with both hands!'

'But people love it when I say stuff like that! I get it all out of a book!'

'Well, tough shit, Herbert Glerbett! It's time you started doing some bloody *good* for a change!'

'Like what?' He's close to tears now. I have him over an Instagrammable barrel and he knows it.

'You're going to . . . going to start posting about . . .' Oh bollocks, now I have to think of something. 'About . . . *puppies!*'

'Pardon me?'

'Puppies! Rescue dogs, I mean! Get down the dogs' home and get some shots of you with some dogs that need adopting! Tell people who they are, and where they can adopt them!'

'Dogs?'

'Yes! And . . . and *trees!*'

'Trees?'

'Yep! Hug some trees, Herbert! Write things on your feed about how we should be caring for our environment!' I point a finger at Herbert. It is a finger of extreme righteousness. 'I want to see Lucas La Forte doing his bit to make the world a better place, not just lounging around in it on expensive things!'

'Er . . . OK. I will.'

'You promise, Herbert?!'

'Yes! Yes! I promise!'

'Good. Because I'll be *checking*, Herbert. I'll be *watching*. And if you don't do what I'm telling you to, I'll tell the world that Lucas La Forte is really Herbert Bilch!'

Herbert looks confused. 'How are you going to do that if you're on a digital detox?'

I instantly freeze.

Bugger, he's got me there, hasn't he?

But then a suitable response occurs to me. 'I have *friends*, Herbert. Friends in high places.' I try to say this as ominously as possible. 'Friends who work for the *newspapers*. They can check on you for me. And they can let everybody know what you've been up to, all the lies you've been telling, unless you're a very *good boy* and do what I say.'

Now he looks terrified again. Good.

'I'll do it,' he tells me in a squeaky voice. 'I'll go and help dogs and trees!'

'No more sports cars?!'

'No more sports cars!'

'Good.' A final thought then occurs. 'Who knows, Herbert . . . if you actually do something good with your Instagram account, maybe you'll get a lot of new, real followers. People love dogs and trees. There are plenty of them.'

'Oh wow. You think?' he says in excitement. 'You think more people will follow me if I do all of that?' A light bulb's gone off in Herbert's brain. It's probably not hexagonal.

'Yes, Herbert. Be a good boy and I'm sure you'll be even more popular than you already are.'

'Dogs and trees,' he repeats, half to himself.

I notice that Mrs Bilch has appeared at the front door again. 'And Herbert?' I add.

'Yes, Andy?'

'Pay your bloody mother back. Every last penny.'

'Yes, Andy.'

'Sell the bloody suits. The dogs and trees will only get them mucky anyway.'

'Yes, Andy.'

I nod in a satisfied manner.

I think my work here – such as it is – is done. There's very little else I can contribute.

'Goodbye, Herbert,' I tell the Instagram Influenza.

'Er, yeah – bye, Andy. It was . . . it was nice to meet you.'

My brow wrinkles. 'I'm not sure I can say quite the same about you, Herbert. But at least we're parting on relatively good terms. And hopefully you'll change your ways from now on.'

As I open the car door and climb in, Herbert digests this. 'Yeah, definitely,' he says. 'After all, as I always like to say, when a change for the better comes along, you have to grasp it—'

'Don't say another fucking word!' I scream at him, and slam the car door closed with all of my might.

Well, that was a truly eye-opening experience.

I'd always known that social media was a place of exaggeration and falsehood, but never actually thought I'd be the kind of person taken in by it . . . not to that extent, anyway. And yet, there we have it.

Back home, as I huffed and puffed over getting the blown hexagonal spotlights out of the bathroom ceiling fixtures and the new ones fitted, I reflected on the reasons why Herbert Bilch managed to fool me in the same way he had done twenty thousand or so other people.

About the only conclusion I could reach was that I must have a tremendous capacity to ignore obvious details when I'm keen on believing in something.

I wanted 'Lucas La Forte' to be real, because I suppose he gave me something to aspire to. Local-boy-done-good kind of thing. I'm sure deep in the recesses of my subconscious I probably thought that with enough time, a bit of luck and some hard work, I too could be wearing expensive Armani suits and sitting on a penthouse balcony.

That's what Herbert's alter ego said to me every day from Instagram, anyway.

I don't know how I really feel about discovering the whole thing was a load of old cobblers. On the one hand, I still feel angry that I wasted my time following Herbert, but on the other, he has shown me just how ludicrous and fake social media can truly be . . . which can only be a good thing for someone on a digital detox.

Maybe the next time I'm desperate to find out what my favourite celebrities are up to, I'll think about Herbert Glerbett and his clear-cut bullshit, and feel a lot better about being unable to.

Now, if you don't mind, I'm going to enjoy urinating under the comforting glow of a fully functional 80-watt hexagonal spotlight.

I don't know what the future has in store for me beyond this moment – as I progress with my Internet-free life – but right now I'm just very pleased I have enough light to piss in.

Which is something I'm definitely going to grasp with both hands.

Chapter Five

GETTING FROM A TO B, AND ENDING UP IN X

I'm not going to pretend that my life isn't significantly more difficult.

It's quite astounding to me just how much of my life – and *all* of our lives in general – have become so reliant on the bloody Internet.

Of course, I didn't realise this until I started the detox. If you'd have come up to me a few weeks ago and asked me how much I rely on being online, I would have probably downplayed it. Not just because I wouldn't have wanted to admit the depths of my addiction, but also because I truly wouldn't have appreciated how much time I did spend on it, on an almost constant basis.

I feel like a moron these days.

Literally, it feels like my IQ levels have dropped off a cliff since the detox began.

I've been so used to outsourcing my general knowledge to Google that when I have to fall back on the contents of my brain, I find that it's a sluggish, stupid thing, with far less recall of facts than it should have.

For instance, I couldn't remember the word you use for describing the way a piece of art looks yesterday.

It's the 'aesthetic' of it. I know that now.

But yesterday, while I was trying to write a proposal for the pie shop job, I just couldn't think of it.

Was it 'anaesthetic'?

'Prosthetic'?

'Atheistic'?

I very nearly described a piece of my own work as either a knockout gas, a fake body part or a complete disbelief in the sweet baby Jesus.

I had to go and dig out an old dictionary from the back of my cupboard just to get the bloody word right. What would have taken me ten seconds on Google instead took me over ten minutes.

Being offline has made me slow down. An awful lot. My life feels like it's being played at half speed. It's very frustrating.

Annoyingly, it's also quite *relaxing*.

This is a strange pair of emotions to put together, and they really shouldn't play nicely with one another, but they seem to be getting on quite well in my head at the moment. Like neighbours who have finally reached an accord over where the fence panels should go.

My head feels far less 'cluttered' than it did before I started the detox. Not having that instant recall of any information I damn well want has made the little grey cells bouncing around in my head calm down considerably. If my brain is smaller thanks to having no Google, it's also a lot more relaxed. Stupidity appears to be calming. Who knew?

I'm sleeping better.

The jaw-clenching has lessened quite a lot.

Even the IBS has calmed down. Although it's going to take far more than a couple of weeks off Facebook to sort that one out.

I'm still divorced from the world – but it's starting to feel like the divorce might have been slightly worth it.

My work has improved as well, I think.

This is because I have no distractions.

I can concentrate properly on the task at hand, without the near-constant binging of notifications and messages. There's a fresh creativity and flourish to my artwork that I'm loving. It's as if the inventive part of my brain – the bit that's been stifled by all that online noise – has found a new lease on life, and is taking full advantage of it.

Take the new logo design I've done for McGifferty's Pies. The old attempt may have looked like a dog turd, but this new one is quite *marvellous*.

The pie I've drawn looks extremely tasty. You'd almost want to reach into the screen and take a bite. And the font! Oh, I do love the new font! 'McGifferty's Pies' is now written in a cheerful, bright, porky font that just *screams* high-quality meat products.

Put the design together with the rather eloquent proposal I've written (which includes the word 'aesthetic' twice, in its proper context) and you have what I believe could be a real winner on my hands.

Paul McGifferty is going to be blown away by all of this. I'm sure he is.

So much so that I've suggested I drive over to their office in the West Country to show it to them. I could have done it over Skype – my detox rules allow me to use the web for work purposes – but no, I've decided I want to do it face-to-face, such is the quality of my work and my pride in it.

This is something of a sea change for me – and is probably another effect of the detox.

I am usually not keen on doing things face-to-face. Not if there's an electronic screen I can use instead. It's so much more convenient, easy and simple. Less nerve-wracking for me, as well.

And before now, going through all the bother of driving over a hundred miles to Weston-super-Mare would have made my toes curl. But the lack of technology has forced me to get out more – and that's no bad thing.

Other than purchasing hexagonal light bulbs from B&Q and having a run-in with a grotty little Herbert, I've also had to jump in the car to go food shopping at Tesco – instead of just ordering online.

I finished *The Lord of the Rings* and needed a new book to read, so I actually went out to a bookshop to find one. I'm sure George R. R. Martin will keep me nicely occupied for the foreseeable future.

Then there was an issue with a late payment for a job I did a few months ago, but instead of just using the live-chat option on my bank app, I popped into the local branch, and sorted it out there.

Basically, I've had to interact with a lot more people since I quit the tech, and I've had to make much more of an effort to get things sorted out.

And you know what? It's not so bad. Not so bad at all.

That's why I feel quite happy to drive over to see Paul at his pie shop. The trip will do me good. And I am very, very proud of my new logo design. It only feels right to deliver it in person.

It is with all this in mind that I set off the next morning in the direction of Weston-super-Mare in my trusty Volvo.

I have never been to that part of the country before, so need help with the directions. I don't own a dedicated satnav, and I don't have access to my phone (it's secreted away somewhere in Fergus's house), so I'm just going to have to do things the old-fashioned way – and use a map.

This feels *right*, though.

It feels like the way I *should* be making this journey.

And it won't be a problem, I don't think. I got on just fine using maps and road atlases before all that technology came along to get me around the place.

OK, I mostly travelled on *pushbike* back then, but the principle still holds.

The map I bought from WHSmith is very clear, very concise and easy to read.

It'll be *fine*.

With an air of positivity about me that I certainly did not have when I went off to that meeting at Fluidity, I set off towards the west, with my logo designs and proposal printed off and on the seat next to me.

Paul McGifferty is going to love it. He's going to give me the job. And very soon, the six branches of McGifferty's Pies will be emblazoned with the best artwork I think I've done for years!

These happy thoughts fill my head as I make my way along the M4, listening to Radio 1 and actually managing to like at least half the songs I hear.

I even have a little sing to myself as I go.

I'm forced to stop singing and turn the radio down, however, when I reach a sudden traffic jam and evidence of a rather large accident up ahead.

This starts to elevate my stress levels before I am even aware of it happening. I've given myself plenty of time to reach McGifferty's Pies, but I could do without this kind of hold-up.

The traffic moves forward in fits and starts, and I start to do that thing we all do when we're in slow traffic – I begin to weave the Volvo slowly out to the right, to see if I can see what's going on.

Usually, by now, I would have reached for my phone, and would be furiously checking Twitter and the Highways England website for more information, but as I can't do that, I am reduced to craning my head upwards and outwards, in the futile hope I might see something to explain why my progress has been halted.

Luckily, there's a police car up ahead, with a bored-looking copper standing next to it.

'Excuse me, Officer?' I ask him, as I bring the car to a stop once more. 'What's happened?'

'A lorry's tipped over,' he tells me. His tone of voice sounds as bored as he looks, so I'm assuming it's not incredibly serious. 'Dumped a load of oil over the road. They're cleaning it up now.'

'Oh no. Do you think it'll take long to get it sorted out?'

He shrugs. 'There's every chance. These things tend to take a while to get cleaned up. Are you in a rush?'

'Sort of. I have a meeting in Weston in about an hour and a half.'

The copper sucks air in over his teeth. Never a good sign. 'You might want to get off the motorway then, mate. It'll be blocked longer than that.'

'OK, thanks,' I say to him, just as the car in front of me starts to pull away again.

Damn it.

That's annoying. I had planned on a nice easy run straight to the town. Now it looks like I'll have to get off the M4 and take to the A-roads.

I grab my clear and concise road atlas off the passenger seat and thumb through it to the correct page. As the traffic comes to a halt again, I study the map and see that my best bet is to get off at the next exit and make my way via the local A-roads to Weston-super-Mare through the Mendips – an area of outstanding natural beauty.

On the one hand this sounds nice. A motorway is a boring thing. I could do with a change of scenery. On the other, though, it's not going to be the easy, smooth journey that I would have had if I could have stayed on the M4.

But what choice do I have?

I can't sit in this tailback for much longer. I'll be late for my appointment.

I spend the next ten minutes getting the car across to the left-hand lane, and breathe something of a sigh of relief when I hit the exit ramp and am travelling at more than five miles an hour again.

To start with, I don't have too many problems. The road atlas remains clear and concise, and I beetle my way down the A-roads of the West Country with some degree of confidence.

Things start to get a little more stressful when I do hit the Mendips, though, especially when I arrive at the charmingly named village of Nompnett Humpwell.

Nompnett Humpwell is one of those bizarrely monikered small hamlets that are littered around the English countryside. The kind with about twelve residents, a tiny church, and an atmosphere that makes you feel like you've travelled back three hundred years in the space of three hundred yards.

The A-road along which I am travelling reduces to only twenty miles an hour as I go through Nompnett Humpwell, and reduces further to about two miles an hour when I come across yet another bloody accident on the road – this one involving a tractor and several discarded hay bales lying across the tarmac.

There are several Nompnett Humpwellians standing around looking at the hay bales – but not actually doing much to clear them out of the way.

I bang the Volvo's steering wheel in frustration.

Of all the luck!

Not one, but *two* bloody accidents have crossed my path today.

I can feel my jaw clenching as I take in the scene before me, and wonder what the hell I'm going to do now.

I can't just sit here while the Humpwellians all scratch their arses and wonder what to do with all of that hay.

I have a sneaking suspicion the answer is probably going to be 'bring the cows over, so they can eat it over the next several months'. Tiny villages like this move at a snail's pace at the best of times, so if I just wait here for them to sort the situation out, I will no doubt eventually become a Nompnett Humpwellian myself.

As being a resident of a village with a silly name is not at the top of my to-do list, I decide to brave the B-road that leads away just off to my left. Consulting the clear and concise road atlas tells me that this B-road connects to another B-road, and then another B-road, in a spiderweb lattice of small, twisty roads that trace their way all over the Mendips.

I should be fine, as long as I take things easy and consult the atlas frequently.

Taking a deep breath, I indicate left and drive on to the B-road.

As I do, I hear the sonorous, deep chime of a foreboding bell somewhere in the hinterland of my consciousness.

If you've never had the joy of traversing the B-roads of the United Kingdom, then allow me to fill you in.

They are a living, hedgerow-covered hell.

They are the Kardashian family of roads. Beautiful to look at – but comprehensively awful to be anywhere near.

Every single B-road is called the same thing. The B3241. Oh, the numbers might change around, but they essentially all just become the B3241 eventually. And the B3241 is always relatively well tarmacked, but has absolutely no lines painted on it and is always just a little bit *too narrow* to allow two ordinary-sized cars to pass one another comfortably.

B-roads cannot be driven at speed. Ever.

They meander and twist so much that any opportunity to put your foot down is impossible, given that at any second you are likely to have to slow down to a crawl, so you and the bloke in that Audi can pass each other without knocking your wing mirrors off.

Also, the B3241 will contain cyclists. Many, many cyclists.

Any pretence you might have held that Britain was not a nation that favoured physical exercise will be utterly blown away, because on B-roads, there are eleventy million of them.

They are all wearing Lycra, they are all called Clive, and you can bet your bottom dollar they are not going to get over to the side of the road so you can get past. Not until they feel like you've had your fill of watching their large arses pumping up and down mesmerically on the way up the slope.

And there are things that also turn up on B-roads that we do not speak of.

Things so abhorrent and ghastly that uttering their very name will bring you out in hives.

I will say the name of these things *once*, so that you may revel in the anxious terror of it. I will not say it again, because I am on a B-road, and do not want to call them to me. They appear when they hear their name, you see. Like large, diesel-powered Voldemorts.

They are . . .

Tractors.

No, no! No more! Never again shall I utter their name! Not while I'm bumbling along on the B3241, with my head half buried in my clear and concise road atlas.

Get stuck behind one of those things and you can kiss your sanity, and decent miles per gallon, goodbye. I have a feeling that if Satan does exist, then he owns a trac— a large thing powered by diesel, and likes to drive it around the B-roads of the Cotswolds at three miles an hour on a sunny Sunday afternoon in July.

Nevertheless, here I am, on a B-road (currently the B3134, but it'll be the B3241 in no time, you'll see) trying my level best to stay calm, consult my map and make it to the other side of the Mendips with enough time to drive the rest of the way to Weston.

At first, while my progress is slow, I do manage to make headway without too much of a problem.

There's a hairy moment when a woman in a Nissan Juke nearly scrapes one bulbous wheel arch down the side of my driver's-side door, but we both manage to slow down enough to give each other an awkward look, before going on with our stressful, B-road-travelling lives.

I only get stuck behind seven hundred and thirty-eight thousand cyclists as well, which is pretty good for a weekday afternoon.

There are no trac— big, fat, diesel-powered monsters, you'll be pleased to know. I am spared that eldritch horror.

In fact, I'm starting to think I might just get through this situation intact and sane of mind, when something happens which brings my progress to a grinding halt.

I have pulled over in a gravel lay-by of the B3241 and am consulting the road atlas to see where I should go next, and everything looks clear and concise . . . until I turn the page.

Suddenly the atlas is no longer showing me the western side of the Mendips, but has decided to show me the roads to the east of Hull instead.

'Thorngumbald?' I say out loud to myself in the confines of the car's cabin. 'What the hell is Thorngumbald?'

For that is what I'm looking at, folks. A place called Thorngumbald. Which is close to the River Humber, and a good two hundred and fifty miles away from where I'm currently sitting.

I flick the road atlas back to the previous page.

Yep. There's the Mendips, in all their Mendipian glory. When I turn the page I should be treated to even more Mendips. Nothing but Mendips as far as the eye can see.

But nope. I turn the page again. Thorngumbald.

One page Mendips. One page Thorngumbald.

Mendips. Thorngumbald.

West Country. Humberside.

Now, one of two things is going on here . . .

Either this road atlas is saying that right in front of me on the B3241 somewhere is an interdimensional portal that will instantly transport me from the south-west to the north-east, or when the atlas was printed it had some kind of serious problem that put the pages in the wrong order.

In feverish hope, I flick through the atlas to the pages that cover the north-east, praying that the Mendips has been transposed to that area – in a direct, unintentional swap.

Nope. More Thorngumbald.

'Fucking Thorngumbald!' I shout, squeezing the steering wheel tightly in one fist.

I'm sure Thorngumbald is a perfectly nice place, with welcoming residents who would certainly offer me a nice cup of tea and a biscuit – but right now I could happily see Thorngumbald blasted off the face of the planet if it would mean that I could have my Mendips back.

I need my Mendips!

What am I supposed to do without the map for them?

I'll have to . . . *gulp* . . . rely on my own instincts.

Instincts that have been dulled by years of inactivity.

My sense of direction has been completely outsourced to Google Maps. What the hell am I supposed to do?

I have to get moving. The meeting is in an hour!

The B3241 was headed in a westerly direction – the direction Weston-super-Mare is in – so I'll just have to keep driving along it, and hope it throws me out at the end of the Mendips and back into civilisation again.

With fear clutching at my heart (and a letter of complaint already forming in my mind, to be sent to the publishers of my not-so-clear-and-fucking-concise road atlas), I drive out of the lay-by and into the realms of the unknown.

Four hours later, I'm still in the Mendips, and it's now starting to get dark.

My sanity has long deserted me.

There have been three tractors.

THREE.

Each one slower, larger and smellier than the last.

There have been nine hundred and forty-seven million cyclists. I have looked at more middle-aged men's arses than a football stadium of proctologists.

The B3241 has become a snaking, unending path towards oblivion.

Any thoughts of the McGifferty's Pies contract have long since departed. Now, all I am consumed by is the need to escape this green hell. This maze of small, claustrophobic B-roads, which never, ever end.

I have stopped for directions. Of course I have.

The people of Bog were very helpful.

Bog is a very small village in the Mendips that makes Nompnett Humpwell look like downtown Manhattan on a Friday night. I arrived there after having been stuck in the B-road maze for two hours, running out of petrol and with tears in my eyes.

Bog has a petrol station. It consists of one pump and a bloke called Cob sitting in a small kiosk that looks like it was built around the time of the pharaohs. Cob is a squat, red-faced little fellow, replete with bushy brown beard and tremendous eyebrows.

Cob of Bog is very helpful indeed. He fills my petrol tank for me while I stare at the ground and twitch a little.

Cob of Bog also gives me directions.

'Well then, you'll want to leave here on the B3457. Then turn left on to the B3327, until you reach the crossroads of the B3445 and the B3961. Take the B3445. That'll get you north of Sidcot and on to the A38.'

Needless to say, Cob of Bog's directions might as well have been written in hieroglyphs and hidden inside the tomb of Nefertiti, for all the good they do me.

Two hours after my stop in Bog, I am still in the B-roads of the Mendips and considering just lying down in one of the nearby fields, waiting for the inevitable heat-death of the universe to end this nightmare.

If only I had my phone.

If only I had my apps.

If only I had any sense of direction whatsoever.

But I have none of these things, so I'm just going to drive around aimlessly until one of the roads spits me out into a place containing street lamps, or my engine seizes up.

I arrive at a crossroads.

It's the crossroads of the B3245 and the B3234.

Have I been down either of these roads before?

Probably.

In the four hours I've been trapped in the Mendips, I must have driven down every single B-road that exists. Twice.

So, what decision do I make this time? In the near-dark. With no map. And no hope.

I have a go at the B3245, because it's only four digits away from the B3241, which it will inevitably turn into in about four hundred yards anyway, so why prolong the agony.

As I do, I notice a small road sign pointing along a rough-looking road that goes off to the left. The sign says 'Nompnett Humpwell'.

I know that place!

I know it!

I went through it twenty thousand years ago, when I started this odyssey through Mendipian hell!

If I can reach it, I can get out of here!

Without thinking any further, I bump the car on to the rough, barely tarmacked road and squeeze the accelerator, sending me in the direction of the friendly Nompnett Humpwellians, and my salvation.

So now I am on what can only be described as a C-road – which is to say it's barely a road at all. More a dirt track, really, with some tarmac thrown on here and there to provide a little light relief. Quite why I believe this clearly unmaintained strip of road will magically take me all the way to the Humpwellians is beyond me. I have clearly lost all sense of perspective, thanks to the hope that has blossomed in my heart because of that bloody sign.

In more sanguine, logical times I would never have taken this route, obviously. The sign has no indication of how far away Nompnett Humpwell is, and – if we're being honest about it – is only *vaguely* pointing in the direction of the half-tarmacked road anyway.

Nevertheless, my course is now set, and I am determined.

This determination stays with me for about the next two minutes, until the C-road veers sharply off to the right and into a thicket of trees. Whatever pretence the tarmac has made of making this seem like an actual road gives up the ghost, and I now find myself driving along compacted, hard earth in the direction of God knows what.

The trees loom around me in the fading twilight like grand sentinels, watching my fearful progress. High in the branches I can see a lonely crow, staring down at me like a harbinger.

I'm not quite sure what a harbinger is, but this crow certainly is one. It's full to brimming with pure, untainted harbinge. The stare it's giving me suggests that I am the first human being to have been foolish enough to venture along the C-road to Nompnett Humpwell in a very long time.

Turn back, the beady black eyes tell me. *Turn back before you go too far, and drive directly into that duck pond.*

Duck pond?!

WHAT?

Yes, right in front of me, slap bang in the middle of my C-road, is a sodding duck pond. And I am going to drive right into it because I've been looking at a stupid crow rather than the road in front of me.

I let out a squawk of terror as I feel the front of the Volvo pitch downwards at an alarming angle. Instinctively I slam on the brakes, but my tyres are entirely unsuited to hard, packed earth, so my forward progress is sadly not arrested.

The front wheels of the car plunge into the waters of the inexplicable duck pond, sending a huge plume of water into the sky. The ducks – of which there are many, and who were probably having quite a nice, relaxing evening until I came along – fly into the air in a flurry of hectic wings and loud quacking.

The car continues its descent into the pond, and I am only spared a trip right into the middle of the damn thing when the car's front end slams into the soft, wet mud at the bottom, stopping it instantly.

I am thrown forward in my seat and am only saved a nasty whack on the head from the steering wheel by my seat belt.

'Jesus!' I cry, my heart about to jump out of my chest. 'Why is there a fucking duck pond?!'

Answers to that question will be forthcoming soon – but for the moment, I just have to live with my ignorance, and try my hardest to get my heart rate back under control by taking a series of very long, deep breaths.

As I do this, a duck lands on the bonnet.

It gives me a look that speaks many ducky volumes.

It is not happy with my sudden arrival and the subsequent disruption of its relaxed evening.

'Duck,' the duck says.

I blink a couple of times.

I think that duck just said 'duck'.

'Duuuck,' it says again, waddling towards the windscreen. 'Duuuuuck duck.'

I've gone mad.

Comprehensively insane.

The Mendips have finally claimed what's left of my sanity.

Either that, or I've entered into a state of shock that is so enormous, I'm starting to hear things.

Ducks do not say '*duck*'. I am no wildlife expert, but I just know they don't. Not once has David Attenborough ever told me that ducks say their own name. I would have remembered something like that.

'Duuuck,' says the duck, disagreeing with me.

When I think back on this day in years to come – and believe me, I will do that *quite a lot* – I will come to the logical and correct conclusion that the duck was merely quacking, and it just sounded a bit like it was saying the word 'duck'.

Right in the here and now, though, no such thoughts are capable of expressing themselves, and I am wholly convinced I have stumbled across a super-intelligent, self-aware strain of duck that has developed powers of speech.

'Duuuuck, duck, duck, duck,' it says, looking in at me with a curious expression on its . . . face? Beak?

Maybe the shock of my car crashing into the pond has made the duck suddenly self-aware.

If I had crashed into a cow shed, would all the heifers inside have started going 'cow' instead of 'moo'? Would sheep go 'sheeeeep' instead of 'baaaa'?

If I'd have whacked into one of the trees that loom around my crashed car and the disturbed duck pond, would they have all started screaming 'tree!' at me?

And how would I have reacted to that?

Would I have sounded or acted any more insane than I currently feel?

'Go away, duck,' I tell the duck.

'Duck, duck, duck,' the duck replies.

'Please stop saying your own name over and over,' I implore. 'I've just had a car crash, and don't think I can deal with a super-intelligent, self-aware strain of duck.'

'Duck, duck, duck, duuuuuuck, duck.'

Perhaps I should try communicating with it in similar fashion? Maybe it'll understand me that way?

'Human,' I say, in a quiet voice. 'Human, human, huuuuuman, human?'

Shock can do funny things to the huuuuuman brain, it appears.

'Duck, duck,' the duck replies. It then turns its back on me and waddles off to the other end of the car bonnet. Clearly, I said something it didn't like. I have failed in my attempts at first contact.

Suddenly, I feel something very cold and wet seeping into my trainers. I look down to see that the water from the pond has made its way into the car cabin, and is now starting to slosh around my feet.

'Oh fuck!' I exclaim, causing the duck to take flight.

Spurred into motion by this latest nasty development, I push the car door open, allowing more of the freezing-cold pond water to gush into the car.

'Aaaargh!' I wail as I climb out, plunging both legs into about a foot of water. The wet mud beneath my feet sucks greedily at my trainers, and I half stumble up the bank to the safety of dry land.

Once I get there I turn back to my stricken Volvo, and take in the full scene for the first time.

The front of the bonnet is completely submerged in water. I can just about see the front headlights still working underneath the surface. There's no doubt that the engine will be full of water by now. The car is a complete write-off.

'Fuck!' I cry in anger and frustration.

'Duck!' the duck replies, having taken up a new position on the bank next to me.

'No!' I shout at it, shaking my head. 'I said "fuck"!'

'Why are you swearing at that duck?' a voice says from behind me.

I spin around to find myself face-to-face with a squat, red-faced little fellow, replete with bushy brown beard and tremendous eyebrows.

I am nonplussed.

'Cob of Bog?' I ask, stunned to see him here.

'I beg your pardon?' he says.

I point at him. 'You. You're Cob of Bog. You gave me directions.'

He stares at me from under those tremendous eyebrows for a second, before the light of realisation dawns. 'Ah . . . no. That's not me. That's my brother you'll be thinking of.'

'Your brother?'

'Yep.'

'You're not Cob of Bog?'

'Nope.' He points a thumb at his chest. 'I'm Ham.'

'Ham?'

'Yep.'

'Ham of Bog?'

Ham shakes his head. 'Oh, no. I don't go down into Bog. I like a quiet life, me.'

This is an *incredible* thing to say. The only way you could possibly have a quieter life than living in Bog is if you were fucking dead.

Ham not of Bog points at my stricken vehicle. 'Why did you drive into my duck pond?'

Which is a valid question at this stage.

'I was . . . I was trying to get to Nompnett Humpwell,' I tell Ham not of Bog.

His tremendous eyebrows knit together. 'You can't get to Nompnett coming this way, young fella.'

'No. I'd gathered that,' I tell him. 'What with there being a duck pond in the way and everything.' Time, I feel, to enquire as to why there is a duck pond right in the middle of what's supposed to be a C-road.

Ham not of Bog shakes his head again, this time ruefully. 'Oh. This hasn't really been a road for donkey's years. Not since they put in that B-road.'

'Which one? The B3241?'

Ham not of Bog nods. 'Yep. That's the bugger.'

'But there was a *sign*,' I say. 'It told me Nompnett Humpwell was along this road.'

'Oh? Well, I can tell you, young fella – that's not right at all.' Ham not of Bog scratches his hairy cheek. 'Sign must've got turned around somehow. Can't get to Nompnett this way, not through my farmland.'

'Duck,' the duck agrees, from Ham not of Bog's side.

I look down at the duck, and then back at my new non-Boggian friend. 'Did that duck just say "duck"?' I ask him.

Ham not of Bog looks down at Duck. 'I don't think so. I think he just quacked, didn't he?'

I nod, happy to have it confirmed that I've not gone *completely* insane. 'Yes. I'm sure he just quacked.'

'Duck, duck,' says Duck in agreement. But I can tell the little bastard is lying.

Ham not of Bog looks at my car. 'I don't think you'll be getting her going again.'

I also look disconsolately at it. 'No. Definitely not.'

'We'll have to pull her out.' Ham not of Bog thinks for a second. 'I know, I'll get Cob to come up here with his tow truck. He's got one down at the station in Bog.'

'Cob of Bog has a truck?'

'Yep. We'll have you out of there in a jiffy, my friend.'

'Thank you, Mr Ham.'

'Ham's my first name, young fella. Surname's Giles.'

Farmer Giles.

Of course, of course.

'How will you get hold of Cob of Bog?' I ask. 'We're miles from any phones.'

Ham Giles now looks at me like I've just stepped off the boat. 'You're kidding, aren't you?' He reaches into his trouser pocket and pulls out an iPhone. 'I'll just text him.'

By the time the sun has gone down, Cob of Bog has arrived and has pulled my poor car out of the duck pond. While he did this, I borrowed Ham's phone and called McGifferty's Pies to apologise for my non-attendance. Paul McGifferty was quite understanding – and agreed to speak via Skype tomorrow afternoon. He seemed to take great pity on me when I explained what had happened. I guess if someone tells you they couldn't get to their appointment with you because they drove into a duck pond, you kind of have to give them the benefit of the doubt.

Ham asked me why I had no phone of my own, so I had to explain the digital detox to him.

He nodded when I'd finished my story. 'Yep. I know what you mean. I spent way too much of my time playing that there *Crossy Road* on the toilet. Gave me piles, it did.'

'Sounds painful.'

'Yep. Sure was. Cob over there still has one of those old Nokia phones. Does nothing except make phone calls and send texts. He's never had piles, as far as I'm aware.' Ham nods sagely and gives me a meaningful look. 'I'd say what you're doing is a bloody good thing there, Andy. Your arse will thank you for it.'

Quite possibly, but my car insurance premium won't.

And neither will my prospects of holding down a job.

Today has been an unmitigated disaster, all thanks to my attempts to live a tech-free life.

I don't get back in my front door until after midnight.

The journey with the AA guy was interminable, as he drove very slowly (for an AA guy, anyway) and liked to listen to late-night Radio 4. By the time we arrived in my street, I'd endured a documentary about tectonic plate movement, a study of Russian art from the nineteenth century, and the recollections of a pumpkin farmer. This last one – you'll be amazed to discover – mainly involved recollecting pumpkins.

I end the day with a large glass of wine. I never normally drink this late, but I've earned it, I think. No one should have to get through an entire day where they miss a job interview, ruin their car and have a run-in with a self-aware duck, without some kind of alcohol to cushion the blow.

As I sit here on my couch, letting the tension of the day slowly seep out of me as the wine seeps in, I try very hard to justify continuing the detox, given the detrimental effect it's had on my work today.

If I don't have a job, I'm likely to be a hell of a lot more stressed and have a lot more sleepless nights than have been caused by my reliance on technology.

I know I made a promise to myself (and Fergus, in a roundabout way) to see this detox through, but for all the good it's doing me physically, the cost might just be too damn high.

As I get to the bottom of the glass, I resolve to keep the detox going for the time being – but it had better not lead me into any more sticky situations!

Mind you, what could be worse than a day spent going insane in the Mendips?

If we peer into the future, we will see that the answer to this question involves a toilet window and the local police force.

You might want to strap yourselves in . . .

Chapter Six

Dating and the Deep State

It has now been a shameful eleven months since my last romantic encounter.

Nearly a year since I had the pleasure of a woman's company.

The woman in question was Christa, and we met on Tinder – back during a time when I was allowed to use such a thing.

Christa was quite nice. I didn't have much time to assess her further than that, as we only went on two dates. The second one did end with a heavy make-out session on the bonnet of her Mazda, though. There wasn't a third date. I can't for the life of me remember why, right now.

Christa was not the first lady I have met this way.

In fact, I've had a series of four dalliances with women – all thanks to swiping right.

All of them were quite nice.

. . .

. . . . . .

Sadly, there's not a lot else I can say, if I'm being brutally honest. Tinder is an excellent way to make the process of meeting women easy, but it doesn't lend itself to deep and meaningful relationships. Not in my experience, anyway.

People rarely tend to actually chat to one another on Tinder – which is definitely part of the problem. I can't tell you how many conversations I've started, only to get total radio silence, or for everything to peter out after a few bland *Hey how are you*s. It's either that, or you just go straight to arranging a meet-up without getting to know one another via a bit of online chit-chat first – at least, that's been how it's worked out for me.

It's all very casual, very throwaway and very temporary. I struggle to think of a meaningful relationship I actually have had – in the last six or seven years, anyway.

Now, I know this is starting to make me sound like an awful misogynist, but let me reassure you, the women in question were just as blasé about the whole thing as me. Tinder is the kind of place you go to for sex, and maybe a little short-term companionship. It's not really the venue for finding the love of your life.

Prior to Tinder, I tried dating on Match.com, and that resulted in a couple of more long-term relationships – both of which ended with me being on the receiving end of the dumping.

The first one hurt.

The second one hurt more.

That's why I was so delighted when Tinder came along. After a couple of heartbreaks, the idea of just engaging in periodic casual flirtations seemed terrific. Much easier on the heart.

And that's been the situation with Andy Bellows and his love life for the past decade.

And right about now I would be spending a lot more time on Tinder – if I were allowed to. It's been too long since I had the thrill of meeting somebody new . . . and hopefully engaging them in some carefree, casual sex.

But Tinder is strictly off limits, as we all know. So, sex – casual or otherwise – is sadly *also* off limits.

And it's not even like I can . . . er . . . enjoy some *gentleman's entertainment* to take the edge off. That's barred from me as well.

I can't remember the last time I actually owned some pornography on physical media. I threw out my last DVD years ago. It was called *Backyard Barbecue Bone Session 3*, as I recall. What barbecuing that actually went on was not done in a safe or hygienic way, I remember that.

So, then, I am left in something of a bind.

I would dearly love to enjoy the company of a new woman, but do not have the capacity to find one.

'Why don't you just go clubbing?' Fergus asks me over a coffee, on one of our periodic trips to the local Costa. This is where we tend to meet up most of the time. It's the only place that does a half-decent flat white. England is full of cafés claiming to make a flat white – only to then deliver you a bloody cappuccino.

'Clubbing? Me?' I shake my head. 'Not a bloody chance. Not my scene at all. I'll just have to accept that until the detox is over, I have no way of finding new love,' I say, with a mournful little sigh.

Fergus thinks for a moment. 'You could try the personal ads.'

I give him a confused look. 'The what?'

'The personal ads at the back of our paper.'

I let out a disbelieving chuckle. 'You still *do those?*'

Fergus nods. 'Oh yes. Right next to the classified ads for cars.' He scratches his nose. 'I mean, there's not many of them any more. Almost everyone does everything online now. But there's still a few people out there who don't. And there's enough of them to fill up half a page or so.'

'Old people, Fergus.'

'What?'

'They'll all be *old* people. They're the only ones who would still use something like a personal ad.'

Fergus sniffs. 'That's a bit ageist.'

I give him a look. 'Are you telling me that they aren't likely to be old people?'

'I don't know for sure. But you don't know until you look.'

He leans over to one side and rummages around in his big, brown leather man bag for a second, before producing a copy of the *Daily Local News*. He opens it up and looks through a few of the pages, before folding the paper in half on a particular open page and handing it to me. 'There you are. Personal ads.'

And would you believe it? He's absolutely right!

There are six of them.

Four I instantly dismiss as being from those of a middle-aged or older disposition. The fifth is from a bloke called Brian, who's forty-two and enjoys having fun and long walks. Possible serial killer potential there, and no mistake.

The sixth and final choice actually sounds quite interesting.

Henrietta is twenty-nine, an antiques dealer and a fan of travelling and cookery. She writes in a very erudite and intelligent manner, and manages to pack a lot of information into the small square of text she's afforded in the paper's column.

What Henrietta is not a fan of is online dating, or the Internet in general.

'I believe the World Wide Web is turning us into soulless robots, and I want to meet someone with a good, kind soul,' she says. 'I'm hoping there might be somebody out there who will see this advertisement who feels the same way.'

She would probably quite like me . . . I am, after all, Captain Detox. And while I don't have quite the dislike of the Internet that she clearly has, I am someone who is currently eschewing the delights of the online world, and that might be good enough for her.

Henrietta also describes herself as tall and brunette, with a slim figure, and the type of person who enjoys intelligent conversation with stimulating company.

There's something about her use of the word 'stimulating' that is quite . . . *stimulating*.

All in all, it actually sounds like Henrietta might be a real possibility for a potential date. This is quite, quite *unbelievable*.

But . . . I can't meet up with her.

'Why not?' Fergus enquires, after I read the advert to him.

'Because it's not 1994, Fergus. This isn't how things are done these days.'

'It's how Henrietta seems to do things. And it's how you do things as well, mate. For the moment, anyway. Why don't you want to give it a go?'

I squirm in the seat a little. 'Well, I have no idea what she looks like, for starters. On Tinder you get a picture.'

'Oh? So you're just about the looks, are you?' He gives me a look of admonishment. 'A bit *shallow*, don't you think?'

I look up to the ceiling in disgust. 'Of course I'm shallow, Fergus. I use *Tinder*.'

'Well, maybe this would be a good opportunity for you to not put looks first for a change,' he suggests.

'Hmmm. Possibly,' I reply, still staring at Henrietta's advert.

Fergus is probably right.

I shouldn't be so shallow.

And I have to admit, there's something quite thrilling about the idea of meeting up with someone on a real, proper, 100 per cent *blind date*.

I haven't been on one of those since I was seventeen and my mate Kevin set me up with his sister's friend Hannah. Hannah was way out of my league, and I never saw her again, but that hour I spent staring at her boobs in the local McDonald's was one of the happiest of my teenage life.

What the hell. Let's give it a go.

'I see by the speculative look on your face that you're considering it?' Fergus says, obviously very pleased with himself.

'Yes. What harm could it do? And when you get right down to it, it's really not that much different from swiping right.'

'Indeed.' Fergus's eyes flash. 'And if it goes well, I can write about it for the paper.'

I point a finger at him. 'I am not meant to be a source of constant material for you, Mr Brailsworth.'

He feigns a look of disappointment. 'But you're so good at it.'

'Yes, well. I'm just going to hopefully go on a blind date with a nice lady from the antiquated personal ads. I'm sure nothing newsworthy will come of it.'

There are two ways I can respond to Henrietta's personal ad. There's an email address set up by the paper that I assume will forward my response on to her. Or there's an actual phone voicemail service I can leave a message on.

I'd like to use the former, but am of course only allowed to do the latter. This requires me to make a proper phone call. I don't think I've done that since the dinosaurs ruled the earth.

Nevertheless, I construct what I intend to say on a bit of notepaper and give the number a call. At the sound of the beep, I recite the few paragraphs I've hastily scrawled down that explain a little about myself. Most of the information is cribbed from an old draft of my Match.com profile I found in my Word documents, and contains the usual platitudes and rather bland pronouncements you always use on dating profiles.

I also mention a brief bit about the digital detox, as I can see that working on good old Henrietta. If nothing else, it should explain why I'm using this ancient personal ads service, rather than the far more normal and up-to-date online method.

The whole experience of leaving my reply to her ad is like stepping back in time. I even have a bemused half smile on my face as I recite my landline number, so Henrietta can call me back if she's interested in a date.

If I'm being honest with myself, I think most of the reason why I'm doing all of this is just to experience the nostalgia of the pre-Internet age of dating. Surely not even Fergus's *Daily Local News* can keep the personal ads up for much longer, and I want to give it a go before it becomes a completely extinct practice. I'm like the man who travelled on the last steam locomotive all those years ago. I'm enjoying the journey, rather than being all that concerned about the destination.

It'll be lovely to meet Henrietta, and who knows what might come of it. But even if it's just one date and I never see her again, at least I will have got to experience something the singletons of yesteryear would have gone through all the time.

Henrietta calls me back in the evening.

She sounds extraordinarily pleasant. Speaking with an upper-class accent that is instantly exotic to my decidedly working-class ears, Henrietta is clearly an intelligent woman, with a bright personality and a very dry sense of humour. I stammer a little during the conversation, but manage to just about acquit myself in an acceptable fashion overall, I think.

Henrietta must think so, as she agrees to meet me for a coffee – not in the local Costa that Fergus and I frequent, but in a cute little café she knows about, tucked away on the high street of a village called Longfield, not too far from town.

Not a village like Bog, I hasten to add. This one is just off the main road, and very easy to get to, thank you very much. Which is just as well, as I doubt my insurance company will be too pleased if I drive the courtesy Polo into a bloody duck pond.

I've never heard of Heirloom Coffee, but Henrietta says they do a very nice Colombian blend there, which instantly piques my interest – not just in the café, but also in Henrietta. She's obviously a coffee lover, and that definitely gives us something in common. If nothing else, we can talk about our favourite roasts for an hour.

I agree to meet her at Heirloom Coffee at 11 a.m. on Sunday morning, and hang up the phone with a smile on my face.

That went very well. Very well indeed.

I can feel a real blossom of excitement in my gut. Far more than before the last date I went on, with Christa. I can only put this down to the fact that I know so very little about Henrietta, beyond what I've gleaned from one phone call and a brief personal ad. With Christa, I knew what she looked like before I'd even met her, and had a good working knowledge of who she was based on a light bit of Facebook stalking.

That's the thing about modern dating. You go in armed with a lot of information about the other person, as they no doubt do with you. It's robbed the experience of some of its mystery.

Not the case with Henrietta, though. I'm walking into the unknown, and that's quite a thrilling prospect.

❖ ❖ ❖

When I venture into Heirloom Coffee, I get a gorgeous whiff of that Colombian blend Henrietta mentioned, and am instantly delighted she suggested the place.

The coffee shop is housed in a very old terraced building along the medieval high street in Longfield, and is just about the quaintest place I've ever been in. It certainly has a lot more personality than the bloody Costa that Fergus and I go to.

Just look at those exposed wooden beams, would you? And that hardwood floor is a wonderful shade of dusky brown. The tables and chairs look like antiques, and are covered in long, lacy tablecloths that must be a right bugger to put on a hot wash.

The walls are painted in a fresh white that contrasts nicely, and several large, arty black-and-white images of coffee cups and coffee machine parts are hung on them. These instantly appeal to the designer in me. They're very well composed, and it's a nice juxtaposition with the rest of the decor.

The place is about half full of very content-looking coffee imbibers. As well they should be, given the rather lovely atmosphere the place has.

Along the back wall is a wide counter, on which is placed a large shiny barista machine – the only truly modern thing in a space otherwise full to bursting with antique British character – and a small cabinet containing all manner of delectable treats, like muffins and flapjacks. Other than these, though, nothing in here breaks the illusion of being transported back to a bucolic, olde worlde period of English history.

It's like a coffee shop you'd find in Hobbiton.

I half expect to walk up to the counter and be greeted by Frodo Baggins, asking me if I'd like a latte or a cappuccino.

As it goes, however, it's not Frodo who greets me, but a pretty, black-haired barista wearing an apron with the café's simple logo on it, and a winning smile on her face. This is fine by me, as hairy exposed feet are not hygienic in a café setting.

'Morning,' I say to her. 'Is it OK to sit anywhere?'

'Yeah, sure,' she replies, maintaining that bright smile. 'Just grab a table, and I'll come over with a couple of menus.' As she's talking, I can see the light of recognition dawn in her eyes.

This is a look I've seen a fair bit of since Fergus's story went into the paper. It appears I have stumbled across someone else who has read the article about my detox.

'Thanks very much,' I say to her, and turn away before she has the chance to question me about it. I'm already feeling nervous about meeting with Henrietta; I'm not sure a chat about my new-found local infamy would help me out right now.

I select a table in one of the bay windows that looks out on to the village square.

Longfield seems like a very nice place to live – if you can afford it. There's no actual sign of the long field itself, but I'm sure it's knocking around here somewhere.

The black-haired barista brings over a couple of menus and places them on the table.

As she does this, her eyes narrow. 'I'm sorry, but do I know you? You look awfully familiar.'

I smile a bit awkwardly. 'Um. Do you read the *Daily Local News*?'

Her eyes widen. 'Oh yes! You're him, aren't you? The guy who's doing the detox!'

'Yep. That's me.'

'I read all about you on the paper's website about a week ago. I was searching for information about detoxing and stumbled across it.'

'Oh, that's . . . that's great.'

The bright smile is gone from her face, and she actually looks a little anguished now. 'Could I ask you how it's going? Only, I—'

At that moment, the café doorbell chimes, indicating that another customer has walked in. And not just any customer, either. This must be Henrietta!

The woman is a tall brunette, wearing a long, flowing mauve dress and a black tailored jacket. She also has a large leather handbag strapped across her chest. Henrietta is pretty much exactly as she described herself in her advert and the phone call we shared.

She's also quite *beautiful*.

Score!

The black-haired barista turns to her, seemingly forgetting about what she was saying to me. That anguished look on her face is gone, and she's all smiles again. 'Good morning!' she says to my blind date.

'Hello there,' Henrietta replies – and I know it's her from the rich, upper-class accent. 'I'm here to meet someone.' She sees me sitting there in the bay window and inclines her head in my direction. 'That gentleman there, I believe.'

I rise from my seat and smile. 'Henrietta? I'm Andy. And I'm very pleased to meet you.'

Henrietta comes over to me and takes my hand, shaking it gently.

I can see now that she is a little taller than me, which is a first.

In fact, Henrietta is not the kind of woman who has historically been my type. But, my word, am I pleased she agreed to meet me today. I may have to alter what my type is after this.

'It's good to meet you too, Andy,' she replies. 'I frankly wasn't expecting anyone to respond to that silly advert. Not in this day and age.' She smiles, lighting up her aquiline features. 'Lucky for me there's at least one man around who doesn't live his life online either.' She cocks her head. 'Temporarily, anyway.'

I nod my head and laugh. 'Yep. That's me.'

This reminds me of the interrupted conversation I was having with the barista, who I see is now walking back over to the counter, probably to grab some menus. I can't help but feel a little bad she didn't get to say more. That look of anguish in her eyes troubled me.

But . . . there's nothing more I can do about that, and I really should turn my undivided attention to the tall, attractive, posh woman who has deigned to meet me for a coffee.

I wonder what her legs look like under that dress?

Henrietta and I sit down at the table, and thus begins the blind date proper.

We both order a drink. Me, my usual flat white, and Henrietta asks for a soy latte with a twist of vanilla, as she takes off the handbag and pops it down by her feet.

When the barista brings the coffees over, I'm amazed to discover that she has actually made me a flat white. This simply does not happen. Not in quaint English cafés, anyway.

I'll definitely be coming back here again.

The first few minutes of the date go by in a relatively run-of-the-mill fashion. Henrietta and I chat briefly about how nice the coffee shop is, and how good our drinks are. We then talk a bit about the weather (as you do) and how warm it's been. All very bland and inoffensive, which is par for the course on a first date.

All of the real conversation is being conducted non-verbally, and I think things are going quite well on that level. I'm getting the impression that Henrietta is warming to me as we chat, and I feel much the same way. If nothing else, I find that accent of hers very attractive to listen to. It's like I'm holding a conversation with the nicer parts of the Home Counties.

We talk about what we both do for a living. She's interested in my job as a graphics designer, and I'm quite intrigued that she runs her antiques business out of her home.

'That must take up a lot of space,' I say with a chuckle.

'Oh, yes. It does. My double garage is bursting with all manner of things.' She arches an eyebrow and grins. 'You should come by and have a look sometime.'

OK, OK. That's good. That sounds *promising*.

All going very well so far.

'How's business?' I ask, trying hard not to blush.

'Not so bad. The antiques game tends to be largely resistant to the vagaries of the economy. I always have customers.'

'Good to know. I suppose things are much the same for me. Companies always need designs to sell their products.'

'That's great, Andy,' Henrietta says, and then arches an eyebrow. 'How do you think we're doing? Is the small talk small enough for you?'

I smile. 'I think so. It may have got a bit too in-depth there for a moment when we mentioned the economy, but I think we're fine otherwise.'

Henrietta laughs a rich, full-throated laugh, and I join in.

We really are getting on very, very well.

Then I look up as the bell above the coffee shop door goes ding. Two police officers walk in, chatting to one other and wearing the relieved looks of on-duty coppers who have found they have enough time in their shift to get a cup of coffee and enjoy a sit-down.

I don't pay much attention to them as they walk in.

The same, however, cannot be said for Henrietta.

That full-throated laugh is immediately stifled with a strange strangled noise as she spots the coppers. Henrietta's eyes narrow and her brow closes in over them like a fresh thunderstorm.

'Um,' I say, slightly taken aback by this change of demeanour. 'Are you OK?'

'Yes. Yes, I'm fine,' Henrietta tells me, though she's now started shifting around on her chair uncomfortably – in a way that Herbert Bilch could probably relate to, thanks to his shenanigans in my Volvo's passenger seat.

What is it with me and making people shifty since I started this detox?

I never used to make people shifty.

But now it seems like I can't hold more than five minutes of conversation with someone without them pretending that an earthquake measuring six on the Richter scale has just struck.

'Are you sure?' I ask. 'Because if I've said or done anything—'

'You've done nothing!' she reassures me, in a deeply non-reassuring tone of voice.

'Oh, OK.'

And yet, my date still looks like the San Andreas Fault has just let go, so something is definitely going on.

Then Henrietta starts throwing tentative glances over at the two coppers, who have just given their orders to the barista and are now leaning against the counter chatting with her.

Hmmmm.

Someone becoming instantly tense and out of sorts the second they see a police officer is *always* a sign of good things, isn't it?

Henrietta then makes a huge play of looking out of the window, into the quaint village street beyond. She plants an elbow on the table and covers the side of her head with her hand.

'Are they watching?' she says in a stage whisper.

'Excuse me?'

'Are they watching?'

'Watching what?'

'Us!'

I look over at the two coppers again, who are now clearly contemplating the purchase of muffins. Nothing about their demeanour suggests they give two hoots about what Henrietta and I are up to.

'No, I don't think they—'

She's fucking gone.

Henrietta has *disappeared*.

Vanished into thin air.

One second she's there . . . the next she's clearly not.

Has she been taken up?

Is the Rapture upon us?

Have aliens beamed her up to their ship for some probing?

Has Henrietta been discorporated by some evil entit—

. . . Oh no. She's just under the table.

I suppose I'd better find out why.

I do hope she's not suffered some kind of *event*.

I lean down, flip up the long tablecloth and stick my head under the table as well, in order to find out what afflicts her. 'Um . . . are you OK, Henrietta? What are you doing?'

'Hiding!'

'Hiding?'

'Yes! Hiding from *them*!'

She stabs a finger over at where the two police officers have apparently decided that the muffins are a go, and are making their selections in a very considered manner.

'You're hiding from the police?'

'Yes. Of course I am!'

Oh, bloody hell. I'm on a date with a criminal.

A crook. A lag. A felon. A villain. A delinquent of the highest order.

'Why?' I venture, now acutely aware that to everyone else in the coffee shop, I appear to be holding a conversation with the underside of an oak coffee table.

'Because they are part of it, Andy!'

'Part of what?'

'*The organisation!*' There's a hectic excitement in Henrietta's voice now as she continues to stare out at the coppers like a hunting dog on point.

'What? The police force?' I hazard.

'That's just part of it! The *organisation* is everywhere!

'Is it?'

'Yes! And it has many names!'

'Does it?'

'Yes! The Illuminati!'

'Oh.'

'The Great Ones!'

'Really?'

'The deep state!'

'Huh?'

'The low men in yellow coats!'

'Pretty sure that one's a Stephen King book.'

'They're everywhere, Andy!' Henrietta continues, wild-eyed – and obviously very keen to impress upon me the importance of all of this. 'And they control the Internet! Everything on it!'

'Even *Crossy Road*?' I suggest . . . for some reason. The game did give Ham not of Bog piles, so anything's possible.

'Of course!' Henrietta grabs my ankle. 'Everything is controlled by them!'

OK . . . so I'm not having coffee with a hardened criminal, it appears, just someone who's clearly a conspiracy theorist of the highest order.

Joy of Illuminati joys.

'That's why it was so nice to hear from someone who doesn't use their Internet too!' Henrietta whispers at me as she peeks out from behind the long tablecloth to see what the coppers are up to.

One has chosen blueberry, the other chocolate – if you're at all interested.

'You mean me?' I ask.

'Of course I mean you! You must know they're out there, watching us! You must see that there's no escape from the deep state! Why else would you have stopped using all that technology?'

'I couldn't have a proper poo,' I say, by way of explanation. 'And my neck hurts.'

'You're my type of man, Andy!' Henrietta exclaims, ignoring this. 'I thought that as soon as I heard from you! Just the right kind of guy to run away with me!'

'Run away with you?!' I reply in shock.

'Yes! And run away from *them*! Get away from their cameras and their spying technology!' Henrietta grabs my other ankle. I'm slightly worried she's about to yank me off my chair and under the table with her. 'We could live off-grid together!' she exclaims. 'It could be so good! Run away with me, Andy!'

Yes, well . . .

I think we can safely say that the only running away I'll be doing when it comes to Henrietta is *from* her.

'Oh God! They're coming over!' Henrietta squeals, looking back over at the coppers. 'Look normal!' she orders.

'Look normal?'

'Yes! Look normal!'

'I'm not sure I can do that with my head under the table,' I point out.

'Then sit up! Sit up and look like you don't care about them!'

Well, that shouldn't be too difficult – I really *don't* care about them.

I do quite fancy a chocolate muffin now, though, if I'm being honest. They look scrumptious.

It's probably best I do stop talking to the underside of the table. I think I've started to draw some funny glances.

I sit up, just in time to see the two coppers take their delicious-looking muffins over to a table in the bay on the other side of the main door, right beside the window. They both sit in seats that look out on to the street, their coffee and muffins on the table in front of them.

They haven't noticed that I've had my head stuck under the tablecloth for the past few minutes . . . but an elderly couple about ten feet away from me have, and therefore have very uncertain looks on their faces.

I offer them a friendly smile and take a sip of my rapidly cooling flat white.

As I do this, I am rather horrified to see Henrietta appear from under the tablecloth on all fours – making her way across the floor, towards the back of the coffee shop at a speed that must be playing havoc with her kneecaps. She deliberately keeps at least two tables between her and the police officers as she goes.

The elderly couple watch her do this for a moment, and then look back at me, as if I have some sort of explanation.

I don't, of course. But I feel as if I should say something.

'We're on a blind date,' I tell them. 'I answered a personal ad in the paper,' I add, as if this in any way clarifies what the hell is going on here.

The old man looks deeply confused, but his wife actually nods slowly and grimaces slightly.

I suppose at this point I should get up and follow Henrietta to make sure she's OK.

Or I could just disappear out of the front door and leave her to it, but I did agree to come on this date with her, so I feel some sense of responsibility about what's going on here.

Rising from my seat, I see that Henrietta has made it to the coffee shop counter, where the barista is watching her, a mixture of befuddlement and amazement on her face.

'Toilet?!' Henrietta snaps at her.

The barista slowly raises one hand, indicating down the hallway just to the left of the counter, and Henrietta takes off down it, all the time throwing looks back at where the two police officers are. Both seem completely oblivious to what's going on behind them. Those muffins must be bloody fantastic.

I hurry over, in time to see Henrietta disappear into the toilet at the end of the corridor.

'Is your . . . your friend all right?' the barista asks me.

'I have absolutely no idea,' I reply truthfully. 'We're on a blind date.'

'Going well, is it?' she asks. Somewhat unnecessarily, I feel. Any date in which one participant tries to escape on their hands and knees cannot be considered to be *going well*.

'Not really, no,' I tell her. 'She thinks . . . she thinks those coppers are after her.'

The barista goes wide-eyed. 'Why?'

I look over at them, and then back to her. 'Um . . . I'm not sure. Possibly something to do with *Crossy Road* and Stephen King; I can't quite figure it all out.'

'Oh . . . right. Should I . . . maybe go and check on her?'

I nod. 'Yeah. If you would. That might be an *exceptionally* good idea.'

OK, I'm passing the buck mightily here, but if the coppers haven't noticed what's going on so far, they will certainly have to respond if I go clattering into the toilet while a woman is in there on her own.

Better to let the barista sort this out, while I attempt to lean nonchalantly on the counter and look at the muffins.

The barista hurries away in pursuit of Henrietta.

A few moments go by.

I think I've decided I'm going to have a white chocolate and raspberry muffin. They look particularly tasty.

'Hey!' the barista calls to me from the corridor. 'I need your help here!'

I rush off down the corridor towards her, casting the muffins from my mind for the moment.

'What's going on?' I enquire.

'She's stuck!' the barista hisses.

'She's what?'

'Stuck! In the *window*!'

'Stuck in the window?'

'Yes! Come and look!'

The barista grabs me by the arm and pulls me towards the toilet.

When she pushes the door open, I am greeted by the sight of Henrietta's bottom, halfway up the wall, above the small toilet cistern. Somehow, her dress has ridden up around her waist and I can see her knickers.

They are large, pink, covered in pictures of Hello Kitty, and THERE ARE COPPERS OUTSIDE. I REALLY SHOULDN'T BE HERE. THIS IS PROBABLY A SEX CRIME.

'Oh God!' I cry in horror.

'I can't pull her out!' the barista exclaims in distress. 'I yanked her leg, but she isn't budging!'

'Get me out of here!' I hear Henrietta cry in a muffled voice . . . from wherever her top half may be. 'Get me out of here this instant!'

'You think we should get the coppers to help?' I suggest. 'Once I've left the toilet, I mean?'

'No! No police!' Henrietta screams.

'I thought of that,' the barista says. 'She wouldn't have any of it.'

'That's right!' Henrietta exclaims. 'You two can pull me out yourselves! No police needed! Come on! Chop chop!'

Henrietta is now thrashing around to such an extent that she's likely to do herself an injury if she doesn't stop.

'OK! We won't get the police!' I shout towards her top end, wherever it may be.

This calms Henrietta down a bit, enough at least to stop her knocking the plaster off the toilet wall with her wildly thrashing feet.

'Well, we've got to get her out,' the barista says. 'I've got a coffee shop to run!'

'Maybe . . . maybe if we take an end each, we can . . . pull her out together?' I propose.

She nods. 'Good idea. You go outside then. There's a fire exit door at the end of the corridor. Turn right once you get out.'

'OK, will do,' I reply.

It's nice to have somebody else telling me what to do at this stage. I feel so much more comfortable in stressful situations when I'm not in charge.

Following the barista's instructions, I clatter out through the fire exit door to find myself in a small courtyard. Turning right, I see the rest of Henrietta – red-faced and dishevelled – poking out of the tiny toilet window.

'Are you all right?' I say to her, going over.

'Get me out!' she demands. 'Get me out before they see me!'

'OK, OK! We'll get you out. Don't worry!'

'Are you there?' I hear the barista call from inside.

'Yes!' I respond, taking Henrietta by the arms.

'OK then! After three!' the barista shouts.

'Yes! After three it is!'

'One! Two! Three!'

I pull at Henrietta's arms as hard as I dare.

'Aaaarggh!' Henrietta wails. Sadly, she doesn't budge an inch.

'No good?' the barista exclaims.

'No!' I reply.

'Try again?!'

'Yes!'

'OK! One! Two! Three!'

'Aaaaarrggghhh!' Henrietta screams. This really isn't doing us any good whatsoever.

'This isn't working!' I shout. 'She's not coming out! I daren't pull any harder!'

'Wait?! What?!' the barista yells.

'I said *I daren't pull any harder!*'

'Oh, fuck it! *I'm* pulling too!'

'Bloody hell!' I exclaim. 'No wonder it's not working!'

'No! Given the fact she's not a Christmas cracker, I'm not surprised!'

'Come on! Come on! Get me out of this window!' Henrietta howls. 'I'm starting to chafe badly! And they'll be out here with us at any moment! You'll see! They'll be wanting to probe us! That's what they do!'

'Oh, give it a bloody rest, will you,' I snap at her.

All I wanted to do was have a fun blind date with a nice lady I met without using the bloody Internet, and I've ended up in an impromptu human tug-of-war with a barista, outside a toilet, with what is clearly a raving conspiracy theorist.

'Don't you tell me to give it a rest!' Henrietta snaps. 'They're real! They're coming for us all!'

'Oh, leave it out. You'll be telling me the moon landings didn't happen next.'

Henrietta instantly goes rigid and stares right into my eyes. 'They didn't!'

'Oh, for crying out loud.'

'It was clearly staged!'

'Was it.'

'Of course it was! The technology just wasn't there for them to do it at that time! They set the whole thing up on a sound stage in Area 51!'

'Yeah, yeah, yeah . . . and I bet the earth is flat too.'

Henrietta laughs in a derisory fashion. 'Of course the earth isn't flat!'

'Oh, good. At least you're not that bad.'

'It is hollow, though!'

'Oh, for fuck's sake.' I roll my eyes and look past Henrietta at the toilet window. 'YOU PUSH, I'LL PULL!' I scream at the barista. I need this to be over. And I need it to be over *now*.

'OK!' she replies. 'One! Two! Three!'

This time, we're in sync with what to do – but it doesn't result in Henrietta being freed from her predicament. She does move about three or so inches in my direction, but that's about as far as it goes.

'Aaaaargggh!' Henrietta screeches, forcing me to stop pulling before I detach her arms from their sockets.

'It's no good!' I shout. 'She's stuck fast!'

'Oh, bloody hell!' I hear the cry come back at me. There's a few moments of silence before the barista responds again. 'That's it! I'm getting the police!'

'No! No!' Henrietta wails. 'Not the police!'

'Good grief, it's fine!' I tell her. 'There's nothing wrong with them. They're here to help us!'

She shakes her head vociferously. 'No! They're part of the organisation! The deep state! They're part of the *machine*!'

'The same machine that faked the moon landings?'

'Yes!'

'Bloody hell. Where do you get all this nonsense from?'

'YouTube!'

'Oh, of bloody course, *YouTube*.'

'Yes! Yes! The truth is all there . . . all you have to do is go and look for it!' Poor old Henrietta is raving now. But that might be because all the blood has gone to her head, since she's stuck fast in a toilet window.

'Look for it, eh?' I respond, half-heartedly.

'Yes! You don't have to be a sheep, Andy! You just have to have your eyes opened to the way the world really is!'

'By going on YouTube?'

'Yes!'

'The place with all the videos of cats flushing toilets?'

'Yes! I mean . . . I mean no!'

'And people unboxing their new *Star Wars* dollies?'

'What?'

'And drunk people falling down holes?'

'Pardon?'

'And "Baby Shark". Do do do do doo do.'

'What are you saying?'

'I'm saying that you think I should look for the truth about the way the world is run somewhere I can also find videos of people jumping naked into piles of horse poo, and eating fifty hot dogs? Possibly at the same time? That's where the truth is, is it?'

'Yes . . . yes, that's right!'

My brow furrows as another thought occurs. 'Hang on a minute . . . if you think the Internet is evil, and that's how this organisation is tracking you . . . why are you on bloody YouTube in the first place?'

'I'm not! Not any more! I left it behind once I saw what I needed to see! They showed me all I needed to be shown! I saw the only videos I really needed to!'

'Charlie Bit Me and "Gangnam Style"?'

'What?'

Sadly, I don't have time to continue this line of thought, because one of the coppers has just appeared at the fire exit door, his mouth surrounded by crumbs of chocolate muffin.

'What seems to be the trouble here?' he asks me, still chewing.

Henrietta immediately goes bug-eyed and starts to wag her finger at the copper like it's a malfunctioning windscreen wiper.

'No! Don't let him near me!' she cries in an imperious voice. 'He wants to hand me over to his evil superiors, probably for some lengthy probing! I saw it! I saw it all on YouTube!'

I give the copper a look that speaks volumes.

He returns the look with one of confusion. 'What's she on about? I've never been on YouTube.'

I sigh and rub my eyes. 'That, mate, is something you should be eternally grateful for.'

Henrietta is freed from her predicament about an hour later, with the assistance of both coppers, two carloads of their colleagues and the local fire brigade.

There's barely enough room in the small courtyard at the back of Heirloom Coffee to fit everyone.

And all through the rescue mission, Henrietta continues to insist that they are all part of some grand conspiracy against her . . . and the people of this country. The only conspiracy I can detect, though, is about getting one person to pay for all the coffees and muffins that are consumed during the rescue process – and I'll give you three guesses who ends up being on the receiving end of it.

The first copper I spoke to – he of the chocolate muffin – sidles over to me, as the barista and I stand there watching a burly fireman slowly lift Henrietta down from the toilet window, which has been widened by the removal of the wooden framework and several bricks.

Funnily enough, Henrietta seems somewhat less perturbed at the intervention of the emergency services now, given that she's being assisted to the ground by a handsome fireman.

There's a joke here somewhere about her possibly not being quite so bothered about a potential probing after all . . . but I'm not going to dwell on it, as I'm tired, hungry and ever so slightly fed up.

'How do you know her?' the copper asks us.

'I met her . . . met her for a date,' I reply.

'A date?'

'Yes. I answered her ad in the personals at the back of the paper.'

The copper looks downright baffled by this. 'They still do those?'

'Apparently,' I say with a sigh.

The copper gives me a slightly awkward look. 'Maybe stick to Tinder next time, eh?'

My face goes flat. 'Yes. Thank you, Officer. I'll bear that in mind.'

He nods his head. 'Good stuff. Well . . . I think we're pretty much done here.' He looks at the barista. 'Sorry about the hole in your wall.'

She gives him a wan smile. 'Don't worry. The insurance will cover it, with any luck.'

'Ah, yeah . . . I'm sure it will. If you need anything from us, though, don't hesitate to give me a shout at the station.'

'Will do.'

'Great. Thanks to the both of you. I hope you have a nice rest of the day.'

We wish him well as he leaves us and goes to help Henrietta as she is escorted out of the courtyard by the hunky fireman.

She seems to have calmed down considerably – no doubt thanks to the uniform and all of those muscles. Though it could also just be because she's knackered.

I know I am.

'Bloody hell,' the barista eventually remarks, slumping against the wall.

'Tell me about it,' I reply.

'That was bizarre.'

'Yes.'

'And you were here with her *on a date?*' she asks, slightly amazed.

I nod my head. 'I was.' I cock my head to one side and think for a second. 'I'm not sure there will be another one. What do you think?'

This makes her chuckle. 'So . . . you answered a personal ad in the *paper?*'

'Yes. I'm not allowed to use Tinder any more.'

'Because of your detox.'

'Because of my detox, yes.' I rub my hands over my face. 'A detox that has led me into meeting way too many bizarre individuals, it has to be said.'

'I'm sorry?'

I wave a hand. 'Never mind.'

The barista stands up straight, giving the new hole in the wall a critical look. 'Well, I guess I'd better clean up this mess as best I can. Get something over that hole before the weather changes.'

I feel instantly guilty. 'I'll give you a hand, if you like.'

'Thank you,' she replies, with a rather tired smile.

'What's your name, by the way?' I ask.

'Grace,' the barista replies. 'And you're Andy Bellows, aren't you?'

'I certainly am.' I thrust out a hand. 'Pleased to meet you.'

'And you.'

'You make a very good flat white,' I add.

'Thank you.'

'This is a very nice coffee shop.' I glance at the hole in the wall. 'Even with a toilet that's probably going to be out of commission for a while.'

'Thanks. Like I said to the policeman, hopefully the insurance will cover it OK.' She smiles. 'And I'm very proud of the rest of the place. All the bits that haven't been smacked about by the emergency services all afternoon.'

'Oh? You own it?'

'Yeah, it's mine,' Grace says with obvious pride.

'Oh. That's nice. Really . . . *nice.*'

This is where the conversation dries up, unfortunately. Normally I can keep the small talk up for much longer, but – as stated – I'm feeling bloody knackered thanks to all of Henrietta's shenanigans.

In fact, when you add today's events to what happened in the Mendips and with Herbert Bilch, it's becoming painfully obvious that living without the Internet is something that's throwing up more problems and difficulties than it's worth. I'm not sure I can cope any more.

It's plainly clear that living a life without technology is not an easy thing to do. The world around me is so geared towards using it, that attempting not to leads down paths of disaster and weirdness – no matter how hard you try to avoid them.

This is an unpleasant realisation.

I knew I was addicted to the online world, but I had no idea to what extent the *actual* world was so reliant on it.

And look at the damage the Internet can do!

Good old Henrietta has obviously been affected by the lies and conspiracies that can be uncovered on the Internet with very little effort. Anything that ends with you suffering friction burns to your midriff and the exposure of your underwear to many members of the emergency services cannot be a good thing.

And let's not forget about Herbert Bilch and his desperation to be followed and loved by hordes of complete strangers on Instagram. That led him to maxing out his mother's credit card and living a constant lie.

There's a growing part of me that truly wants nothing to do with being online any more. My digital detox is starting to expose me to facets of the Internet and social media that I do not like one little bit.

Unfortunately, the part of me that feels like this is being comprehensively drowned out by the rest of me – which would rather not end up in another duck pond, or on a date with a mad conspiracy theorist.

I hate to say it, but for all the problems the Internet throws up, there are more problems it solves. On balance, the good outweighs the bad – I *think*.

Dating on the Internet is certainly a good thing. I've managed to prove that today.

OK, you may not find the woman of your dreams, but you're also less likely to end up standing in a courtyard, arguing about YouTube with someone who wears Hello Kitty knickers and thinks the moon landings didn't happen.

I would like to think that Henrietta is alone in her wild and crazy way of thinking . . . but all the evidence I've seen in the dark recesses of the Internet proves that this probably isn't the case.

Don't believe me? Search for the Flat Earth Society on YouTube sometime.

If you need to chew on something while you do it, I recommend a nice chocolate muffin.

Chapter Seven

State of Grace

I wake the next morning – after a solid nine hours of uninterrupted sleep – and instantly feel highly annoyed.

I had a very stressful day yesterday. Hanging out with the emergency services is never what I'd call a relaxing experience. How can I possibly have followed that up with a nice, deep sleep?

It's *ridiculous*.

It should have taken me ages to get off to sleep – but nope, I was fast asleep almost the instant my head hit the pillow.

I crunch through my morning cereal still feeling highly annoyed.

You see, I came to a decision last night. Just before I drifted off into that deep sleep.

I'm going to give up the detox.

Again.

But this time I at least feel like I've given it a good go.

And I know some people might be disappointed – not least of whom will be Fergus. But I've reached a point where I just don't think I can carry on with it. My life has become too bloody difficult.

After I've finished my cereal, I am going to take a shower, have a nice cup of coffee and then log on to my laptop and have a look at the world again for the first time in weeks. Then I'll go to Fergus's house to get my box of goodies back. I will apologise to him for ending the detox, and explain the reasons behind it. I will be firm and unwavering.

Then I can get back to living my life of convenience and ease – without having to worry what might happen to me the next time I step outside of my flat.

Who knows what catastrophes I will be avoiding by giving up?

A run-in with a horny Afghan hound, for instance. Or accidentally setting fire to my pubic hair. How about being arrested for molesting a traffic cone? Or being chased down the high street by an elderly woman dressed as Hitler?

All of these things – and many, many more – are quite possible if I continue with my offline lifestyle any longer.

And yes, I have to accept that if I'm going to avoid such potential future disasters, I may have to put up with a few health issues. But I don't remember the IBS really being *all that bad*. And I'm sure the jaw problems were really more about the stress I was under at the time, trying to get that Fluidity contract.

I'm pretty sure that if I go back to my proper lifestyle, things will be a bit better now.

And besides . . . I'm not responsible for anyone else, am I?

This is my life, and I can live it however I choose.

I don't owe anybody anything, and if I want to make the decision to give up the detox, then I am perfectly entitled to do so. There's literally nothing stopping me from just—

Ding dong.

I look up at the clock on my kitchen wall.

Odd time for someone to be calling. The postie never comes before 1 p.m. these days, and I have a very clear and very concise 'No Cold Callers' sticker that prevents unwanted guests at the door.

With a faint feeling of curiosity (and, let's face it, a degree of trepidation; I am British, and am therefore automatically uncomfortable at the prospect of having to speak to strangers on my doorstep), I rise from the breakfast bar and walk over to the door.

When I open it, I am relieved to see it is not a Jehovah's Witness or someone trying to sell me mops.

No.

It's Grace.

From the coffee shop.

Colour me amazed.

She's now dressed in jeans and a cream shirt instead of her work clothes, but it's definitely her.

'Hi,' I say, in a very surprised tone.

'Hello,' she replies, offering an awkward smile.

'It's Grace, isn't it?' I ask.

'Yes. That's me. Grace.' She shuffles a bit. 'And you're Andy.'

'Yes indeed.'

You'd think we'd met a year ago and not yesterday from the way this conversation is going.

'What can I do for you, Grace?'

A sudden sinking feeling strikes me.

She wants to sue me.

Yes. That must be it.

Grace wants to sue me for the broken toilet window.

She could sue Henrietta, but she seemed more than a little off-balance. It'd be far easier to squeeze cash out of the seemingly normal sap responsible for arranging the date in the first place. One that led to a large and possibly structurally unsound hole in her back wall.

'I just . . . I just . . .' she begins, but can't seem to get the words out.

I just want to wring you dry of all the money you have, you bloody idiot.

That's what she's about to say, but she's obviously so angry at me that it's taking her a moment to compose herself.

'I just wanted to ask you about your detox,' Grace eventually blurts out, all in a rush.

'My detox?' I reply, amazed. Maybe I'm not about to be taken to the cleaners.

'Yes. I just wanted to know . . . to know . . .'

There are tears in her eyes. That strange anguished look I saw on her face before Henrietta came in to the coffee shop.

'. . . to know . . . is it working? Is it helping? Do you feel better?'

Oh God. She's crying now. Standing on my doorstep and crying.

What the hell do I do?

I've never had a crying woman on my doorstep before. It's new territory for me.

'Would you . . . like to come in?' I venture.

Grace looks down at the floor for a second, before looking back up at me and nodding. 'Yes please.'

I step back and let her into the flat – and instantly regret it. The place is a pigsty.

Of course it's a pigsty. I am a single man in his thirties. There'd be something wrong with the universe if it wasn't a pigsty, to be quite frank.

Still, at least the kitchen area isn't too bad – other than the dirty dishes in the sink, soaking in a load of freezing cold, scummy water.

I'll just escort her over to the breakfast bar, thus avoiding the sink area, and clear away my bowl of muesli as swiftly as possible.

'Sit down here, Grace,' I say, in as soothing a voice as I can manage. 'Would you like a cup of tea?'

She nods again, producing a tissue from her pocket and wiping her nose. 'Yes please. I really am sorry about this.'

'No. No. That's fine. I can't promise the tea will be anything like you'd make in your lovely coffee shop, but it might make you feel a bit better.'

I threw the compliment in there just in case there are any lingering notions about suing me. A bit of light flattery can never hurt in these situations.

'I'm sure it will.'

Another thought occurs while I'm popping teabags into two of my cleaner mugs. 'How did you find me?' I ask Grace.

She looks a bit sheepish. 'I looked your address up on your website. It's in your contacts section.' Her eyes go wide. 'I'm not trying to stalk you or anything!'

'No! I'm sure you're not!'

'I read your article in the paper,' Grace continues, 'and really wanted to speak to you. I knew your address, so I thought I'd pop by. I thought you might be able to . . . able to help me.'

'No problem at all,' I tell her. She's obviously quite upset about something, and I don't want to make it worse by making her feel unwelcome.

If today does end up with me having a knitting needle shoved into my privates by my new black-haired stalker, it won't be because I was rude.

'Yesterday was awful, wasn't it?' I say.

'Yes. It certainly was.'

'Is that why . . . why you're here? Why you're . . . um . . . upset?'

Grace shakes her head. 'No. It was all fine, really. I rang the insurers, and it looks like they will cover the cost of the window. And I don't think having the police and fire brigade swarming around the place for so long will do any real damage to the shop's reputation . . . at least I hope not.' She wipes her nose with the tissue again.

Eep.

I know I actually have nothing to feel guilty about – Henrietta was the one who caused all of the trouble yesterday – but I feel it all the same. Character flaw.

'Here you go,' I say in what I assume is a comforting voice, as I place a cup of tea reverentially in front of her.

We all know the power of a freshly brewed cup of tea. It should have her feeling as right as rain in no time.

'Thank you,' Grace replies, and takes a sip. 'I'm here because I've been having a really bad time of it lately.'

I lean against the breakfast bar and take a sip of my own tea.

Mmmmm. Calming. 'I'm sorry to hear that,' I tell her.

'Thanks.' Grace looks up for a second, obviously composing herself before carrying on. 'When I read your article in the paper, it really struck a nerve . . . because I'm the same as you.'

'What? How so?'

'Addicted to the Internet.'

'Really?'

'Yeah. I spend way too much time on there. I know I do. I've lost my social life . . . a lot of my friends. I don't go out.' She looks pained for a moment. 'Hell, even coming here today took just about all the nerve I had. My life consists of working at the coffee shop and sitting at home on my bloody computer.'

I'm stunned.

I am a thirty-six-year-old single man with a pigsty for a flat.

I am also very much not an alpha male. I have watched every season of *Star Trek: The Next Generation*, can give you the complete history of Batman without breaking a sweat and have beaten *Dark Souls* on the PlayStation 4 six times.

It makes sense for someone like me to have an addiction to the Internet.

Grace, on the other hand, is quite clearly a beautiful raven-haired woman with her own extremely picturesque coffee house and a vibrant clientele. This is not the kind of person you'd expect would be chained to her PC.

Now, I know this is *grossly* stereotypical of me. I apologise for that. But I'm just having a very hard time imagining that Grace is like me.

Or like I *was*, anyway.

Grace catches the expression on my face. 'You don't believe me, do you?'

'Well, I, er, um,' I splutter, not really knowing how to respond.

'It is true, though. The first thing I do in the morning is look at Instagram. I follow more influencers than I care to mention.' She grimaces. 'OK, I'll mention it. There's over a hundred. A good two dozen of them are just baristas. There are more pictures of steam wands on my feed than is healthy for any one human being.'

'Well, that's not too bad,' I try to argue. 'You do run a coffee shop.'

'True, but they're only a small handful of the dozens and dozens of people I've found myself obsessively following in the last three years.'

'None of them are called Lucas La Forte, are they?' I say with a wince.

'No. Why?'

'Never mind. Not important. If it's just Instagram you're talking about, though, it can't be all that bad?'

For some reason, I am determined to prove that Grace does not have an issue with her Internet use like I have. I have no idea why I feel like this, but I do.

'It's not just Instagram, Andy,' she tells me solemnly. 'I'm on Facebook for hours and hours every day, watching videos and chatting in groups. Most of them seem to involve people either trying to sell me make-up or teaching me how to bake cakes. Then there's *Minecraft*.'

'You play *Minecraft*?'

'There aren't many hours in the day when I *don't* play *Minecraft*.'

'I've never played it myself. Is it any good?'

'Yes, Andy. It's like electronic crack.'

'Isn't it just building stuff?'

'Yep. More or less. But you can build *anything*. You can create *anything*. And then share it with people like you . . . probably on Facebook and Instagram.'

'Why?' I blurt out.

'Why what?'

'Why are you so addicted?'

She narrows her eyes. 'Why are you?'

I shrug my shoulders. 'I'm lazy,' I tell her matter-of-factly. 'I'm also not massively keen on having to communicate with people, if I'm honest. And I get bored easily. I need constant distraction.'

Grace blinks a couple of times. 'That's all very self-aware of you.'

'Yep. That's me. As self-aware as a duck.'

'I beg your pardon?'

'Never mind. It's just my brain. It does things like that from time to time. Anyway, you never answered my question. Why do you think you spend so much time online?'

This is actually a hideously personal thing to ask, but I'm almost feeling slightly annoyed that Grace has turned up at my door like this, needing to share her own problems. I have enough of my own to be dealing with.

Also, I get very awkward when someone says they need my help. I'm not temperamentally prepared to help people. I'm the one who usually needs the assistance.

For evidence of this, please think back upon strange women trapped in windows, and duck ponds.

I'm not very good at being awkward around people I don't know very well, and it tends to morph into frustration.

Blimey, I *am* being very self-aware, aren't I?

Is this an offshoot of the detox I hadn't thought about? Has my brain been so starved of stimuli that it's begun to critically evaluate the meat sack it's being carried around in?

And is that a good thing or not?

Grace is looking at me with an expression that could go one of two ways. Either she's going to get understandably mad at the tone of voice I'm using, and get up to leave – or she's going to let me get away with it (for now) and give me a response.

When she goes for the latter option, I breathe a small sigh of surprised relief.

'I wasn't always like this,' she tells me, picking at a chip in the handle of the mug in front of her. 'Never used to use the Internet much at all.'

'What changed?'

That anguish is back once more, only this time Grace isn't even trying to hide it. 'My sister died,' she says in a small voice.

Oh, very well done, Bellows. Well done indeed, you complete buffoon.

Any irritation or embarrassment I was feeling has been instantly extinguished. And rightly so.

'Oh God, I'm so sorry, Grace,' I say. 'I should never have asked. I—'

'No. It's OK. It's probably good for me to say it out loud to someone' – she tries a smile – 'instead of just writing about it on a bloody forum.'

'Well, OK, but it's really none of my business. I'm so sorry.'

'No, it's fine. You weren't expecting a mad woman to turn up at your door this morning.'

'You're not mad. Clearly,' I tell her.

Grace smiles briefly, then takes a very deep breath before continuing. 'When Megan died – that's my sister's name – I . . . *went in on myself*. Stopped going out. Stopped communicating with people. Her death hit me really hard.'

'I'm sure.'

'And that's when I started to spend so much time on the web. It was . . . *easier*, you know? Megan left Heirloom Coffee to me, so I had to spend a lot of my time keeping it running, but whenever I wasn't there, I was at home, on the Internet. Still am.'

The haunted look in her eyes is truly awful.

'And I've been miserable for a long time, because of it,' she carries on. 'Never felt so unhappy in my life. So alone. I feel like the world is passing me by.' She looks squarely into my eyes. 'And that's when I read the article about you. About what you were doing. It sounded like such a good idea.'

'Did it?'

'Yes! Of course! I've been thinking about trying to cut down on my Internet usage for a while now, but just never had the guts to do it. It felt like giving up too much. Giving up the only thing I had. And I wanted to speak to you, because I just wanted to find out . . .'

'Find what out?'

She gives me a shy look. 'Whether it's working or not?' She sits up. 'Is it, Andy? Do you feel better? Has life got better since you gave it all up? Has it all been worth it?' The tears are back in her eyes again. 'Only, I feel so bad right now . . . and I need to know if there's something I can do to make . . . make myself feel better. I need to know if doing a digital detox like you will be good for me.'

Oh boy.

Oh boy, oh boy, oh boy.

What the hell do I say to that?

How on earth can I tell Grace that I'm *giving up*? That it's been one disaster after another? That I don't care what health improvements I've had – it's still too much to deal with, and I want it to end?

I thought I had problems with my online addiction, but a bad neck and an attack of the shits is nothing compared to the grief of losing someone you love!

So, what the hell am I supposed to say?

How do I burst her bubble? How do I tell her that it hasn't worked for me?

'Yes, it's working,' I reply, in a bland voice.

What?

What?!

What are you *doing*?

'I feel much better than I did,' I continue – scarcely believing the words that are coming out of my mouth.

Grace is obviously someone in need of help. She needs to hear that quitting her online addiction will make her feel better about herself – and who am I to tell her it won't?

She's not me. Her situation could be completely different to mine. Just because I've had problems, it doesn't mean she will. She doesn't look like the kind of person who would be dumb enough to drive into a duck pond or go on a date with a conspiracy nut. The detox could be the best thing for her.

She's clearly very unhappy living online. It's having a horrible effect on her. I bet the detox would help her out immeasurably.

You could say the same thing about yourself, Bellows – so why are you quitting?

That's different.

Is it? Because she's clearly in as much emotional pain as you were physical. If you think the detox would be good for her, why isn't it still good for you?

'Oh, that's so good to hear, Andy!' Grace exclaims, bringing me sharply back to the real world, outside my own stupid head. 'My brain is always buzzing, you know?' she says. '*Fizzing.* I never seem to relax. Can't sleep most nights. Does that go away?'

'Yeah. It does.'

And that's the truth. I *do* sleep better. My brain *does* feel calmer.

'Do you feel healthier as well? The story said you were suffering with muscle pains and stuff like that.' Grace puts one hand on the back of her neck. 'I get terrible shooting pains in my neck and back.'

'Yeah, they're better too.'

And that's *also* the truth.

Blimey, saying it all out loud really does hammer home just how much of an effect the detox has had on me.

'Great!' Grace says, now extremely animated.

Oh Christ, I've given her *hope.* What an awful mistake to make.

'And do you miss it all?'

'Miss what?'

'Being online? Social media, games, the Internet?'

I nod my head. 'Yes. I do. A lot.'

And this is the biggest truth of all, of course. I do miss it all. *Hugely.*

Although, if I'm being brutally honest, I didn't think about going on Twitter once this morning when I got up. Or Facebook, for that matter.

Nor have I for *days*, if I really think about it.

169

Blimey (again).

Grace is now standing up, leaning across the breakfast bar. 'But it's worth it? Worth missing out on all that stuff? Because you feel better? You feel *happier*?'

'Yes,' I repeat – and now I have no idea whether I'm lying to her or telling the truth. This is all dreadfully confusing.

'So, should I join you then?'

'*Join me?*'

'Yes! On the detox? Can I join you doing it?'

'You want to do it *with* me?'

'Yes! If you don't mind? I'll probably need a bit of help with it – but I can lend you some moral support as well.'

Say *no*, Bellows!

We don't want to do the detox any more, remember?

We want to go back online again!

We want to play *Call of Duty* again!

We want to swipe right on Tinder, get directions on Google Maps and order Mexican on Uber Eats again!

'Yes. OK, Grace. That would be lovely,' I hear myself say.

. . . Because, what's going here? When you get right down to it?

I have a rather beautiful woman in my kitchen, who I clearly have a lot in common with, asking me to help her detox from an unhealthy online lifestyle. This will probably mean spending a fair bit of time with her – with that smile, that gorgeous black hair, and the skills required to make a decent flat white in a country largely bereft of them.

Of course, as we've already discussed, staying on the detox may also lead to me getting probed by an Afghan hound while my pubic hair is on fire . . . but I fear I am now prepared to take that risk.

'Great! Thanks, Andy! I'm really grateful you're happy to help me out,' Grace tells me, having no idea that she's probably going to have to watch the Afghan hound defile me, and drive me to the hospital with third-degree burns.

'No problem. Really happy to.'

'Great.'

'Yeah.'

'So . . . how do you do it?'

'Do what?'

'Detox?'

'Oh. I have a leaflet here somewhere . . .'

I go rummaging in the kitchen drawers and manage to find the annoying pamphlet Dr Hu gave me. 'Here, have a look at this.' I hand over 'Digital Detoxing and You', and while Grace reads it, I make us a fresh cup of tea.

By the time I plonk it down in front of her, she's got to the end, and looks a bit sick.

'That's appalling,' she says, handing it back. 'Written by some-one who is clearly a serial killer.'

This makes me laugh. 'Yes, that's what I thought. But if you can ignore the tone, the information is pretty much correct. It's what I've been sticking to.'

Grace swallows hard and looks deeply worried.

I can sympathise. It's exactly the same response I had when I first realised the extent of what the detox was.

'Gosh. That's . . . that's *everything*, isn't it?' she says, pulling out a necklace from under her blouse. She starts to fiddle absently with the small golden locket hanging on the end of it.

'Yes,' I reply. 'It's a massive shock to the system, I can tell you.'

'I feel a bit light-headed even considering it.' Grace grimaces. 'Don't you feel . . . like . . . *divorced* from everything?'

'Yep. It's like you've had the world taken away from you. Or at least . . . that's what it feels like at first.'

'But it gets better?'

'Ye-es,' I say uncertainly. I want to be encouraging, but I also don't want to barefaced lie to her.

'OK, that's good,' Grace says, nodding. I'm not sure she really believes me, given the way she's continuing to fiddle nervously with that locket.

'What's that?' I ask, trying to change the conversation.

Grace looks down and laughs ruefully. 'Sorry. It's a habit I've picked up. Any time I'm feeling a bit on edge, I start twiddling with it. Probably shouldn't. It's very old.'

'Where did you get it?'

'It was my grandmother's. When she died, it was passed down to my mother, and when she died, Megan had it. It came to me after . . . well . . .'

Oh, bloody hell. She's lost so many people!

'It's very beautiful,' I say, voice a little thick.

'Thank you. It opens up.' Grace plays with the clasp for a brief moment. Her hands are shaking as she does so. I guess that's because she's still digesting the horror of what the detox entails, but I'm sure there's also an element of being nervous about sharing so much of herself with someone she's only just met.

'Here, these are pictures of Megan, Mum and Gran inside.' Grace shows me the opened locket, and there are indeed tiny pictures of three very similar-looking raven-haired ladies. You can tell instantly that they are related to Grace from their features. 'Gran's picture was taken in the sixties, Mum's in the eighties and Megan's about a year before she died.'

'It's very nice. A . . . a nice thing for you to have.'

'It's my most precious thing. My family's only heirloom.' Grace smiles warmly as she closes the locket again and tucks it back in her blouse. 'Megan named the coffee shop after it.'

'Where's your father?' I ask, hoping against hope that she's not about to tell me he's dead as well. I'm finding all of this heartbreaking enough.

'He lives in New Zealand. When Mum passed, it affected him deeply. He just . . . well . . . ran away.'

Oh, great. So, not dead. Just on the other side of the world.

Grace sees the expression on my face. 'Don't think badly of him, please. He's honestly a good man . . . just not very strong. I still speak to him all the time on FaceTime.' Grace's eyes go wide. 'Oh no! Would I still be able to do that if I'm on a detox?'

'Yes! I'm sure!' I reply quickly. 'There are no real rules here, Grace. Just try to do what you can. And it's only for a few weeks, anyway.'

'Fair enough.' I can see her visibly relax hearing this. 'What about you? Where are your family?'

'My mum and dad live in Scotland. Moved up there a few years ago. They weren't . . . running away from anything. They've just always loved the place and wanted to go there in their retirement. Can't blame them really. The pace of life up there is much more laid-back.'

'Do you see them much?' she asks.

'Probably not as much as I should,' I answer honestly. 'Scotland's a ball-ache to get to at the best of times.' I scratch my cheek. 'Actually, I think I speak to them more on FaceTime than I do in real life, as well.'

I wince a little internally as I say this. I really should get in touch with Mum and Dad more. Grace's sad story proves that your parents won't be around for your whole life, and I have been quite neglectful of them recently.

Oh, great.

Now I get a little more guilt to add to the pile, alongside what happened at Heirloom Coffee with Henrietta.

'So, do you think you still want to try the detox?' I ask Grace, once more neatly diverting the subject of conversation. Sadly, I've managed to divert it back to the thing I was previously trying to divert it *away from*, proving that I probably need some kind of satellite navigation system for my brain as much as I do for my car.

Grace seems to think about it for a second, before nodding her head once. 'Yes. I do want to try it. I need to get back out into the world. I need to stop hiding away. And I'm not going to do that if I'm glued to my bloody laptop.' She reaches into her jeans pocket and pulls out her phone. 'Or this thing.' Grace thumbs the screen and turns the phone around to show me. It is covered in apps. Far more even than were on mine. The ones that take the most prominence at the top of the screen are Snapchat, Instagram, Facebook and Pinterest. Behind all of them is a picture of her and Megan. You couldn't sum up Grace's predicament better than with this single image if you tried. 'Just look at the state of that screen, would you? All those apps!' she says with disgust.

'Yeah. Mine was a lot like that too.'

Grace turns the phone back to her own face and looks at it angrily. 'No more,' she says in a determined voice. 'No more of *you*.'

And with that, she quickly gets up from the breakfast bar, walks over to the sink and drops the phone into the dirty water, where it sinks underneath the saucepan still half covered in the remnants of last night's bolognaise sauce.

'Er, why did you do that?' I ask her as she turns and looks at me triumphantly.

'Didn't you get rid of all of your tech?'

'Yes. I put it in a box.'

Grace stares at me for a moment with a blank expression on her face, before looking down at the sink. 'Bugger,' she says. 'And I've got four months left on my contract.'

It's nearly midday before Grace leaves my flat, carrying her phone in a sandwich bag full of rice.

I agree to pop round to the coffee shop in a couple of days, to see how she's getting on. I figure by that time she'll be seriously contemplating giving up on the detox, having been bereft of tech for forty-eight hours. She'll probably need some encouragement to stick with it at that point.

I have to marvel at my change of heart over the whole thing.

I was fully prepared to give up my own detox right before Grace called at my door, but now I know somebody is attempting to do it alongside me, it has given me a renewed resolve.

Is it just because misery loves company?

Or is it because, deep down, I know the idea of cutting my time spent on the Internet is a good thing, regardless of the problems it also causes?

Or is it just because Grace is a pretty girl? One I'd probably like to spend more time with?

I just don't know.

But when you get right down to it, it doesn't really matter. What matters is that I *am* going to continue with the detox, and that makes me feel good about myself.

I don't actually like to quit. I don't like to let people down. And I sure as hell don't like to think that my life is controlled by anyone – or anything – other than *me*.

I'm sure there's a chance I will still meet with some kind of disaster – simply because I'm so inadequately prepared to live a life without the comfort and convenience of the online world – but at least there's someone doing the detox alongside me now. Someone who is calm in a crisis. If I can't stop myself being chased down the street by a pensioner dressed as Hitler, then hopefully Grace can.

And maybe in return I can help her get her own life back together again.

One with you in it, Bellows?

Maybe?

Hopefully?

We'll just have to see, I guess.

Chapter Eight

TURNING A CORNER

When I do get to Heirloom Coffee two days later, I can see that I have arrived just in time.

Grace looks harried, tired and twitchy.

'How's it going then?' I ask her as I sip my flat white. It's still very good, even though it's been made by someone who's clearly extremely *on edge*.

'I feel like someone's cut one of my legs off,' she replies as she feverishly cleans a coffee cup. 'No. Not my leg. My *head*.' Grace slams the cup down on to the counter, before picking up another one and going to work on it just as hard. 'You've made me cut my head off, Andy.'

'Sorry about that,' I tell her, suppressing a smile. I know exactly how she feels, of course. That feeling of dislocation and disconnection is extremely hard to cope with.

'Do you know how awful it is not knowing what your favourite people are up to?' Grace continues. 'I haven't a clue what Chrissy Teigen is doing this morning. Or Selena Gomez. They could both be *dead*, for all I know.'

'Not all that likely, but I get your point.'

'And what's happening in the bloody *world*, Andy? I tried to watch Sky News this morning, but it just went on and on about an MP being caught with a prostitute. For a good *fifteen minutes*. I'm used to getting all the news I want in *seconds*. I usually don't have to wait for Kay Burley to stop banging on about some Tory's adventures in a knocking shop before hearing about the weather!'

'Things do take longer when you're not online,' I concede.

Grace bangs the second cup down on the counter. 'Yes! They certainly do!'

'It gets easier,' I promise.

'It had *better*! I don't want to live in a world where I don't know what make-up Kylie Jenner is wearing out tonight.' She thinks about this for a second. 'No. I don't want to live in a world where I *care* about what make-up Kylie Jenner is wearing out tonight!'

'It takes a while for your brain to rewire itself,' I say. 'The damn thing gets used to being fed certain information on a regular basis. It doesn't like it when it gets starved.'

Grace thinks for a moment. 'That sounds about right.'

'The trick is, you just have to start feeding it something *different*.'

She nods. 'That's a very clever way of putting it.'

I shrug. 'Is it? Thanks!' I think for a moment. 'Maybe my brain's started to function more efficiently now I'm not bombarding it with rubbish all the time. Yours could too!'

Grace gives me a look of mock outrage. 'What are you saying about my brain, Andy?'

'Oh God! Sorry! I didn't mean your brain was . . . you know . . .'

She smiles and puts her hand over mine briefly. 'Relax. I was only messing about. And I like your idea of feeding my brain something else . . . but the question is, what?'

'I've been reading lots of books,' I suggest.

'Hmmm. Yeah. That sounds good. But I'd like to do something a little bigger and more meaningful than that. Something that occupies my mind, but also gives me a real sense of what life is like without being so insular.'

'What do you mean?'

Grace goes a little wide-eyed. 'I need to *get out*, Andy. Now I'm not online, I just feel so restless at home. It's frankly a blessing to come into work! And I'm surrounded by temptation when I'm in my house as well. I want to spend as little time there as possible at the moment.' As Grace talks, the locket comes out again, and she starts to twiddle it. 'It's strange. Home has always been my haven, because I've been able to communicate with the world from it, using all of my lovely technology. But now? I feel *hemmed in*. Even after only two days. I *have* to get out!'

'Well, that's got to be a good thing, hasn't it?' I reply. 'You said you were tired of just being stuck at home?'

Grace now looks confused. 'I think so . . . I'm not sure. On the one hand, I'm desperate to be away from my house, but on the other, I'm terrified of going out . . . thanks to being such a shut-in over the past few years.'

I nod my head. 'I can understand that. Doing a digital detox is something that comes with both its good points and bad. I've learned that fast. It forces you to confront things about yourself that can be . . . *challenging*.'

'Maybe that's what I need!' Grace says with some excitement.

'What?'

'A *challenge*!'

'Really?'

'Yes! Something that gets me out of my house and challenges my fears about going out into the world.'

'Like what?'

Grace lapses into silence and continues to twiddle with her locket. Then she looks down at it, and a smile spreads across her face. 'Tell me Andy . . . have you ever been to Bath?'

◆ ◆ ◆

The answer to that question is 'no'.

Bath is not a place I've ever had the chance to visit. For no other reason than I've never had any call to go there, it's quite a long journey away on some fairly questionable A-roads and I've never really had a thing for bathing in public. This is largely due to the fact that I have odd-shaped toes. They are gangly toes. Toes that require being covered up at all times. The last thing the good people of Bath need is to see the toes of Andy Bellows.

'Are you telling me you've never visited Bath because of your *toes*, Andy?' Grace asks me from the passenger seat of my rental Polo.

'More or less, yes,' I reply, noticing a sign that says we're only ten miles from the city now.

'I don't think you're required to actually *have a bath* in Bath, you know.'

'But it's right there – in the name,' I argue. 'You can hardly go to Bath without taking a *bath*, can you? It just wouldn't be right.'

'Well, I don't particularly want to have a bath in Bath today, Andy, so I guess we'll just have to fly in the face of convention on this one.'

'Fine by me. My toes can remain hidden.' I frown a little. 'To tell you the truth, I'm not so keen on getting my knees out in public, either.'

'Well, rest assured I will not be requiring a look at your knees or your toes on this entire trip.'

'Excellent. So, what are we going to do then?'

'It's like we discussed, remember?'

I do remember . . .

. . . and I'm still not sure this is a good idea *at all*.

Grace's proposal in the coffee shop was quite simple: that she and I should take ourselves off to a large city, and try to negotiate our way around it, using absolutely nothing but our wits.

No electronic devices. No apps. No Internet. And no maps.

Gulp.

Having already driven my car into a duck pond the last time I tried to get around without technology, this is naturally something I am very wary of doing.

'This will be different,' Grace confidently told me. 'Because you won't be doing it alone.'

Which is more than fair enough, I suppose. Grace should be able to stop me from entering into too many disasters. She's already managed to navigate us straight to the outskirts of Bath, using only road signs, without any deviations or issues whatsoever. It's quite remarkable.

And why Bath?

Quite simple, really.

Bath is where the jeweller's that made Grace's locket used to be. They were called Hackett & Mostrum Fine Jewellery. Grace's grandmother told her when she was young that they shut down a long time ago, but Grace wants to find the building where they were and see what's become of it.

Obviously, she also wants to find out how well she can cope with being out and about in a busy city, instead of being parked at home in front of a screen. And I have to confess, I'm interested to see how I get on with it, as well.

I'm now several weeks into the detox and have settled into a routine that isn't too traumatic. But that's largely because I haven't really done that much with myself. I've been working, reading, taking walks and watching a lot of TV – but that's about it.

The combination of feeling uncertain about the world now I'm divorced from so much of it, and the fear of stumbling into any more catastrophes, has left me a little *inert*.

I think a day out in Bath might be just as much of a challenge for me as it will be for Grace.

And the plan is quite simple. We're just going to drive into the city centre, find a place to park and . . . have a wander.

I cannot remember the last time I just *had a wander*.

Even on all those walks I mentioned, I have a route laid out in my head that generally takes me towards the leafy common about a mile away from my flat, or up past the shopping centre and around the playing fields of the local school. I certainly don't venture off the beaten path of either.

I have lived a life of refined order – up until I started the detox, anyway. Technology has a way of regimenting your existence, which only becomes truly apparent once you have to do without it. It's almost as if all that reliance on computers starts to turn you into a bit of a computer yourself.

Not a good one, though. Maybe a ZX Spectrum.

So, today is going to be a huge stretch for me. So much so that I very much doubt I'd be doing it if I were alone. But with Grace alongside me, it shouldn't be too bad . . . with any luck.

'So, where do we park?' I ask as we drive into the city centre and into an inevitable stream of traffic.

'No idea,' Grace replies. 'How about that place over there, across the river?'

'Really?'

'Yeah. Why not?'

'Well, we don't know how much the hourly rate is, or if it's a safe car park to use.'

Grace looks a little perplexed for a moment. 'No, that's true.'

'It could be really expensive and could have a problem with anti-social behaviour.'

'Or . . . it might not,' she replies optimistically.

'Yes. But the point is we just *don't know*.'

Ordinarily I would have googled the car park to find these important things out. But, as it stands, I know nothing about it. What if we drive in there, find out it's really pricey, and then we want to leave, but can't, because you have to get a ticket to get out of the car park, which means paying a vast amount of money?

Or what if we leave the car and come back and it's had a wing mirror knocked off? Or someone's slashed the tyres? Or taken a poo on the bonnet?

'Do you really think someone is likely to take a poo on the bonnet, Andy?' Grace asks me with a look of horror on her face.

'I don't know. But that's the point. I have no way of knowing. This could be poo bonnet central for all we know.'

Grace pats my hand on the steering wheel. 'I think it'll be OK. Why don't we just drive over that bridge and see what's what, eh?'

Gulp.

'OK. I guess so.'

And that's precisely what we do.

The car park is half full – this being a bog-standard weekday, outside of the tourist silly season – and it turns out that it's only mildly expensive.

I don't see anyone lurking in the shadows who looks like they might want to curl one out over the bonnet badge, but they could just be very good at staying inconspicuous.

It is with a rising sense of uncertainty that I pop the ticket on the dashboard and shut the car door.

It looks like a rather nice place to park the car, to be honest – next to the fast-flowing River Avon and quite close to a park just along the river's edge, but who am I really to judge, just based on what my eyes can see?

I need search engines, God damn it. And maps. And possibly police reports about incidents of public defecation in the centre of Bath.

'You OK?' Grace asks me when she sees the disconcerted look on my face.

I stare back at her for a moment, before common sense reasserts itself. Nobody is going to be pooing on my bonnet.

'Yeah. I'm fine. I just feel a bit . . . well . . .'

'Lost?'

I nod my head. 'Yeah. That's it.'

Grace smiles. 'Me too. I have sweaty palms.' She looks around. 'I'm surrounded by more people and places than I know what to do with.'

Grace looks quite vulnerable in that moment, so I do something that feels ever so natural, while at the same time ever so strange.

I take her hand.

'Come on, let's see what trouble we can get ourselves into,' I say, praying she doesn't whip her hand out of mine and give me a disgusted look.

Happily, Grace does neither, and we set off from the car park, hand in hand, wondering where the hell we're going to end up.

. . . On the receiving end of an angry chihuahua, it turns out.

I only went up to the little old lady to ask her for directions.

That's a normal thing to do, isn't it?

Perfectly acceptable in polite society?

To enquire from one of your fellow citizens as to the where-abouts of a popular tourist attraction – in this case the famous Roman Baths?

Grace and I have spent a good hour wandering aimlessly through the streets, fast coming to the realisation that Bath is sign-posted in an extremely haphazard manner.

It is after we've returned to the banks of the River Avon for the fourth time that I decide it might be a good idea to ask someone for directions.

No small feat for a person who has historically done all he can to avoid conversing with complete strangers.

The little old lady looks like the easiest person to talk to. Certainly more so than the bloke in the black suit having a massive argument with somebody on the phone, and the guy jogging along the edge of the river in a pair of purple Lycra shorts that look like they're cutting off the circulation to his man parts.

However, when I approach the old woman with my best ingratiating smile and ask her where the baths are, I'm surprised and dismayed to find that secreted in the voluminous tartan bag she has held tightly in one hand is the world's most irritated Mexican dog.

'Excuse me, could you tell me where the Roma—'

Arf arf arf arf arf arf arf!

'Jesus Christ!'

The little sod's head has poked out from the bag and it is barking at me in such a high pitch that I think it breaks at least one of my cochleae.

'Eh?! What?' the little old lady says as loudly as possible, over the barking of her enraged pet.

'The Roman Baths? I was wondering if you knew where they—'

Arf arf arf arf arf arf arf arf arf!

I back away from the little old lady a few steps. It looks like she has a very firm grip on the handles of that bag, and therefore the chihuahua is not going to jump out and savage my poor face – but I'm not taking any chances.

'You want to do what with my bath?' the old woman shouts at me at the top of her lungs, still trying to be heard over the dog.

I shake my head. 'No. I don't want your bath. I just want to know where the baths are!'

Arf arf arf arf arf arf arf arf arf arf arf!

The woman looks mortified. 'You're not getting in a bath with me, young man!'

Oh, bloody hell. She's clearly deaf as a post.

No wonder, really. I feel like my hearing has been irreparably damaged by just a minute of the chihuahua's caterwauling. I can only imagine what years of it would do.

'Never mind!' I shout at her, backing away further. 'I shouldn't have bothered you!'

'You want to do what with my *mother*? She's been dead for fifty years!'

Arf arf arf arf arf arf arf arf arf arf arf arf arf!

Oh, for the love of God.

I turn tail and hurry back to where I've left Grace sitting on a bench. She is doubled over in hysterics. As is only right and proper.

'Well, that went well,' I say, plonking myself down next to her.

'Absolutely!' she replies, trying to get the giggles under control.

'What do you suggest we do now?'

She wipes a tear away. 'I don't know. Maybe follow the river up? It's got to go somewhere, hasn't it?'

I nod my head. 'Sounds like a plan.' I scratch my chin. 'And this jeweller's is definitely near where the baths are, is it?'

'Where it used to be, yes. I have no idea what it is now. But it's on one of the small side streets close to it. Union Passage, I believe it's called.'

185

'Hmmm. A small side street in a city apparently *full* of small side streets. Should be fun trying to find that.'

Grace laughs again and pokes me in the ribs with her elbow, playfully. 'I'm sure you'll be able to find another helpful stranger, Andy. You seem to be very good at it!'

'Very funny,' I reply with mock chagrin, and get up again. 'Come on . . . let's get out of here before the little bastard breaks free of that tartan and comes for my throat.'

We follow the river northwards and are delighted to soon find signposts that point in the direction of the Roman Baths. These take us through a series of streets lined with the sandstone-coloured buildings that the city is famous for, and I can't help thinking that there are certainly worse places in the world to spend a day. Bath really is quite a beautiful city.

It gets pretty damn breathtaking once you reach the baths themselves, I can tell you.

If you wanted to show off the best of British architecture to travellers from distant lands, you could do a lot worse than bring them here to see the Roman Baths, Bath Abbey and the surrounding environs. It's frankly stunning.

'You look like you're enjoying yourself,' Grace remarks as she looks at me gawking up at the abbey's Gothic main tower.

'It's pretty impressive, isn't it?' I reply, still gawking.

I think half the reason I'm so caught up in the place is that I had no idea what I'd be seeing until I actually saw it.

This is very rare for me. Usually, I have thousands of pictures on Google to show me what a landmark looks like, before I get anywhere near it.

But I had no idea just how amazing the centre of Bath looked before I arrived, and therefore I'm all the more impressed by it.

It's a little hard to take my eyes off it all.

Sometimes, there's nothing like a pleasant surprise to lift your spirits.

And I do believe that this is probably the first pleasant surprise I can remember having for a very long time.

'It is very pretty,' Grace agrees, 'but unless they decided to open a jeweller's in the belfry, I think we'd better start looking a bit closer to the ground.'

'Sorry,' I reply sheepishly. 'Eyes on the prize, eh?' I look around. 'Where do you think we should start?'

Grace shrugs. 'No idea. Perhaps we should just wander around here for a bit. See what pops up. You never know, we might stumble upon this Union Passage while we're doing it.'

'All right. Let's have a meander, then,' I say, feeling a bit light-headed.

Maybe it's just that I stared up at the abbey for too long – or maybe it's that I'm feeling in an extremely good mood all of a sudden, thanks to the joy of discovery.

The idea of just ambling around at random, hoping to stumble across the right street, is something that should fill me with unease. But it doesn't. In fact, I'm relishing the prospect.

And that thrill of discovery certainly doesn't end with the magnificence of Bath Abbey. Not by a long shot.

Bath is full of fun little surprises around almost every corner. Most of them containing fudge.

I love fudge.

I mean, who doesn't?

And if you want fudge, then come to Bath. Because there is fudge everywhere. More fudge shops than you can shake a fudgy stick at.

And teacakes.

Lots of those too.

Basically, if you have a sweet tooth, then Bath is the place for you. You don't have to go far to find a purveyor of things fudgy and teacakey. You can even have both at the same time, if you're young, healthy and in no danger of having a coronary episode.

With bags of fudge in hand (mine a nice toffee and chocolate; Grace's a strange minty thing I won't be going anywhere near), we start to explore the streets around us, hoping to find the one where Hackett & Mostrum used to ply their trade in the finest of jewellery.

Needless to say, this does not come about *quickly*.

While it's a refreshing change to just bimble about a bit with no clear plan, it does mean taking an inordinately long amount of time to actually get anywhere.

Years of apps and Internet search engines have put everything I need at my fingertips, and it's made me ever so impatient. I'm not used to things taking a long time to sort themselves out.

So, while I start our search for Union Passage with a smile on my face and a full bag of fudge in my hand, by the time the small cellophane bag is emptied of its fudgy contents, I am becoming quite annoyed.

'Bloody hell,' I snap under my breath as our progress down another small side street is held up by a gaggle of Asian tourists.

The poor sightseers are doing absolutely nothing wrong. But there are an awful lot of them, and none of them seem to want to get out of my way.

'Excuse me,' I say in a strained voice as one of them steps backwards into my path to take a picture of what appears to be the front of an estate agency.

Quite why this gentleman feels the need to have a picture of Quimley's of Bath is beyond me. Perhaps he likes the name. Or maybe there's a five-bed detached on the outskirts of town he's interested in. Either way, he's in my way, and I'm not happy about it.

'I said *excuse me*,' I repeat, earning me a befuddled look. I tut as loudly as an Englishman dares in public and slide past the man, pushing him out of the way slightly.

'Are you all right?' Grace says to me as she draws alongside me, once we're past the group of happily snapping tourists.

'Not really. My feet hurt, I'm out of fudge and we're still no closer to finding this bloody street.'

'It is getting a bit frustrating, isn't it?' she agrees. 'We don't seem to be getting any closer. We could really do with a map.'

'Yes, we could,' I agree, my hand unconsciously coming up in front of my face.

I notice that Grace is making the same gesture.

'Oh, bloody hell,' I say, shaking my head ruefully.

'What?'

'We're both holding up our hands like we've got our phones in them,' I point out.

Grace looks down at her own slightly cupped hand and goes a bit wide-eyed again. 'Jesus Christ.'

I consciously lower my arm in a very deliberate fashion and take a deep breath. 'Time for some more directions, I think.'

'Agreed. But who from? I don't see any deaf old women with mental dogs around.'

I stare back at the gaggle of Asian tourists. 'Back this way, I think.'

Grace looks down the street. 'You think they'll know any better than us?'

'Not them,' I reply as I set off back towards them, 'but maybe what they were taking pictures of.'

Quimley's of Bath is the kind of estate agent's you come to if you are extremely rich, extremely posh and possibly in need of something with crenellations along the roof.

I have no real idea what a crenellation is, so am not supposed to set foot in a place like this, but Grace and I need to find this bloody jeweller's, and if anyone's going to know something like that, it'll be an estate agent's that looks like it's been here since the dawn of time.

Speaking of things that look like they've been here since the dawn of time, I walk up to the only inhabited desk on the tiny shop floor, behind which sits a dusty skeleton.

Oh no, sorry, my mistake. It's an old man, not a skeleton. He is quite dusty, though. That three-piece suit he's wearing looks like it was tailored about five minutes after the shop opened.

'Good afternoon,' I say.

'And a fine and tremensicle afternoon to you too, sir!' comes the hearty reply, in a booming voice.

Is 'tremensicle' a word, though?

I mean, it *could be*. But I've never heard it before.

Mind you, as stated, I have no idea what a crenellation is either, so we'll just have to hope this ancient entity has a better grip on his vocabulary than I have on mine.

'I was wondering if you could help my friend and I?' I ask the dusty old man, who has now risen from the enormous mahogany Chesterfield desk and is coming around to stand in front of us with a speed that belies his obvious age.

Vampire!

What?

It's a bloody vampire!

What are you talking about, brain?

He's skinny, tall and ancient, but moves like greased lightning – and he talks like he's Brian Blessed! Clearly a vampire! Run, you fool! Run before we are taken by the creature of the night!

I do not run, I am proud to say. However vampiric this gentleman may appear to be, I am fairly sure he isn't actually one of the undead. They probably wouldn't allow them in Bath. They wouldn't go with the sandstone and fudge. You've never seen a vampire munching on a nice square of fudge before, and if you can't munch on a nice square of fudge, I'm pretty damn sure Bath is not for you.

'Why, I'd be delighted to help, young man! What serviceables may I render unto you and your lovely companionation? Perhaps you are in the market for a fresh domicillary locale?'

OK, there's at least *three* words in there that aren't real. This guy may not be a vampire, but he's sure as hell sucking the life out of the English dictionary.

'We'd just like some directions,' Grace replies, while I stand there, giving the old man a deeply suspicious look. 'Mr . . . ?'

The old man flaps his thin hands around at high speed. 'Oh! Where are my mannerations?!' He sticks out one hand to Grace. 'My name is Algonquin Quimby.'

'Quimley,' I automatically correct, given the name that's on the door to this place.

'I'm sorry?' the old man responds.

'It's Quimley's of Bath. You must be Mr Quimley, surely?'

It's his turn to give a suspicious look. 'Ah, no, sir. That would be the name of the man I entered into purchasement of this agency from. Gerald Quimley. A fine chap. His departure from this world was just too tasty.'

What?

'I beg your pardon?' I say, swearing that this man has just pretty much told me he sucked the life from the previous owner.

'Too *hasty*, sir. Mr Quimley died far too young.' He gives Grace an indulgent smile. 'The surname similarities are merely a coincidence.'

I'm officially creeped out now. I swear he said 'tasty'. My confidence that this old boy is not a blood-sucking fiend from beyond the depths of hell has been severely rattled.

'Can you tell us where Hackett & Mostrum Fine Jewellery is?' I blurt out, keen on leaving this establishment post-haste, before he starts to look at my neck in a hungry fashion.

Again with the rapid-fire hand-waving. 'Ah! Poor Mr Hackett and Mr Mostrum! What fine gentlemen they were. I myself bought many a jewelletic treat from them over the years.' He holds up one palsied-looking hand to my face. 'The ring on my third finger is one of their most spectacular creations. Truly magnificent.'

It is an impressive ring. Clearly pure gold, with a red ruby set into it.

A blood-red ruby.

Right, we need to get out of here.

'Do you know where their shop was?' I hastily ask, moving my head back a bit, away from that cadaverous hand.

'Why of course!' he tells me, lowering the hand and offering me a smile that starts off warm and comforting, but descends into blood-curdling when it stays on his face a nanosecond too long. 'You simply turn right out of this shop, truculate down the passage until you reach the main road. Turn left until you see Old Bond Street on your right, across the road. About thirty paces along you will find that which you seek – a terracement building with the most *wonderful* blue window frames and white facade.' He looks sad. 'Though I fear the jeweller's itself is long gone. I believe it was turned into a restaurant, offering delictationaries from the Mediterranean, some years ago.' Quimby looks wistful. 'I had Mr Hackett and Mr Mostrum to dinner when they had to close their wonderful shop down. It was the last time I saw them.'

Yeah, I bet it was. Right before you swooped back to your coffin for a snooze to digest their giblets.

'Thank you so much,' Grace tells the old man, and again shakes his hand. 'You've been most helpful.'

Bath Dracula smiles at her in a way that could be described as pleasant, but could equally be described as predatory.

'Yeah, cheers,' I add, starting to hustle Grace towards the door.

If I can just get it open, we might be safe. If he makes a lunge at us, I might be able to throw one of the Asian tourists in his path and make our escape. We should be able to get away, no problem.

I can't move for ages after I've had a Chinese – I'm assuming the same is true for the undead.

'Not a problem at all!' Quimby responds. 'And if you feel the desire to purchase a new domicile in the wonderful encumbrances of the Bath region, then do let me know!'

'Yeah, will do!' I tell him, eyeing up which person looks small enough for me to pick up without doing my back in.

Once we're in the street, and safely back past the sightseers, Grace turns and gives me a horrified look. 'That was a bit rude, Andy!'

'No, it bloody wasn't. I just saved your life.'

'What are you talking about?'

'He was clearly a vampire. Haven't you seen any Hammer horror movies?'

'That's a horrible thing to say! He was just a helpful old man.'

'A helpful old *lightning-fast* man, who talked about having old friends for dinner. Clearly Nosferatu. No doubt about it.'

Grace rolls her eyes and gives me a look. 'You're not that good with people, are you?'

I look back at her with disbelief. 'Well, of course I'm not. I've spent most of my life talking to a computer screen. People *terrify* me, Grace. Especially the ancient ones who can only be destroyed by a stake through the heart . . . or possibly a light bit of decapitation.'

Grace doesn't say another word. She just slowly takes my hand, in the manner of someone trying to help one of the enfeebled. 'Let's go and find this jeweller's – or whatever it is now,' she says.

I nod. 'That's probably for the best.'

And in fact, it only takes us a few more minutes to find where Hackett & Mostrum once proudly stood. Mr Quimby's directions prove to be very accurate. But then, if you'd been alive for several centuries, you'd probably have a good handle on your whereabouts as well, wouldn't you?

'He wasn't a vampire, Andy, stop it,' Grace says, looking at the expression on my face.

'I wasn't thinking about that.'

'Yes, you were.'

Quite disconcerting that this woman can read my mind so easily.

. . . And is also quite lovely.

'Looks like we've found the right building,' I note, trying to change the subject from creatures of the night who run estate agencies in their spare time. 'There are the blue window frames he spoke about, and it's definitely white.'

So white, in fact, it rather pops out from the rest of the terraced shops it sits among. Most of them have a more subdued grey or beige colour scheme, and their bay windows are nowhere near as noticeable as the terrace we've been directed towards.

'It's a Greek restaurant,' Grace says as we halt in front of it. She sounds a little disappointed. I trust this is because there's no evidence that this in fact was the jeweller's in question – rather than that she has something against souvlaki.

'Looks like it,' I agree. 'I've never eaten Greek food before.'

This is not a particularly helpful thing to say, given Grace's obvious disappointment. There is literally nothing about the frontage of Christos' Greek Taverna that suggests it was once a place where one could buy a nice silver necklace or gold locket.

'Ah well, that's that then, I suppose,' Grace says in a small voice.

I look from her sad face back to the restaurant, and back to her face again.

She's probably right.

What else can we do?

It's not like we can jump on the Internet and find anything more out about the place. That would at least have made the trip seem more worthwhile.

Just go inside.

What?

Go inside, you dolt. Ask a few questions. See if anyone knows anything.

I stand there and blink a few times.

Of course. That's exactly what I should do, isn't it?

No matter how scary that still feels.

If today has shown me anything, it's that I have been sorely deprived of decent, interesting human interaction in the past few years thanks to my addiction. OK, I've nearly been bitten by a rabid, tiny dog and had my blood sucked by what was clearly a vampire (no matter what Grace says), but I've shared more words with complete strangers today than I have in a very long time.

I'm suddenly struck by a huge sadness, thinking about all the people I may have missed out on over the years. All the friends I might have missed out on making. All the dogs I may have missed out on patting. All the vampires I might have missed out on turning me into an immortal creature of great power, with huge amounts of sexual attractiveness.

'Let's go in,' I tell Grace, in a determined fashion. 'Maybe they can tell us something about the old jeweller's.'

'Do you think they'd know?'

'I have no idea, but there's only one way to find out.' I cock my head to one side. 'And even if they don't, I'm hungry. How about you?'

Grace nods. 'I am quite peckish.'

'Good.'

I take Grace's hand again, which is shaking a little. It shouldn't feel like a brave thing to do – walking into a restaurant to ask a few questions and maybe grab a bite to eat – but for us, it is.

This entire day has been an exercise in facing the unknown.

Hell, that's what the last few weeks of my life have been about.

And I think I'm starting to get *better* at it.

Inside Christos' Greek Taverna – which is virtually empty, as it's only just opened for the late-afternoon business – the decor is much what you'd expect if you've ever been to Greece. The colour scheme is universally blue and white. The walls are whitewashed, with arched ceilings that have been tastefully covered in what look like old fishing nets and crab pots.

The place screams rustic Greek charm.

We are approached by a barrel-chested gentleman who is as short and healthy-looking as Quimby was tall and emaciated. This man is obviously not a vampire. I doubt they grow many vampires in Greece. Too sunny, and probably too full of recipes that require a lot of garlic.

'Hello,' he says in a friendly tone, with a slight Greek lilt to his accent. 'Table for two, is it?'

'Maybe,' I reply. 'We'll probably eat in a minute, but just have something we'd like to ask you.'

The man immediately looks a little terrified. 'Are you from the council? Only we had our hygiene rating done only last month.'

'We're not from the council,' Grace tells him.

This doesn't make him look any calmer. 'Oh no! You're from the *Bath Gazette*, aren't you?' He holds up his hands. 'The thing with the tortoise happened a long time ago, and we had nothing to do with it!'

OK, now I desperately need to know what the thing with the tortoise was.

'We're not from the *Bath Gazette* either,' Grace says.

The man relaxes a little. 'Oh. What do you want to ask, then?'

Ask about the tortoise. Ask about the tortoise.

'We wanted to ask you if you knew anything about the jeweller's that used to be here,' Grace says. I try not to look disappointed. This is what we're here for, after all.

'Ah, yes. It was a jeweller's before my father bought the place,' the man replies. 'Why do you want to know about it?'

Grace delves into her shirt and pulls out her locket. 'This was made here. It's very important to me, and I wanted to see where it was fashioned. I was hoping there might be something left of the jeweller's, but it looks like it's all gone.'

The man beams. 'Not quite, miss. Not quite.'

The restaurant owner – who identifies himself as Christos – leads us out the back and past the kitchen. 'We don't normally let people back here, of course. So please don't tell anybody!'

'Of course we won't!' Grace promises.

I'm not so sure. Maybe I can blackmail him with it, so he tells me about the bloody tortoise.

Christos then leads us up a set of narrow stairs at the back of the building to a second floor. There, he pulls out an old set of stepladders from what looks like the airing cupboard, and carries them over to a place just underneath a wooden loft hatch in the ceiling.

197

'My father put everything that was left from the old shop up here. I have been meaning to clear it out for storage, but never got around to it. Lucky for you!'

It takes him a few moments to get the loft hatch open, and he disappears up into the darkened space, flicking on a light switch somewhere to provide enough illumination.

'Come on up! But please be careful!'

Now, if it were Quimby the estate agent beckoning me up into his loft space, I'd run a mile, but Christos seems a lot more trustworthy – and part of the human race.

I let Grace go up first, and as I follow her, I hear her gasp in surprise.

And no wonder.

Just look at this lot, would you?

The loft is full of antique furniture. I feel like I've stepped on to the set of a Charles Dickens movie – one that's unfortunately been caught up in an earthquake.

Several desks, stools, chairs, sideboards and glass-fronted cabinets are piled up around the small loft space – all in remarkably good condition, considering. Yes, they're covered in about a ton of dust, but other than that, they look in good nick. Hackett & Mostrum obviously knew how to buy quality furniture for their business.

'I keep meaning to take this lot to the antique dealer's, but never get the chance,' Christos confides. 'Look in the drawers.'

He pulls one open next to him. Inside is a pile of small, delicate-looking tools, made from wood and metal. Grace picks up what looks like a set of thin, exquisitely made pliers. The smooth dark wood handles each have a tiny metal stamp laid into them that reads 'Hackett & Mostrum – Fine Jewellers'.

'Wow,' Grace remarks, turning the pliers over in her hand. 'These are amazing.'

'They could have been used to make your locket,' I reply.

Grace doesn't say anything, but there are tears forming at the corners of her eyes. The notion that she could be holding a tool that helped make her most valuable possession has obviously struck her hard.

Christos smiles and gestures to her. 'You keep them, eh?'

Grace gives him a startled look. 'Oh no! I couldn't. They're yours!'

Christos shakes his head. 'No. You should have them. I have enough here anyway. You keep them. Maybe your boyfriend is right . . . maybe they did make your locket with them!'

Boyfriend.

Oh my.

I've suddenly gone a bit light-headed again.

'Thank you so much, Christos!' Grace says, and gives him a hug. Not an easy thing to do, given our cramped confines.

You'll notice she doesn't correct him by telling him I'm not her boyfriend.

Seriously, I feel *really* light-headed now.

I need to get down from this loft – and I probably need something to eat.

'Er . . . table for two then, Christos?' I ask him, once Grace has let him go.

He beams again. 'Certainly, Mr Bellows! You must try our dolmadakia!'

Must I?

OK.

But I'd better find out what it is first . . .

And so, we come to the last challenge, in a day that's been full of them.

To be exact: deciding what to eat in a restaurant that has food you're completely unfamiliar with, when you have no access to Google to fill you in.

I should be terrified. There are things on this menu I've never heard of. I should just order a Greek salad and have done with it – instead of taking a jump into the unknown and ordering something that might come battered and full of wobbly stuff.

But I'm not terrified. I'm *excited*.

My day out in Bath has proved that if you just let life come at you every now and again, you might be pleasantly surprised – *and* you might find you enjoy yourself a lot more.

If you don't get eaten by a vampire, that is.

If we'd have had Google, we would probably have just looked up the old shop on the Internet and been satisfied with that. Maybe there would have been a few pictures, and even a Wikipedia entry – and we would have thought that was good enough.

But then we wouldn't have met Christos, Grace wouldn't be the proud new owner of a pair of exquisitely wrought jeweller's pliers with a long history, and I wouldn't currently be tucking into my battered octopus . . . which is absolutely *delicious*.

'How do you feel?' Grace asks me as she takes a sip of retsina.

I think for a moment.

'Free,' I tell her, simply.

She smiles. 'Me too. I think today has been a great success, don't you?'

I nod. 'If nothing else, I've discovered the joys of battered octopus,' I say as I cram another ball of the golden food in my mouth.

'Thank you for coming with me, Andy,' Grace says, reaching out a hand to take mine.

There's been a lot of hand-holding done today, but this time it feels different.

It feels . . . *more*.

'It was my pleasure,' I say, in a voice that I'd like to think is thick with emotion, but is probably just thick with battered mollusc.

'It's not really so hard, is it?'

'No. It's actually quite soft,' I say, around a mouthful of food. 'A bit chewy though.'

Grace gives me a look. 'That's not what I meant, and you know it.'

I do know it . . . I'm just trying to avoid talking about it.

Because it *is* hard.

One day in Bath doesn't necessarily change that.

Feeling free does not also stop you from feeling *lost*. The two emotions can sit beside each other quite comfortably, it turns out. After all, you could describe a man lost in the desert as also being free, couldn't you? He may not appreciate it, and would rather you just gave him a bottle of water, but you *could* do it.

If anything, today's jaunt around the sandstone city has made things more difficult. Because now I know that without all that digital claptrap, I can live a more spontaneous, interesting life.

Before today, I'd have struggled to tell you what real-world advantages there are to a digital detox . . . but now I know.

That doesn't stop me yearning for the opportunity to look at what's happening in the world on Facebook, though. It's just not that simple.

Grace is looking into my eyes, searching them for what I'm feeling. I hope she has a better handle on it than I do.

After a few moments' pause she squeezes my hand. 'One day at a time,' she says in a quiet voice. 'There's nothing about this that's easy.'

A much better handle, as it turns out. One with a slip-free rubber grip.

One day at a time.

That's a fine piece of advice, isn't it?

And a way of living that's never really occurred to me before.

Why would it? Being online means you can pretty much plan every facet of your life, months in advance.

One day at a time.

One hour at a time.

One minute at a time.

Blimey.

That sounds as wonderful as it does scary.

'One day at a time,' I repeat, and squeeze Grace's hand right back.

Chapter Nine

The Following

'One day at a time, eh?' Fergus says in an amused voice, from over the flat white Grace has just prepared for him.

'Yes.'

'I can't think of anyone I've ever met who is less suited to that philosophy, my friend.'

I sneer at him. 'Well, that's kind of the point, isn't it? This digital detox is meant to change me for the better. Maybe this is one of those positive changes.'

'Like coming here instead of Costa,' Fergus says, looking around Heirloom Coffee.

'Yep. The coffee is much better.'

Fergus nods in the direction of Grace, who is currently serving a couple at the counter. 'And the service too, eh?'

I blush. 'Yes.'

Fergus grins the grin of a man who has been in a solid relationship for many years and knows nothing of the horrors of new romance. 'So, things going well with her then?'

'How do you mean?'

Fergus rolls his eyes. 'Are you *dating* her, Andy?'

I shake my head. 'We've just been hanging out together. As friends. It's nothing more than that.'

'Isn't it? That's too bad for you.'

'No . . . I don't mean . . . We're not . . .' I give an exasperated gasp. 'We're trying to help each other through this detox right now, Ferg. Getting romantically involved probably wouldn't help matters.'

'Yeah. You just keep telling yourself that, pal.' He gives Grace a quick look again. 'But you might want to tell her as well. The way she keeps flicking glances at you suggests she thinks differently.'

'Really?' I say, voice a little too eager.

While the rational part of my brain insists that I should probably keep things platonic between Grace and me while this strange period of my life plays itself out, the rest of me just wants to throw caution to the wind and kiss her.

But, despite Fergus's opinions, I'm not sure Grace is ready for anything like that. Or willing, for that matter.

Let's face it, we're both going through a rather traumatic change to our personal circumstances. Do we really need the anxiety of trying to start a relationship at the same time? Surely it's better for each of us to sort our own mental health out before doing anything like that?

Grace and I have not discussed this with each other at all on the several occasions we've met up since the day in Bath, but I feel like there's a tacit agreement there that doesn't really need to be openly talked about.

One day at a time.

And if there's anything romantic between us, it'll happen in due course.

Of course, this eminently sensible way of thinking does not stop me sounding like an excited schoolboy when Fergus points out the way Grace is looking at me.

'Yes, Andy. She definitely likes you,' he says, still in that irritating, amused tone of voice. He sips his coffee again. 'She also makes the best flat white I've had in ages. You should probably marry her at your first opportunity.'

'Very funny,' I remark. 'To change the subject – which I feel would be best for us all right now – what was it you wanted to chat to me about?'

Fergus's eyes light up and he puts the coffee cup down, spilling some of its contents into the saucer. 'Ah! Well, Mr Bellows, I have a proposition for you!'

I groan internally. 'What?'

Fergus looks annoyed. 'Don't be like that. This is a *good* thing.'

'What is?'

He sits up straight. 'A follow-up!'

'A what?'

'A follow-up, Andrew! Another story about your digital detox!'

My jaw goes slack for a second. 'Why?'

Fergus looks incredulous. 'Because you've done so well!'

'Have I?'

'Well, of course you have! You've got . . . what? Another couple of weeks left?'

'Just over that, actually. Sixteen days.'

Not that I've really been counting . . . not at all.

One day at a time, remember?

'And look how far you've come!'

I scratch my nose. 'I don't think I've really come all that far, Ferg.'

'No? How are you sleeping?'

'Fine.'

'And the IBS?'

'It's . . . also fine.'

'Work going OK?'

'I guess so.'

Actually, I've been on a massive creative kick recently. The art-work has been flowing out of me faster than ever before. And it's all really good stuff.

'And you feel happier, right? Better up here?' He taps his head.

I think about this for a moment.

I don't know if 'happier' is the right word to use. I'd probably steer more towards 'calmer'. My brain doesn't feel like it's perma-nently set on maximum overdrive any more. There are times now when I can just sit there and empty my mind of thought. That sounds like it should be an easy thing to do – but trust me, it isn't for a tech-head.

But I can do it now, and it's very relaxing.

To just 'be' for a few minutes a day.

'I certainly feel better in my head, yes,' I tell Fergus truthfully.

'And . . . you know . . .' He jerks a thumb over at Grace, who is now talking to the other barista who works for her as they both deal with customer orders at the enormous coffee machine.

'Yes, yes. I get your point,' I say, hoping that Grace doesn't notice his rather overt thumb-jerking.

'Well . . . I'd say all of that warrants a follow-up article, wouldn't you?'

I open my mouth to protest, but then close it again just as quickly.

It probably does, doesn't it?

Because I do feel quite proud of myself, you know.

These last six weeks have been difficult, but I have soldiered on through them without breaking the detox *once*. I have done something that I once considered quite impossible, and I've done it without breaking any limbs or damaging any internal organs.

OK, I've had a few run-ins with misfortune, but none of them have resulted in long-term psychological or physical damage, and

I can certainly say they've been a mild price to pay for the sense of self-satisfaction I currently have.

And I am *immensely* self-satisfied right now.

I am sleeping very well.

My neck pain has completely gone.

I now shit once a day, and when I do it's quite a pleasurable experience.

Do you know how alien that feels for someone who suffers (or rather suffered) from irritable bowel syndrome? I now *look forward* to having a poo.

Madness. Sheer, unbridled *madness*.

And I've even reached the point where my disconnection from the online world has become an annoyance, rather than a tragedy.

I've discovered that I'm not actually that bothered about what people I've never met are talking about on forums. I no longer give two hoots about what the local community is talking about on Facebook. The whereabouts of celebrities on Instagram is entirely inconsequential to my life, and whatever is trending on Twitter no longer matters one jot.

About the only things I still miss about my previous lifestyle are the convenience of it all, and the ability to find out information that I actually need to know.

Ordering goods and services is still a massive headache. Getting a takeaway is more trouble than it's worth, and shopping in general is now a task I loathe on every single level.

And boy do I miss the ability to just look something up quickly. Whether it be the spelling of a word, or the time a TV show is broadcast, it takes me twenty times longer to seek out the answers I need.

But . . . I'm pretty sure all that is worth it, because I now look forward to having a poo.

I have reached a state of equilibrium in my life that pleases me no end.

As I think this, I unconsciously look over at Grace, who is now handing over a couple of lattes to the couple at the counter.

'You really think people want to read another article about me?' I ask Fergus.

'Of course! Why wouldn't they? You're a success story!'

'OK then,' I say. 'Why the hell not?'

Fergus grins and whips out his mobile phone. He thumbs the screen, and then places it between us on the table. 'Why don't you tell me how it's all gone, Andy? In as many words as you need. Don't leave anything out. Tell me *everything*.'

I take a deep breath, and begin to talk.

◆ ◆ ◆

The article – which Fergus entitles 'Logged Off and Loving It' – appears in the paper four days later.

In it, Fergus does a pretty damn good job of summing up how my life has changed since the detox started. He certainly does a good job of detailing all the escapades I've been through since leaving the technology behind. Although, he spends a lot more time talking about the new relationship I've formed with Grace than I think is entirely necessary.

When I point this out to him, he's incredulous. 'You're kidding, right? People *always* want to read about relationships, Andy. Every good story ever written is about a relationship. It's great that your mental and physical health has improved . . . and what better way to underline that than the fact it's helped you meet someone new?'

'But we're *not dating*, Fergus. I told you that!'

'Meh . . . doesn't matter. Human interest is human interest, Andy. And Grace adds a whole new dimension to the story that gives it even more life!'

Which is hard to argue with, I suppose.

Grace has certainly given my life a whole new dimension – one where I spend a lot more time outside in the sun. After the trip to Bath, both Grace and I have developed a shared love of getting out and about that is keeping us away from both technology and the insides of our own heads.

We've been on walks together in the country, taking advantage of the warm weather, and have been actively considering the purchase of walking sticks from Trespass – which you know means we must be serious about it. I never realised how much I adore hedgerows – when I'm on foot, anyway. Big, bushy green hedgerows, covered in bees and butterflies. Lovely.

A small but perfectly formed peacock butterfly landed on Grace's nose the other day as we lay down for a rest on the grass. It was quite the most exquisite thing I think I've ever seen.

It's a good job Grace was willing to be in the story. Fergus had to do a bit of convincing, but as we've readily established, he's very good at that type of thing.

She asked Fergus not to go into any detail about her own detox – which is more than fair enough. I may be willing to let the whole world in on my travails, but it doesn't mean she has to.

It's a bit of a shame she didn't want it mentioned, though, as she's been doing remarkably well with it. Far better than I did in the first few weeks. She hasn't written off her car even *once*.

If she's had any wobbles, she's managed to keep them hidden from me. All I see is someone who's discovering the outside world again for the first time in ages, and dragging me along with her.

I find myself unquestionably happy to be dragged.

◆　◆　◆

Five days after Fergus's story went in the paper, when I officially have a week left of the detox, Fergus sits down opposite me in Heirloom Coffee again and looks at me with wide eyes.

'I think you've started something here, Mr Bellows,' he tells me breathlessly.

'What do you mean by that?'

'Well, the morning after the paper went out, I started to get phone calls and emails about you. About your *story*. I've also had quite a lot of people contact me on social media . . . though you wouldn't have seen that, of course.'

I suddenly feel deeply worried.

Why would people be contacting Fergus about *me*?

What did I say?

Did I *offend* someone?

Maybe I said too much. Maybe I went into too much detail about what I'd been going through.

I knew I shouldn't have talked about the duck pond incident or what happened with Herbert Bilch and Henrietta. No actual, real names were used, but maybe those involved still recognised themselves, and are angry at me because of it?

I thought I was quite nice about Bath. I didn't say anything controversial.

Have I angered the fudge people?

I don't want to anger the fudge people. They have access to a lot of hot fudge that I'm sure could be turned into a deadly ballistic weapon if the need arose.

Have I pissed folks off, without meaning to?

'No! Nothing like that, Andy!' Fergus assures me when I confess my concerns to him. 'They *love* you!'

'They *do*?'

'Yes! Every person who's been in touch has done so to say how much they admire what you're doing.'

'What, even driving the car into the duck pond?'

Fergus laughs. 'Not the specifics, mate. Your entire *journey*. I knew it would make a great second story as soon as you were done talking, and I was bloody right!'

'What . . . what have they been saying?'

'Oh, that they can see themselves in you. That you've shown them how reliant they are on their phones, and how it's been bad for them. That they want to do the detox as well. That you're a bloody inspiration . . . you know, that kind of thing.'

'An inspiration?'

'Yeah!'

Dear Christ in heaven. Me? Andy Bellows? An *inspiration to people*?

I've often been flabbergasted by humanity, to the point of panicked incredulity. This revelation is not helping matters.

'Like I say, I think you might have started something here, pal,' Fergus says in an excited voice.

'Started something?'

'Absolutely! A movement.'

'A movement,' I repeat in a slightly nauseous tone.

'Yes. There's not a lot else you can call it when dozens of people get in touch in such a short space of time.' Fergus shows me his phone screen. It's covered in Twitter, Facebook and email notifications. 'Just look at that little lot, would you?'

'A movement,' I say again, staring down into my empty coffee cup.

I don't want to start a movement.

I don't want to be a part of a movement.

The only kind of movement I want in my life is a smooth easy one, while I'm sitting on the toilet.

In my limited experience of history, I know that no one who starts a movement ever comes out of the other end in good shape.

They usually get killed by the authorities, their own followers or a cyanide capsule.

Hitler created a movement. It didn't turn out well for anyone. They wrote books about it and everything.

'Oh, bloody hell,' I gasp and sit back in my chair, looking at the ceiling.

'What's the matter?' Fergus asks me.

'What's the matter? You've just told me I'm like Hitler and you ask what's the matter?'

'Hitler?'

'Yes! He started a movement!'

This is a strange and irrational train of thought, but please forgive me, I've just been told that dozens of people want to know more about me. That they are interested in my story.

Dozens of brains with the name 'Andy Bellows' currently at the forefront of their thoughts.

I feel sick.

'Everything OK, guys?' Grace asks, having no doubt come over to say hello to Fergus.

I look up at her, ashen-faced. 'I'm Hitler, Grace,' I tell her.

'What?'

'I'm Hitler. Fergus has turned me into Hitler.' I grab her arm. 'I don't want to take a cyanide capsule!'

'Andy? Are you all right?'

'I think he might be having some kind of nervous breakdown,' Fergus opines. 'Maybe I should have broken the news to him a bit more gently.'

'What news?' Grace asks, pulling up an empty chair from one of the other tables.

Fergus then explains what's been happening, while I sit there trying not to think about the word 'Nuremberg'.

'Ahh . . .' she remarks when Fergus finishes. 'That is quite a thing, isn't it?'

'It certainly is!'

I do wish Fergus would stop looking quite so happy about all of this. It's not him parked at the front of dozens of brains, is it?

Grace plays with her locket while she shoots me a couple of concerned looks. 'I mean, I understand it, obviously. I did exactly the same thing, when you get right down to it. The original story you wrote is what led me to Andy's door after all.' She unconsciously puts a hand out and squeezes my arm. 'But that many people? That's a lot for him to deal with.'

'They liked you too, you know,' Fergus points out.

Now Grace joins me in the realms of panic. I can't say I'm upset about this. A trouble shared is a trouble halved, after all.

'Me?!' she cries, eyes wide with horror.

'Oh yeah. I think it's the fact you got in touch with him that gave them the inspiration to do it themselves.'

Now Grace contrives to look guilty.

'You know that makes you Eva Braun, don't you?' I tell her in a quivering voice, still reeling from how bizarre all of this is.

Grace stares at me. 'Didn't he shoot her?'

I nod slowly. 'I think so. You don't have to worry, though . . . about the only gun I can get hold of is a plastic wheel lock.'

That doesn't seem to make her feel any better, to be honest. 'I'm sorry, Andy,' she says.

I look horrified. 'No! You don't have anything to apologise for!' I turn an evil stare on Fergus. 'This is all *his* fault!'

'*My* fault?' Fergus exclaims, pointing a finger at his own chest.

'Yes! You wrote the stories, Fergus!' I denounce. 'You're the man who put it out there!' I gasp as a revelation strikes me. 'You're fucking Goebbels!'

'Goebbels?!'

'Yes! Fucking Goebbels!'

'Can we quit with the Nazi comparisons now, please?' Grace implores. 'It's making my head hurt.'

'Sorry,' I tell her, but I continue to give Fergus a look that speaks Nazi volumes.

'The question is,' she continues, 'what do we do about this?'

'Do about this? What do you mean?' I ask, now turning the look on Grace. Did Goebbels have an assistant?

She holds up her hands. 'You have to reply to them, don't you?' she asks, and then looks back at Fergus/Goebbels. 'Doesn't he?'

Fergus shrugs. 'Yeah. It'd be nice if he talked to them. Probably a very good idea.'

I'm staggered. '*Reply* to them? *Talk* to them?'

Both Grace and Fergus nod.

I stare at them both. 'Have you gone completely bloody mad, the pair of you?'

They give me blank looks.

'I can't talk to those people!'

'Why not?' Fergus asks.

'Because . . . because . . .' I stab two fingers towards my own head. 'Because I'm *me!*'

'What do you mean by that?' Grace asks, confused.

'You've both *met me*, haven't you?' I say to them. 'OK, one of you has known me a lot longer than the other, but it doesn't take long to discover that I am not . . . not a *people person*. The concept of communicating with dozens of strangers is not something my brain can contemplate.' I think for a moment. 'Or my digestive system, for that matter.'

'But you have such a great story to tell,' Fergus complains. 'You've got a lot of wisdom.'

'Wisdom?!' I cry in a high-pitched voice. 'I ended up on a date with someone who thinks the earth is hollow, and my Volvo's engine has only just recovered from having several gallons of pond water pumped out of it!'

'It's your example they're interested in, Andy,' Grace says in a very calm voice. She's trying to talk me down off the ledge I'm rapidly escalating towards jumping off. 'The way you've changed your lifestyle completely is quite inspirational. It inspired me. And I feel a lot better for it.'

Unfortunately, this is very true. I've only known Grace a few weeks, but she looks like a very different person from the scared, lost woman I opened my front door to.

But that wasn't because of anything *I* did. She chose to join me on the path of the digital detox. That all came from her, didn't it?

'But I wouldn't have done it without your example, Andy,' she tells me. 'Without you, I'd never have dared give it a go. I needed your story to show me that I had a problem, and that I needed to do something about it.' She points at Fergus's phone, which is now on the table and flashing with new notifications on a frighteningly regular basis. 'And maybe those people feel the same way.'

'She's right, mate,' Fergus adds. 'Pretty much everyone who's contacted me has said how they wish they could get off the Internet . . . use their tech less. Live a calmer life. Just like you.' He smiles. 'Hell, even I've been thinking I could do with a little less screen time myself.'

I look from Grace to Fergus, and then back to Grace again, my face a ball of anguish. 'But I don't want to be an inspiration for anyone, guys. I don't think I'd be very good at it, and I don't want to end up in a bunker.'

'But you *are* good at it, Andy,' Grace tells me with a warm smile. 'Whether you like it or not.'

'She's right about that too, mate,' Fergus agrees. 'And there are people out there, like Grace, who would clearly like to follow you on your path.'

Gosh.

What a strange, strange thing.

And by strange, I mean *stomach-clenching*.

Then a thought occurs. One very salient thought that will put the kybosh on this whole thing good and proper – thank God.

'There's no way I can communicate with them, though!' I say, possibly more triumphantly than is strictly necessary.

'What do you mean?' Fergus asks.

I waggle my eyebrows. 'I can't go online, can I? I can't go on social media! And I'm only allowed to use emails for work!'

Ha!

It's the perfect get-out clause!

Fergus looks a bit deflated. He knows I'm right!

All of those poor people will just have to get along on their own, without the assistance of Andrew Bellows. This is no doubt for the best, as there probably aren't enough duck ponds in the local area for them to drive into.

I'm still on the digital detox, so there's no way for me to speak to these people, even if I wanted to!

Marvellous!

'We could arrange a meeting?' Fergus suggests.

Somewhere, far off, the *Jaws* music starts to play.

'What?' I snap, coming out of my exultant mood in a split second.

'You know . . . a meeting. A meet-and-greet. So they could come and see you in person.'

Grace – who I would hope would be on my side in this debacle – nods and looks very interested in the notion.

I should have slammed the front door in her face.

'You want me to *meet* these people *in person*?' I say, feeling my legs turn to jelly as I do so.

Fergus nods. 'Yes. I think that would be lovely.' He scratches his chin. 'It'd make a good third story for the paper too.'

'We could do it here,' Grace remarks.

I whip my head around to look at her so fast I'll need ibuprofen in the morning for the whiplash. 'Here?!'

She nods. 'Yes. The café is big enough to accommodate a lot of people . . . if I move some of the tables out the back.'

Fergus claps his hands together. 'Ha! That's *perfect*, Grace! On so many levels!'

'Perfect?!' I whine in a voice that is in danger of breaking into a million pieces.

'Absolutely! I can reply to all of your new friends to let them know they'll be able to come and have a chat with you about your detox.' Fergus gives me a thumbs up. 'Well done, mate. I wouldn't have thought of that unless you'd pointed out that you can't go online!'

I must get out.

I must run away.

These people are clearly demons from hell disguised as my friends – bent on putting me through the torments of Hades until my soul explodes or my bottom falls off, whichever comes first.

I shake my head rapidly back and forth. 'I can't. I can't do it.'

'Of course you can!' Fergus argues. 'You're a lot better with people than you think you are.' He opens his arms expansively. 'And think how good the business will be for Grace! All of that coffee being drunk by all of those people.'

I see Grace's eyes light up.

You complete *bastard*, Fergus!

He knows that I have feelings for Grace – and I would probably do anything to make her happy.

'Business has been slow since the whole thing with Henrietta,' Grace points out. 'People get a bit twitchy when the police turn up somewhere. And the repairs did cost an awful lot . . .'

Oh well, that's fucking it, then, isn't it?

How can I say no?

I'm going to have to do this stupid meeting with a bunch of people I've never met before, because I'm being forced into doing it, thanks to my so-called best friend and the woman I'm in love wit—

No!

No, no, no!

I didn't say that!

I didn't say it!

I'm not in love with her!

Honestly!

She's my *friend*. Just my friend!

I am *not* in love with Grace!

'All right, I'll do it!' I splutter, not entirely in control of my own brain, thanks to the revelation it's just thrown at me at one thousand miles an hour.

'You will?' Grace says, with no small degree of excitement.

Fergus laughs. 'Of course he will! He knows it's the right thing to do!'

I will visit you, Fergus Brailsworth! I will visit you in your sleep and do unpleasant things to your person!

'I'll spend a few hours getting in touch with all these fine people,' he continues, 'to let them know that Andy will be here to talk about the detox . . . and offer some advice.' He snaps his fingers. 'I'll pop an advert in the paper too!'

Oh, heavens to Murgatroyd.

What have I done?

◆ ◆ ◆

Mind you, it can't really be all that bad, can it?

OK, so Fergus had a lot of people contacting him about my story, but that doesn't mean they're all going to want to travel to meet me.

After all, it's quite easy to find information about digital detoxes online. There's no need to actually speak to someone about it.

At least, I'm assuming there's a lot of stuff online about them, anyway. Obviously, I can't check. But given that you can find reams of information about a deep-sea creature called the flying buttocks, I'm pretty sure digital detoxes will be covered at some length as well.

I'll now wait while you go and google 'flying buttocks'.

. . .

. . . . . .

Done?

Let's carry on then.

There's a very good chance that not many people will turn up to hear me speak at all, which is just as well, as I have no idea what to say. Everything pertinent to my detox is included in Fergus's annoyingly detailed stories, so anything I add will just be repetition. I might as well stand there and recite the articles verbatim, while the few people who turn up to Grace's coffee shop sit there and drink their cappuccinos.

I am not looking forward to seeing Grace's face when she sees the poor turnout. I can't blame her for being excited at the prospect of a large crowd that Fergus put in her head, but I'm just not that interesting. I'm not that much of a draw.

I wish she could see that.

I also wish I could run away from the entire thing.

Maybe visit, and get lost in, another one of the country's many attractive cities. York maybe, or possibly Edinburgh.

Yeah. That'd be nice. A trip to Edinburgh. Just me and Grace again, wandering through the streets, looking for fudge and avoiding vampires dressed in tartan.

I could add a visit in to see my mother and father too. That'd be lovely.

I've talked with them both a lot on the phone recently (and actually listened to what they've had to say properly for the first time in years, given that I haven't also been fiddling around with my iPad at the same time).

I'd love for them to meet Grace. I think they'd all get along like a house on fire.

This daydream fills my head nicely as I drive to Heirloom Coffee on a sunny Thursday evening – a few days after Fergus contacted all of the people who'd emailed and messaged him.

It is a day of some importance for me.

It is the last day of my digital detox.

Yes indeed, I have made it through to the end.

I have completed my task.

It's a surreal feeling, to be completely honest with you. On the one hand I am delighted that tomorrow I will be able to go on Facebook for the first time in two months and play a few cheeky games of *Call of Duty* multiplayer, but on the other hand, I almost feel . . . I don't know . . . regretful? Sad? A little melancholic that my online-free life is about to end.

I've learned quite a lot about myself in the past eight weeks, and have improved my general sense of well-being a great deal . . . so I can't pretend that bringing the detox to a close will be 100 per cent positive.

Don't get me wrong, though. I do intend to bring it to an end.

Two months in the wilderness is probably enough for Andrew Bellows.

Jesus only bloody managed forty days, and he was the son of God.

This meeting tonight seems like an extremely good way for me to bookend my experience of a digitally free life. I can speak to the three or four people that do turn up, try to give them as much advice as I can with my limited conversational skills, and send them on their way.

Then I can get up tomorrow morning and get on with life again.

I just miss it all too much, you know?

The last week has dragged *massively* as I've counted down the time to the end of the detox. My head has been filled with all of the exciting things I'm going to do once I'm allowed back online.

But then I think again of wandering around Edinburgh with Grace, the same way we did in Bath, and I feel deeply confused again.

That day out has become emblematic of all the positives that have come from the detox, and every time I fantasise about scrolling through my Twitter feed – finally plugging back into the world around me – the trip to Bath intrudes, and reminds me of what I might be missing out on when I do end the detox.

And then there's a question that I don't want to know the answer to . . .

What will happen with me and Grace when I do end the detox?

Right now, we have something in common that binds us to one another – but what happens when that commonality disappears?

Grace has said she's going to take one day at a time with her own detox, so she hasn't placed an end point on it like I have. That means she could want to carry on with it indefinitely. What will it do to our relationship if she's still living a tech-free life, but I'm back using it again? Will our friendship last? Or will she drift away from me?

Can I stand that?

But then again, can I stand feeling so disconnected from the world any longer?

Do I have to lose one to have the other?!

Just think about holding her hand as you turn a corner, you fool. Anything else is likely to spark off the irritable bowel.

I try my hardest to do this as I drive up the village street to where Heirloom Coffee is. The calming thoughts stay with me for about thirty seconds, until I actually drive past the window of the shop and look inside.

OK, it's not packed to the rafters, but there are certainly more than three or four people in there. I count at least twenty. Maybe even *thirty*.

My heart instantly starts to pound.

I have to be very careful turning in to the car park at the back of the terrace that Heirloom Coffee sits in. My hands are a little quivery, and I don't want to crash into the post office on the corner.

Thirty people.

All of whom I assume have come to look at Andy Bellows.

I should have worn a nicer shirt.

And jeans.

And been three inches taller.

And have larger pectoral muscles.

And a better haircut.

Gulp.

I park the car carefully and climb out of it *very slowly*. On legs that feel more rubbery than a comedy chicken, I make my way around to the front of the row of medieval houses, and walk towards the café's entrance.

Nice deep breaths.

Think about Grace's warm hand in yours.

Try not to think about needing a poo.

Oh no. I need a poo.

That's not good.

That's *never* good.

The irritable bowel syndrome that has been kept under a decent amount of control recently is rearing its ugly head again as I draw ever closer to Heirloom's front door.

Why did I agree to do this?

Because of Grace, you fool.

Damn it.

Damn it all.

I really need a poo.

I push open the door and try to affect a pleasant smile as I do.

Have you ever tried to affect a pleasant smile when you really need a poo? It's rather like trying to look relaxed while white-water rafting.

With lips curled into what probably resembles more of a snarl than a smile, and buttocks clenched against the rising tide, I walk into the coffee shop and find a small sea of faces staring back at me.

All of them with looks of recognition.

For someone like me, who is very uncomfortable and anxious in large crowds, having everyone in the room look at me like they know me is akin to a soft, plump rabbit stumbling into a den of foxes.

The smile drops off my face, and I desperately search for someone familiar. Luckily, Grace and Fergus are standing over at the counter, both smiling the kind of smile that comes from people who are not about to suffer a brown-trouser accident in front of a group of strangers.

I twiddle over to them as fast as possible.

I know you wouldn't usually use the word 'twiddle' to describe how someone walks, but trust me, when your bowels are about to let go in public, about the only thing you can do is twiddle. Twiddle as fast as possible, and hope it's not too late.

'Hey, Andy,' Grace says as I reach her.

'Evening, pal,' Fergus adds.

'I need the toilet,' I say in a rush, and twiddle my way past them and the counter, down the short corridor to the single toilet cubicle at the back of the shop.

Inside, things occur that need no description. You've already had to suffer through one toilet escapade of mine, so I don't feel the need to trouble you with another.

Suffice to say, I emerge from the toilet about five minutes later a good couple of pounds lighter and somewhat calmer of mood.

Calmer, that is, until I see all of those expectant faces again.

'Are you OK?' Grace asks me.

'I think so,' I reply, trying to ignore my stomach, which is still rolling like an angry ocean. 'Are all of these people here to see me?'

'Yep!' Fergus says. 'Had a better turnout than I was expecting. Shall I introduce you?'

No, Fergus.

I do not want you to introduce me.

I only want to do two things right now – kiss Grace and kick you in the testicles.

But as I don't have the stomach for either, I guess you'd better just let these poor people know who I am, so we can get this palaver over with. 'Yeah, go on then,' I tell him, steadying myself against the counter.

'Hello, everyone, thank you for coming,' Fergus tells the crowd – who are all sat nursing a variety of coffees. The profits for the café will be good this evening. 'This here is Andy, as I'm sure you're all aware. We figured the best way we could do things is if you guys just ask him whatever questions you may have about his detox . . . so hands up anyone who has one to ask.'

For a moment, everyone just sits there, and I breathe a small sigh of relief. If they're as reluctant to come forward as I am to be standing up here, then this meet-and-greet will go a lot faster.

But then, almost at once, every single person in the café puts their hand up, and I know I'm in this for the long haul.

I feel Grace come and stand beside me, and reach one hand over to gently grasp my arm and give it a squeeze.

I don't think there's many things I couldn't do if it came with a gentle encouraging squeeze from Grace – up to and including white-water rafting.

From the crowd of expectant faces, I pick out a heavy-set and pleasant-faced woman sitting just in front of me. 'Er, yes, what would you like to know?' I ask hesitantly.

The woman shuffles in her seat a bit, looking somewhat surprised that I chose her, but after a moment she composes herself and says, 'Hi, Andy. I'm Josephine.' She seems to compose her question in her head for a moment before finally asking it. 'Are you happy now?'

Oh.

What a thing to ask.

I should have chosen somebody else . . .

I stand there for a moment, swimming in a sea of uncertainty about what I should say.

Do I say yes, and probably give her the answer she wants to hear? It might be the best way to go about things. Definitely the *easiest*.

Or do I tell her the messy, complicated truth?

Then I concentrate for a moment on the feel of Grace's hand on my arm, and I know what I should say.

'I'm happ*ier*,' I tell the woman, heavy accent on the last syllable.

She nods, and then looks at me intently – clearly expecting more.

I stare back at her for a second, understanding that I'm not going to get away without going into further detail.

But I don't want to tell her more, damn it!

This is my *life* we're talking about, and I don't really want to let a bunch of complete strangers in on my every thought and emotion about the last two months.

But looking around the room, I have no doubt that I'm not going to be allowed to just give one- or two-word answers. More is expected from me.

Sigh.

Just lie. Tell her – and the rest – what they want to hear, and maybe we can get this done with a minimum of fuss.

I don't want to lie.

Oh? Does the idea of laying yourself bare sound like more fun to you?

No.

Well, there you have it then. Tell them all that the detox is wonderful, and then get out of here. There's every chance our bowels are going to want to have words again before this evening is over, so the faster we can get this ridiculous Q & A session over with, the better.

You make a good point, brain. Let's do this.

'I'm very happy!' I tell Josephine, plastering on a fake grin for all I'm worth.

Her face lights up when I say this, and I know that I have done the right thing.

Even though I also absolutely know that I have done the *wrong thing.*

'Yes. It's been a wonderful couple of months, and I feel like life is so much better for me now!' I add, and am delighted to see that the entire café is smiling along with me as I say it.

This isn't so bad.

It turns out public speaking is quite good fun – as long as you're saying things that people want to hear.

And saying things that people want to hear is precisely what I do over the next hour or so. And for every answer I give, the mood and general atmosphere of the café lifts.

When I'm asked whether I miss being online or not, I say that I don't miss it all that much – and that makes them happy.

When I'm asked whether I feel healthier or not, I say that I most certainly am in every sense of the word – and that makes them happy.

When I'm asked about how I fill my days without technology, I say that I easily find things to do – and that makes them happy.

And what makes them happy, makes *me* happy.

It really is quite a marvellous feeling.

I've entered into some kind of reciprocating loop, where the more lies I tell, the more they smile, which means I smile more, and therefore tell more lies.

And I'm not *completely* lying, after all. The detox *has* done me a huge amount of good. I do feel healthier, and I have found lots of things to keep me occupied without being online. The day out in Bath was a great deal of fun – as are all the walks in the country.

So what if I'm not also talking about the bad aspects? These fine people don't need to know that I still crave my social media every single day, or that I find a great deal of my life to be dreadfully inconvenient without technology.

And they definitely don't need to know that the only reason I agreed to speak to them in the first place was because I've developed feelings for someone who may – or may not – feel the same about me.

And there's no way in hell I'm telling them that I have every intention of going back online first thing tomorrow morning.

Those smiles would probably drop off their faces at the speed of light if they knew just how much I still want to be online. That for all the good the detox has done me, it's also left me out in the wilderness.

These people clearly want – and even need – to go down the same path that I have taken. And they want to hear that the path is an easy one to traverse once you're on it.

From what I can gather from this evening's conversation, they all suffer greatly in one way or another from too much time spent online – whether it be Internet shopping, or on social media, or playing online video games, or falling down the YouTube rabbit hole.

All of them have rather gaunt looks on their faces that only lift when I tell them my next white lie about how wonderful my life is, now I'm free of the shackles of the Internet.

And who am I to tell them the path is hard? That it comes with a lot of pitfalls?

I'm self-aware (duck) enough to know that I'm the kind of person who naturally gravitates towards pitfalls at every available opportunity. Perhaps for these fine folks things will be easier. I certainly don't want to put them off, just because I'm an accident-prone wally. I very much doubt they'd encounter the same duck-pond- and toilet-window-related disasters I did!

This is exactly the same mentality I had when I first talked to Grace about the detox – and that seemed to work out well for both me and her, so it stands to reason it's the right way of handling things now as well.

So, tonight I am Mr Positive, and my audience clearly loves me for it.

From the back of the room, I spy a hand go up, and my heart sinks. I have been avoiding looking at the owner of that hand all night. I have done this because the owner of the hand has trouble written all over him. He is a young man of a slight build and a rather pinched expression.

I am going to describe what this young man is dressed in, and I'm interested in what your reaction will be. I know we're not supposed to judge people by the way they dress themselves in this enlightened day and age, but in this case, I hope you'll agree it's impossible not to.

The young man wears a bobble hat upon his head. The bobble hat has the *Star Trek* logo on it. Underneath the hat I see curly brown, and rather unkempt, hair. The young man wears glasses. Thick-rimmed and round, they create a magnification effect on his eyes that is visible even from across the café. The eyes themselves are permanently fixed in narrow slits of suspicion. The poor chap has a problem with acne that a month spent in a bath of heavy-duty spot cream probably couldn't solve.

Upon his person he wears a cagoule. The top half is bright blue, the bottom half is bright red.

Yes. Those are brown corduroy trousers.

No, I don't know why a fully grown man in 2019 would be wearing green Crocs and yellow socks either.

Now . . . what do you reckon?

Am I being entirely unfair in not wanting to draw this young man's attention all night? Or do you think that I might have a point?

We're about to find out, as he's the only one with his hand up now. Everyone else appears to be satisfied and happy with what I've had to say tonight, but this cagoule-wearing chap has more he wants to know and there's not a damn thing I can do to get away from whatever questions he may have.

You've probably worked with a variation of this kind of fellow before. You know . . . he's the one who, after a three-hour meeting, will always have more questions to ask. No matter that it's now

5.47 p.m. on a Friday afternoon. No matter that the topic has been covered in great detail from every conceivable angle.

No, this chap will have more questions to ask, and will continue asking them until someone senior enough in the meeting has the fortitude and guts to shut him up, so everyone can go home. And God help you if there's no one senior enough in the room to do this, as it means you're going to be there until at least 6.41 p.m.

On a Friday evening.

You might as well have Chinese torturers come in and start whacking bamboo splinters up your fingernails at that point.

I point a reluctant finger at my cagoule-wearing friend. As I do so, in my peripheral vision I see several other members of the audience suppress groans.

Yes. They've all been in that meeting, haven't they? They've all known what it's like to get home at 7.52 p.m. on a Friday.

'Yes?' I ask him in a tremulous voice.

The young man pushes his glasses up on his nose and fixes me with a stare.

'Are you going to continue with your detoxification, Mr Bellows?' His voice is reedy and clipped. It couldn't really be anything else.

'I'm sorry?'

'Your detoxification? I note from both the articles written by Mr Brailsworth, that the period of time that you have elected to be on the detoxification will officially come to an end tomorrow.'

I groan inwardly. I was hoping no one would ask this. I was hoping that everyone would just enjoy hearing me being incredibly positive about how great the detox has been – while tacitly understanding that I am coming to the end of it.

'Yes, that's right,' I tell Mr Cagoule in a gritty tone of voice.

'Well, it's very apparent from what you have said tonight that the detoxification has been extremely positive, and with no downsides, so I have to assume that you will be carrying on with it indefinitely?' He pushes the glasses up again. 'There doesn't appear to be any reason for you not to, does there?'

Yep.

I should never have let him bloody speak.

'Well, I . . . er . . . I . . .' What the hell do I say? 'Er . . . what's your name?'

'Colin.'

Of course his name is fucking *Colin*. What the hell else would it be?

'Well, Colin, the detox has been as wonderful as I've described to you all here tonight, extremely accurately. But . . .'

But what, Bellows?

What is this *but* that you're about to drop on the sea of happy faces you've created here this evening?

What *but* could you possibly be about to come out with that will satisfy young Colin and his cagoule?

Because if you're about to say that you're going to stop with the detox tomorrow, you'd better be prepared for a lot of *buts* coming your way instead.

But you said it's great . . .

But you said it's made you feel so much better . . .

But you said your life is a lot more fun . . .

But you said you feel more relaxed and happy . . .

There will be more *buts* than a farm full of incandescently angry goats . . .

. . . probably angry at the fact I've missed one 't' off the word 'but'.

I've gone and painted myself into the legendary corner, haven't I?

There's simply no way I can tell these people I'm quitting the detox tomorrow without disappointing all of them. And probably making them angry.

I wouldn't want to make them angry . . . especially not Colin, who looks like the type of man who would have many sharp pencils secreted about his person.

I once heard the legend of a chap who killed three men with a pencil. Who's to say he wasn't wearing a bobble hat and a cagoule, eh?

'But . . . it should be coming to an end tomorrow, as you say, *Colin*,' I say to my potentially pencil-wielding friend, 'but . . . but I could hardly stop it now, could I?'

No! No! Don't say these things!

'No . . . I will of course be carrying on with the detox, for as long as possible.'

Every word drops out of my mouth like a hardened turd.

Hardened turds that seem to please the small crowd in front of me no end. Even Colin – pinched of face and suspicious of glance – smiles and sits back in his seat, no doubt satisfied that he got the answer he was looking for.

I look around to see that Grace is also smiling broadly.

Oh, for the love of God!

I just want to play *Candy Crush*! I just want to download some pornography! I just want to spend two hours arguing with a complete stranger about how bad the last season of *Game of Thrones* was!

But now I can do none of those things, because I have promised this room of complete strangers – and the woman I have stupidly fallen in love with – that I will remain on my bloody detox for the foreseeable future.

Aaaarrggh!

I spot Fergus out of the corner of my eye. He's trying very hard not to look triumphant, but he's not doing a very good job of it. More Andy Bellows on a detox means more opportunities for stories for his bloody paper, and he knows it.

'Thank you, Mr Bellows!' Colin the Cagoule says – and then does something that actually, physically, makes my skin crawl.

He rises to his feet *and starts to clap*.

For an excruciating moment, he stands there alone, clapping away to himself. But then the others all start to get to their feet as well, and they start to applaud too.

It's like someone is throwing darts at my head.

Fergus then starts to clap too . . . far, far too enthusiastically for my liking.

I look at Grace.

She does not clap.

Instead, she gives me a half-amused, half-worried smile and gives my arm another gentle squeeze.

For once, though, her touch doesn't really help.

How can it? I'm standing in front of a bunch of people I've just spent the last hour lying to about my life, and now they are applauding me for it.

It's excruciating.

It's unbelievable.

It's . . . probably everything I deserve.

I have made my analogue bed, and now I really am going to have to lie in it.

Chapter Ten

FROM TECH-HEAD TO FIGUREHEAD

Loggers Off.

That's what Fergus called them.

The people who came to see me that night.

The Loggers Off.

Awful, isn't it?

And I'm not just talking about the potentially incorrect grammar . . .

By giving the group a name – a collective way to describe them – Fergus has made them a *thing*. An *entity*. A creature of many terrible facets – all of them pointed directly at *me*.

Fergus's second follow-up story went in the paper the day after I consigned myself to a life of seemingly never-ending digital exclusion. He got an exhaustive interview with Colin the Cagoule, who went into great detail about how much he admired my stance on a tech-free life, and how he was definitely going to follow my example. It appears that Colin lost his job thanks to his own online obsession. There's only so many times you can fall asleep at your desk because you've been up until the wee small hours discussing how great a Starfleet captain Sisko was, before somebody pulls the plug.

I'm sure Colin's ex-colleagues were delighted that he got the sack, because it meant they could go home at 4.30 p.m. on a Friday afternoon. But for him, it was an understandable disaster. He had so many more questions to ask, you see. So many more Friday evenings to inadvertently ruin.

And people who read Fergus's article *loved* Colin, of course. Which in turn just made them love me more, by association. Why couldn't Fergus have made Colin out to be a less sympathetic character?

The Loggers Off began to grow in number. *Hideously* quickly.

In the fortnight that has passed since that meeting in Heirloom, Fergus has informed me that well over *two hundred people* have contacted him about wanting to become part of the 'movement'.

It's a bloody good job I can't access social media, because if I could, I think I might have a heart attack – given what my best friend is telling me. He created a Twitter account called @ LoggersOff – which has apparently gained four hundred followers already. It took me about *three years* to get to four hundred followers. I'm insanely jealous. Apparently of myself.

The Facebook page has been equally as popular. If I ever do go back online again, it's always going to come packaged with a fair amount of low-level embarrassment, knowing that such things exist . . . technically in my name.

Some of them have just joined to hear more about what a digital detox is, but some of them have apparently already declared they are starting their own version of one.

There's a hashtag. #LoggingOffWithAndy.

It seems strange to go on social media just to declare you're *leaving* social media – but of course nothing happens these days unless you have *mentioned* it on social media. It's a rather strange *Catch-22*-like state of affairs.

I wonder how they're going to feel once they can't do that any more? Just pop on Facebook and tell everyone what they're up to?

I wonder how many of them are going to last the full sixty days? How many will crash and burn quickly? And how many may make it a permanent thing? I have no idea.

The local TV news has picked up on my story too.

I did a short interview to camera two days ago with a pretty young woman called Christie, who confided in me when we'd finished that she thought she spent far too much time on the Internet and might join the Loggers Off herself.

Fergus has contacted a printing company to see if he can get some T-shirts made. He's asked me to design the logo for it.

I've agreed to this, because he promised that the paper would pay me quite handsomely for it.

I am my own worst enemy.

There's been an air of inevitability about this recent chain of events that makes my teeth itch. There are clearly a great many people out there who are struggling to live in the digital age. Men and women suffering with a variety of mental and physical health problems, all stemming from too many hours spent looking at a screen. And in me they have apparently found – oh, good God in heaven – a *figurehead*. Someone whose example they can follow.

This, I hasten to add, is not because I am worthy of such followship.

It's because I am unlucky enough to have a best friend who is a journalist and is unnaturally good at his job.

Even I read the stories he's written about me and think I sound like a pretty good chap who's probably worth listening to.

The utter bastard.

There's another meeting scheduled in a few days at Heirloom (as advertised both online for the folks who haven't started their own detox yet, and in the paper for those that have), and Grace is getting a bit stressed about it, because she doesn't think she's going to have enough chairs for everyone to sit on. She's also increased her coffee bean order from the wholesaler's by 25 per cent to cover the amount of people she thinks will turn up.

Along with the T-shirts, Fergus has also asked the printing company to make a 'Loggers Off' sign that Grace can hang in the shop.

He says he's going to give any money he makes from the sales of the T-shirts to a mental health charity.

The utter, utter *bastard*.

And of course, with all of this going on, I am still not on the Internet. My detox continues apace – whether I like it or not.

And it feels so much worse now, because I have no idea when it's going to end.

When will this Loggers Off thing lose steam?

It must eventually, of course. Everything does. Our culture is fad-based, and fads are not usually long-term pursuits. But the more Fergus tells me about how many people are logging on to join Loggers Off (oxymoron that it is), the more I become worried that it's not going anywhere soon.

And yes, of course I've been tempted to break the detox and go online to see the bloody Twitter and Facebook pages. In fact, I've been more tempted than at any other point in this whole process, I think. But I've managed to resist, simply because I know I might not like what I find if I do. Fergus tells me everyone's being overwhelmingly positive . . . but I'm not sure I entirely believe him.

The Internet does not allow for universal praise. If you don't believe me, just post a picture of the cutest puppy you can find, and there will be some people who will criticise it for not being fluffy enough, or having doe eyes that are just a bit too runny.

I know full well that there will be some trolls on the Loggers Off social media accounts who will be ripping into me no end – and I can't take seeing any of that.

So, I have not broken my online fast, and have no intentions of doing so.

Frankly, out of sight is out of mind to a certain extent with all of this, and I am able to live my life day to day without obsessing about it *too much*. Especially when I have something else to concentrate on.

And today, I am concentrating on linguine with chilli, crab and watercress – followed by chocolate and honey semifreddo.

These are the two recipes I have decided to cook for dinner this evening.

Usually, I would be eating a lamb and chicken shish from the local Turkish grill (it's a new Friday-night tradition in these here parts), but tonight I am making a special effort, because I have a guest for dinner. The person who has had the most impact on my life in recent weeks.

No, not Fergus! About the only thing I'm planning on cooking up for him in the near future is a slap across the chops. He thoroughly deserves one, given that he's made me a local celebrity, has improved my work opportunities no end and is helping a very worthwhile cause by donating money to it. He's evil personified, as I'm sure you'll agree.

I am – of course – talking about *Grace*.

Yes, I have finally plucked up the courage to ask her around to my place for a meal.

Our platonic relationship has been going very well, and there's been a part of me that hasn't wanted to spoil it by trying to take things to the next level. But then this morning I was in Heirloom working on a logo design for a leisure centre when Grace came over, looking decidedly harried and telling me how rushed off her feet she was.

I instantly felt guilty, because I'm responsible for this. It isn't easy running an independent coffee shop at the best of times, but when you're planning on a sizeable event like another Loggers Off meeting, it makes it all the more difficult.

'I don't know whether I'm coming or going,' she told me. 'I won't get out of here until bloody late, so God knows what I'm going to do about dinner.'

'You could come to mine.'

The words were out of my mouth before I had a chance to think about them. This is just as well, as I probably wouldn't have said them otherwise.

Grace smiled shyly. 'That'd be lovely, Andy, thanks.'

And thus the die was cast . . .

I spent the rest of the day worrying about what the hell I was going to cook.

A chicken and lamb shish really wouldn't cut it. Nor would my standard go-to recipe of battered chicken bites with super noodles and a dollop of habanero sauce.

I am to cooking what Homer Simpson is to parenting.

No, I have to make a proper effort tonight – hence the linguine with chilli, crab and watercress, along with the chocolate and honey semifreddo.

Nigella is to blame.

I went into Waterstones at lunchtime and picked up her latest.

I chose the above two options from the book because the first one sounded relatively straightforward, and the second sounded just exotic enough to impress.

Needless to say, the first *wasn't* easy in the *slightest*, and the second may sound exotic, but is a galloping bastard to actually make.

I have been at this shit now for *five hours*.

My kitchen looks like several war zones have been through it, on their way to the pub.

The linguine thing wasn't exceptionally hard in terms of the actual ingredients, but cooking crab is roughly as hard as performing brain surgery with boxing gloves on. It's all about the cooking time, you see. Not long enough and it's mush, but too much and you've cooked yourself something that you can erase pencil marks with.

But I got it right eventually, and putting it together with the pasta, the chilli and the watercress wasn't too hard. I just chucked it all on the plate and remained hopeful.

My version of the recipe doesn't look entirely the same as Nigella's, but we'll put that down to the lack of decent lighting and prep time, and hope it's going to at least taste nice.

The fucking semifreddo is another thing entirely.

I had no idea what a semifreddo was before attempting to make one, otherwise I would never have bothered. It's essentially a big block of frozen cream, covered in chocolate and honey – which sounds like it shouldn't be too hard to make, right?

Wrong!

Do you know how incomprehensibly difficult it is to shape cream into a block? To wrestle a liquid into a solid? If you've never attempted to make a semifreddo then you don't, and please don't pretend otherwise.

There are currently *six* semifreddos going hard in my freezer.

Yes . . . six.

There are so many because I have no idea whether any of them will actually stay solid once they come out.

It's the cream-whipping, you see.

Cream-whipping makes crab-cooking look about as easy as running a tap.

I have whipped so much cream today that I frankly never want to look at the stuff again as long as I live.

My right arm could wank off an elephant.

Some of the cream went globby. Some of the cream went slooshy. Bits of it went crumbly.

Crumbly!

How in Captain Fuckabout can you whip a liquid into a crumbly?

It's *against the laws of physics, people.*

It took me hours just to get the cream whipped into a consistency that could be considered worthy of freezing. And even then, I'm not sure whether I've done it right – hence the multiple semifreddo attempts currently cooling off on the bottom shelf.

I'll just have to hope that at least one of the buggers comes out OK, so I can drizzle it in the honey and runny chocolate I bought from M&S in my rushed bout of last-minute shopping this afternoon.

Everything else is done, though. The table is laid with crockery that only has a few chips in it. There's a bottle of Pinot Grigio in the fridge, and I even bought a candle, which is currently sitting in the middle of my IKEA dining table, wondering what all the fuss is about.

I'm wearing my nicest jeans, a black shirt and an expression of faint hope.

Maybe tonight, I can try to kiss Grace.

The thought of this makes my toes curl.

It feels like the right time to move things to the next level.

As stated previously, Grace has settled into her own detox well, and is very much enjoying all the excitement around Loggers Off – despite the admin problems it's thrown up for her.

She did have one wobble recently. Though that's to be expected after a few weeks. It happened the other day when Shayna – Grace's assistant barista – told her that Chrissy Teigen's website has 50 per cent off her make-up range. I had to forcibly hold Grace back from ripping the Samsung Galaxy out of the hands of a nearby customer.

Other than this incident, though, she's been coping magnificently.

The time spent wandering around the local countryside has helped, I'm sure. Grace loves to be out and about as much as possible. She's clearly trying to make up for all that time spent locked in her house, in front of the computer screen.

And on those walks we take together, we talk a lot. About everything and nothing. About our lives before we met, and our lives now we're on the detox.

I feel like I've bonded with her more than I have with any other human being, and it's come about via a lot of in-depth conversation – only interrupted by the occasional stile or disconcerting cow. I could talk to her for hours.

I think both Grace and I are in a place now where I can probably make a move.

I'm guessing (hoping) she must feel the same way, otherwise she wouldn't have agreed to come to dinner tonight.

This will be the first time I've had her over to my flat since we met. Up to now, we've been hanging out with each other in the great outdoors, or over at Heirloom. Nothing as intimate as an evening spent in my own home. Tonight will mark a real change in our relationship.

With any luck I can do a good job of wooing her with the crab linguine and the semifreddo.

Then maybe I'll get that kiss . . . and more besides, if I'm an extremely lucky boy.

I try to ignore my own semifreddo's reaction to this train of thought, and busy myself tidying the kitchen.

Ding dong!

That'll be her now!

A little earlier than she said she'd arrive, but no matter. The linguine is being kept warm in the oven, and the semifreddo should hopefully be freezing nicely, so I am in a calm state of mind as I go over to the front door.

As I do, I am reminded of the first time I opened it to Grace. I am hoping and expecting to see her looking a lot happier tonight than she did back then.

'Just in time, I've got the meal all read—'

This is not Grace.

Unless Grace has split herself into two entities, both male, one wearing a blue and red cagoule.

Actually, make that *three* entities. The other male one is holding a small dog.

'*Colin?!*' I say, in a horrified voice.

What the hell is he doing at my door?

'Hello, Mr Bellows,' Colin replies, offering me an ingratiating smile. 'How are you?'

'Er . . . I'm . . . I'm fine, thank you.'

I look over – and down – at Colin's companion as I say this.

Said companion is about five feet tall, has curly dark hair of a tight, wire-wool consistency, and is all about the teeth.

The chubby little fella has virtually no top lip, so his large and brilliantly white main incisors are presented for all the world to see.

He looks like Dennis the Menace and Bugs Bunny made sweet, sweet love, and this was the result.

He is also wearing a *Death Curse Intransigent* T-shirt. A game that I have still not as yet purchased, or even had a go at – given that you have to play it online.

The little man is holding the aforementioned small dog.

This dog is a pug.

The pug is dressed like a wizard.

A little blue pug wizard looks up at me from his owner's arms with doe eyes that are probably just a little bit too runny.

Incredible stuff.

'That's lovely to hear,' Colin says, nodding appreciatively. 'Sorry to trouble you on this lovely Friday evening, but I felt I should come to you, because my partner Wilberforce here really needs your— *Puggerlugs! No!'*

The dog jumps out of Wilberforce's hands and powers right past me into the flat.

'Hey!' I cry in surprise as I dodge out of the dog's way.

'Puggerlugs! Come back!' Colin entreats, before his small companion rushes past me into the flat to chase down the puggy wizard – who is now over at the bookcase by the TV, turning in circles on the spot. 'I'm so sorry, Mr Bellows!' Colin exclaims, a look of vast apology on his face. 'Puggerlugs can be a little devil sometimes!'

'Apparently so!' I cry, still trying to process this extremely strange turn of events.

'I'd better go and render my assistance,' Colin tells me in a harried voice. 'I warned Wilberforce that we should have left Puggerlugs at home, but he's so attached to him!'

And with that, Colin the Cagoule also barrels into my flat and over to where Wilberforce is trying to corral Puggerlugs into one corner.

'Look, you two . . . sorry, three . . . can't be in here!' I bellow – possibly for the first time in my life. Despite the fact it's my surname, I am not a natural bellower. But I have made a lot of effort this evening, and I don't intend to have it ruined by two unwanted gatecrashers.

I sprint over to Colin and Wilberforce just as the little toothy man is trying to grab Puggerlugs back up into his arms. This fails completely, and the pug wriggles away, heading for the footstool that sits in front of my couch, at a vast rate of knots.

The instant the dog arrives at it, he pops his two little front legs up on the footstool, gaining a strong grip on the jumbo cord material it's made out of.

The dog then starts to have sex with my footstool.

Less than three minutes ago, I was having a lovely daydream about what might transpire with Grace here in this flat tonight. Now I am watching a pug dressed as a blue wizard shag my footstool.

If anyone doubts that the universe is a place of complete chaos and total uncertainty, this jolly well proves it, as far as I'm concerned.

Things would be bad enough if the pug was undressed, but the wizard outfit adds a whole new level of surrealism to proceedings that I can scarcely comprehend. Just look at the way the little wizard hat on the top of his head is jiggling about, would you?

'Get him off there!' I cry, jumping over to where Colin and Wilberforce are now crowding over my footstool and around their little dog, both with dismayed looks on their faces.

'Oh dear. He doesn't normally do this, I can assure you! He's usually a very good dog!' Colin exclaims.

'He's not being a bloody good dog now!' I spit, and bend down to pull the little bastard away from the footstool before he has a chance to really get going on it.

This earns me a growl and a baring of teeth. Both are quite horrifying.

'Jesus Christ!' I exclaim in terror, and back off before the pug can lacerate my hands with those tiny sharp teeth.

'He must be stressed out!' Colin says in a hectic voice. 'He knows how anxious we are at the moment, and it's obviously translated down to him! Puggerlugs has always been a stress humper!'

'Well, just bloody stop him doing it before he translates something on to my jumbo cord!' I demand, still trying to keep my distance from those ghastly little teeth.

Colin looks at his friend. 'We'll have to sing the song. It's the only way!'

Wilberforce nods feverishly in agreement.

I whip my head from one to the other. '*Song?* What song? What the hell are you both on about?'

'We have a special song we sing to Puggerlugs when he gets like this,' Colin tells me. 'It never fails to work. He loves it so very much!'

'Well, bloody sing it then!' I cry as I see the dog start to build up speed.

Colin and Wilberforce both nod to one another, and the little man with the big teeth then pulls out what looks like a kazoo from his back pocket. He blows on it once to produce a note.

Then they both take a deep breath and start singing in perfect harmony.

'Puggerlugs! Puggerlugs! Stop being bad!'

I've clearly gone fucking insane.

'Puggerlugs! Puggerlugs! You're making us sad!'

Stark staring bonkers.

'Puggerlugs! Puggerlugs! To you we entreat!'

Completely off my bloody chump.

'Puggerlugs! Puggerlugs! Be a good boy, and get a lovely treat!'

As if on cue, at the end of the song both Colin and Wilberforce hold out small doggie treats in their hands, dangling them temptingly in Puggerlugs's direction.

This seems – quite incredibly – to do the trick.

The little wizard dog slides down off the footstool and gently plucks the treats from first Wilberforce's hand, and then Colin's. He then sits attentively for a moment, before allowing Wilberforce to gather him up in his arms again.

Colin visibly relaxes. 'Blimey. That was a hairy one, I can tell you.'

'Was it?' I respond in disbelief.

'Yes. We did well to calm him down that quickly.'

'Did you?'

'Most certainly.'

'Colin?'

'Yes, Mr Bellows?'

'What the hell are you both *doing here*?' I snap.

Colin gives me an ingratiating smile. 'I came to ask you to speak to my partner, Wilberforce. He's not one for large gatherings, so I couldn't bring him along to Loggers Off.'

'How did you find my flat?'

'Your website, Mr Bellows. Your address is on it, in the contacts section.'

I groan. I really should have done something about that – or got somebody else to do something about it. It's one thing for someone like Grace to turn up at my door, but it's quite another for Colin the Cagoule, his odd little friend and their humping dog to do so.

Grace!

She'll be here any minute! I can't have her walking in to discover these two!

'Look, you guys really can't be here. You'll have to leave,' I tell Colin in an urgent tone.

Both of their faces fall.

'But I promised Wilberforce that you would speak to him,' Colin tells me. 'He's been struggling like I have recently – with being on the computer too much. I hoped your advice would help him . . . help both of us.'

And then Colin does something so profoundly loving that it quite takes my breath away. He gently puts one arm around the little man's shoulder, and gives him the gentlest kiss on the side of his head, before turning back to me. 'Life has become so very difficult for Wilberforce, Mr Bellows.'

Seeing this clear gesture of concern and love forces my stance on this massive interruption to my evening to soften instantly.

Colin obviously thinks his companion could do with meeting me – no doubt about my detox – and it's equally obvious he cares a great deal for the little man. Enough to track me down for help, anyway.

This can't have been easy for either of them. Or Puggerlugs. No wonder he's stress-humping.

I sigh and sit down on the couch.

'So, tell me more, Colin,' I say in a resigned voice. 'Why exactly have you brought your boyfriend to me?'

Colin looks awkward.

Sorry . . . *more* awkward. There's an inherent awkwardness to Colin and his cagoule that probably began at birth.

'Well, much like myself, and all the other people at your meetings, Wilberforce here has an issue with how much time he spends on the Internet.'

'Is that when he's not stopping his dog making sweet, sweet love to items of furniture?'

'Aha. Yes,' Colin replies, looking a little sick. 'But when he's not doing that, the Internet consumes Wilberforce . . . even more so than it does me.' His face crumples. 'We don't go out any more, Mr Bellows. We don't see friends. We don't walk Puggerlugs much. That's why he has so much . . . so much *unspent energy*. And the stress of it all is becoming too much to cope with. Wilberforce and I snap at each other. We argue a lot. Puggerlugs here is stressed out most of the time. It's becoming intolerable.'

I look at Wilberforce, who now has an expression of such anguish on his face that I feel like crying.

Oh, bloody hell.

'He really does need to get offline,' Colin continues. 'But it's hard for me to convince him, as I am almost as bad as he is. Which is why I brought him to meet you. I was hoping you could give him a few words of encouragement . . . as the head of Loggers Off. To help him take the leap with me. To convince him a detox is the right thing to do, and to show him that it's not that hard.'

I rub my hand across my forehead and sigh. 'Sure, why not?' I tell Colin, and indicate for them both to sit on the couch with me.

'Excellent!' he replies, and looks at his partner. 'Wilberforce? Mr Bellows is going to talk to you now.'

Wilberforce smiles, nods and comes to sit next to me, with Puggerlugs still firmly grasped in his arms.

The look on Wilberforce's face is very expectant as he awaits my sage advice.

Oh God. I don't want this. I don't want complete strangers to look at me expectantly. Especially ones suffering from psychological issues brought on by excessive Internet usage.

I'm a graphic designer, for crying out loud. What do I know about helping people with their issues?

I can barely handle my own.

'Hello, Wilberforce,' I say. 'How are you?'

Wilberforce turns his head away from me shyly.

Colin perches himself on the footstool. 'I'm sorry, Mr Bellows. Wilberforce has a bit of trouble talking to strangers.'

'No problem, Colin.' I look at Puggerlugs, who returns the stare a little uncertainly.

'That's a lovely wizard outfit he's wearing, Wilberforce,' I say to the little man. 'He looks a bit like Gandalf.'

If Gandalf had had some kind of allergic reaction to eating berries, possibly.

But this puts a broad smile on Wilberforce's face. 'Are you . . . are you a fan of *The Lord of the Rings*?' he asks me, which is the first thing I've heard him actually say, beyond that silly song he performed for his strange little dog.

'Yeah, I am,' I reply. 'The detox gave me the chance to read it properly for the first time.'

'That's wonderful,' Wilberforce replies. 'It's my favourite story.'

'Mine too now . . . I think,' I say, before taking a breath. 'Colin here says you could probably do with going on a detox, like the one I've been doing?'

'Probably, yes. I do tend to spend a little too much time online.'

'Er . . . how much time would you say?'

Wilberforce thinks for a moment. 'I'd estimate my time on the Internet to be between twelve and fourteen hours a day.'

'Good grief!'

Colin leans forward. 'Wilberforce here is what you might call "independently wealthy", Mr Bellows. He doesn't need to work. He takes very good care of us.' Colin looks upset again. 'This is just as well, given what happened with my job.'

I swallow nervously. 'Well, that is interesting. And do you think you'd like to do a detox, Wilberforce?' I ask him.

The little man looks thoughtful for a second, flicking his tongue over his two enormous front teeth. 'I'm not sure, Mr Bellows. Colin tells me I need to cut down. And I always listen to Colin. He knows what's good for me.'

Colin smiles a bit indulgently. 'I like to think so. It's a problem we sadly both share. If I must do something about it, then so must Wilberforce. Our partnership was born of our shared online passions many years ago, and we really should move away from them together.'

'What kinds of things do you both do online?' I ask, knowing I might be opening a rather large and squelchy can of worms.

'Oh, the usual,' he tells me. 'We very much enjoy strategy games such as *World of Warcraft* and *DotA*.'

'And light aircraft appreciation,' Wilberforce adds.

Colin smiles again. 'Ah yes. We both enjoy our light aircraft very much. Many a happy hour we've spent in flight simulators. We once flew all the way to New Zealand and back.'

'And the forums!' Wilberforce says. 'We are both members of many film, television and computer game forums.'

'Indeed!' says Colin excitedly. 'We also follow a great many of the same people on social media. Wonderful, interesting people.'

'Yes!' Wilberforce agrees. 'Twitter is wonderful! I once got retweeted by Sir Ian McKellen!' he says, in a voice filled with the purest of pleasure.

That might explain his love of *The Lord of the Rings*, I guess.

'It's so nice to follow people we admire online,' Colin continues. 'Makes you feel closer to them.'

I nod my head in recognition.

These two men are not so dissimilar to myself, when you get right down to it. They seem to have fallen into a lifestyle almost identical to the one I lived. I have probably played many of the same games they have. Have followed the same people on social media. Have probably even spoken to the two of them on the same forums, at some point.

Yes, these two are not so different from me at all . . .

'And of course, there are the pugs,' Colin adds. 'So many websites, Instagram pages and Facebook groups dedicated to pugs.'

Wilberforce nods happily. 'Pugs! Lovely little pugs as far as the eye can see!'

At the mention of his breed, Puggerlugs immediately starts to wriggle in his owner's arms again.

'Puggerlugs! Calm yourself!' Wilberforce squeals as the little dog starts to thrash around wildly.

'Oh no! We may have overexcited him with all the mention of pugs!' Colin remarks. 'I'm afraid it doesn't take much these days to get him riled up!'

So riled up, in fact, that he squirms out of Wilberforce's arms, leaps off the couch and clamps himself around my right leg with a vice-like grip.

'Fuck about!' I scream, and try to get to my feet.

It's like I've been attacked by a facehugger from *Alien*, only instead of leaping at my face, he's gone straight for my shin bone.

I'll give you three guesses what he does next.

'Aaaaarggh! Stop him!' I wail as the little dog starts to hump my leg like it's going out of fashion.

'Puggerlugs!' Colin yells, rising from the footstool.

'The song!' Wilberforce bellows. 'We must sing the song again!'

'Yes!'

Wilberforce whips out the kazoo and plays the single note as I start to hop around the living room, shaking my leg for all I'm worth, trying to dislodge the tiny, horny terror.

'Puggerlugs! Puggerlugs! Stop being bad!' they sing. *'Puggerlugs! Puggerlugs! You're making us sad! Puggerlugs! Puggerlugs! To you we entreat! Puggerlugs! Puggerlugs! Be a good boy, and get a lovely treat!'*

'Aaaaarggh!'

'It's not working!' Colin howls.

'No it's fucking not!' I agree as I lean against the wall, holding my leg aloft in front of me. This bloody pug grips like a boa constrictor covered in superglue.

'You'll have to sing with us!' Colin implores.

'What?!'

'Sing with us, Mr Bellows! It needs more people. It's the only way we'll get him off!'

'I don't want to get him off, Colin! That's the bloody point!'

Wilberforce again blows on the kazoo.

'Puggerlugs! Puggerlugs! Stop being bad!' they sing.

'Puggerlugs! Puggerlugs! Stop being a twat!' I also sing, misremembering the words.

'Puggerlugs! Puggerlugs! You're making us sad!' they continue.

'Puggerlugs! Puggerlugs! Stop fucking my leg, you little bastard!' I . . . er . . . 'sing'.

'Puggerlugs! Puggerlugs! To you we entreat!'

'Puggerlugs! Puggerlugs! Ahhh! Gerrof gerrof gerrof!'

This is a fucking nightmare!

This is the most awful thing that's ever happened to me!

This couldn't possibly get any worse!

'Hi, Andy! I saw your front door was open and – *bloody hell!*'

I look over and my face falls apart in sheer embarrassment and horror. 'Hi, Grace! Come on in and join the party!'

She looks understandably traumatised. Who wouldn't? After all, how else are you supposed to react when you walk in on your potential love interest being sexually molested by a pug dressed as a wizard, while two men crowd around him, singing a weird song at the tops of their lungs?

'Puggerlugs! Puggerlugs! Be a good boy, and get a lovely treat!'

'Yes! Give him a fucking treat!' I scream. 'Give him all the treats! Just get him to stop shagging my leg before he translates himself all over me!'

I fear that however well the linguine and the semifreddo may turn out, this disturbing scene will have killed any potential passion that tonight may have held in store for Grace and me.

'Why . . . why is that dog humping your leg, Andy?!' Grace exclaims.

I think for a moment. 'Because somebody thought a digital detox would be a good fucking idea?' I venture as I lower my leg again.

If the leaflet I picked up from Dr Hu's office had come with a note at the bottom that said, 'Warning: This detox may result in strange dogs dressed as Gandalf having sex with your right shin', I doubt I would have bothered with the whole thing.

'Can you . . . can you get him to stop?!' Grace exclaims.

I look over at Wilberforce and Colin, who are both now holding up dog treats again.

'I'm honestly not sure!' I screech. 'Lads! Any ideas?!'

'We all give him treats!' Wilberforce suggests, rummaging around in his pocket and producing a small bag. This he holds out in Grace's direction.

'Take one!' I tell her.

'I don't want to!' she argues – quite understandably.

'Please, God! Take a treat and wave it at the molester on my leg!' I wail.

'OK! OK!' Grace grabs a treat from the bag with a disgusted look on her face.

'Hold it out to him!' Colin tells her as he and Wilberforce crouch down to do the same. She follows suit, and I'm instantly reminded of the three wise men at the crib of the little baby Jesus – only this baby Jesus is snorting like a pig and thrusting like an eighties heavy metal frontman.

Luckily . . . thankfully . . . by the grace of God, and by the grace of Grace . . . Puggerlugs sees what they are all holding out for him, jumps off my leg and goes over to snatch the treat from Grace's hand.

After he does this, Wilberforce gathers him back up in his arms again and steps backwards.

I slump against the wall, trying very hard not to think about the fresh stain on the leg of my jeans.

Grace stands upright again and takes a deep breath. She then points at Colin and his boyfriend.

'Are they staying for dinner?' she asks.

I look at her in horror. Partly at the thought of these three hanging around while I serve up my crab linguine, and partly that Grace would even think that I would have invited them.

'No!' I cry, suddenly spurred into motion. There's no way I'm going to sit there and masticate on a semifreddo while a horny pug attempts sex with any more of my body parts, or furniture.

'Colin!' I snap at the two interlopers. 'I think it's time for you, Wilberforce and Puggerlugs to leave!'

'Yes! Yes! I'm so sorry, Mr Bellows!' Colin wails.

'We are so very sorry!' Wilberforce adds.

'That's fine, that's fine! No real harm done,' I tell them. 'But please leave, the both of you.'

Wilberforce scuttles towards the door, his rampant dog gripped tightly against his chest.

'Goodbye!' he says to Grace, who unconsciously takes a step backward as he passes. This doesn't seem to offend Wilberforce in the slightest, and he powers his way back through my front door without another word.

Colin follows swiftly behind, offering his goodbyes to Grace as well. He follows Wilberforce out of the door, leaving Grace and I staring at each other in utter disbelief.

'What on earth was all that about?' Grace says.

I throw my arms out. 'I literally *have no idea*,' I tell her.

'Mr Bellows!'

'Jesus Christ!' I scream.

Wilberforce has reappeared in the doorway.

'Mr Bellows . . . do you think I should do a detox?' he asks me.

'Yes!' I tell him. 'You should definitely do a detox, Wilberforce.'

'Thank you!'

'And get Puggerlugs neutered while you're bloody at it!'

'Come away, Wilberforce!' I hear Colin screech, and the little man disappears from view once again.

I'm taking no fucking chances this time. I leap over to the front door and slam it closed with all of my might.

'Oh my God!' Grace exclaims, and sits down hard on the couch.

'I know, right?' I reply, leaning against the door.

'Did you know they were coming over?'

'No! They just turned up, and – well, you know . . .'

'What did they want?'

'Advice.'

'About detoxing?'

'Yep.'

'What was the dog sex about?'

I have to think about this for a second. 'It's a long, complicated story, Grace. One that I will only be able to tell over partially frozen Italian cream.'

'*I beg your pardon?*'

With another one of my patented world-weary sighs, I stand upright and indicate towards the kitchen. 'Come with me and I'll explain.'

And, by the time we do move on to the chocolate and honey semi-freddo, I have indeed explained in as much detail as I possibly can.

The meal has gone well so far. You'll be pleased to know the linguine came out a treat.

'Oh, that's actually quite sad, isn't it?' Grace remarks as I inspect the first three semifreddo attempts. She's sitting at my breakfast bar – which doubles as my dining table – sipping wine, while I try to sort out the dessert.

'Yes, it is,' I mumble, as I attempt to upend the third semi-freddo – the one that looks the most solid. It plops on to the plate in a relatively satisfactory condition, so I pick up the honey and start to squeeze it over the top. 'Wilberforce and Colin clearly have quite a few issues. That's what happens when you shut yourself off from the real world.'

'No argument here. I was starting to go down the same path.'

'Probably a good job you don't own a pug then,' I tell her, and park her half of the now-complete semifreddo in front of her, and take my seat again.

She smiles. 'This looks very nice.'

'Thank you. If you enjoy it, I have another five you can take home with you.'

Grace laughs and picks up a spoon. 'So, how does it feel?'

'How does what feel?'

'To be someone people look up to?'

'What do you mean?'

She pops a spoonful of the dessert into her mouth and talks around it. 'People just don't turn up at your door looking for advice like that unless they look up to you, Andy.' She grins. 'Colin and Wilberforce are Andy Bellows stans.'

I give her a withering look. 'Please don't use words like that.'

'Sorry . . . I mean, they're *fans* of yours. All of them are. All the ones that turned up at the café the other week. All the people Fergus has talked to online.'

I shake my head vociferously. 'No. They're not fans of *mine*. They're just . . . people who are a bit interested in detoxing, that's all.'

'Two people tracked you down to ask your advice directly,' Grace rebuts. 'Hell . . . make that *three* people. I did it too! And people just don't turn up to random events at coffee shops because they're *a bit interested* in something.' She points her spoon at me. 'They came to see you, Andy. *You*. They're your fans . . . whether you like it or not!' She takes another mouthful of dessert, a thoughtful look on her face. 'And I guess I'm one of them too.'

My face has gone extremely red, and extremely hot. If I try to eat any more of this semifreddo it'll probably melt before it gets anywhere near my mouth.

'Stop it, Grace,' I tell her, flushing.

'Stop what? I'm just being honest. My life has improved so much since I met you.'

'Well, getting offline has probably done you a lot of good,' I mumble.

Grace slides off her seat and leans in closer to me. 'I'm not talking about the detox, Andy. I'm talking about meeting *you*.'

'Meeting me?'

Jesus. It's suddenly got very hot in here. How is my semifreddo not just a puddle of liquid?

'Yes. The best thing about the detox has been making friends with you.'

'Thank you. I feel the same way.'

Grace plunges her spoon back into the semifreddo and leaves it there. 'And I think I'd like to be more than friends with you now,' she says, leaning even closer to me.

'Would you,' I say in a thick voice.

'Yes. A little less conversation, a little more action please.'

Grace kisses me. Her lips are cold and sweet from the frozen dessert.

I've not been too sure about the exact nature of my relationship with Grace, or where it might be heading, but she's obviously had no such worries.

I kiss Grace back, and the coldness of the semifreddo is pleasantly replaced by the warmth from our bodies.

We spend a good few minutes right there at my breakfast bar, kissing each other passionately while the semifreddo melts into a sticky goop.

And then Grace starts to lead me away from the kitchen by the hand, over to somewhere we can be more comfortable.

'Which one is your bedroom?' she asks me in a husky voice.

I point a slightly shaky finger. 'That one,' I tell her.

'Come on then.'

By the time we're in the bedroom, I have forgotten completely about Colin, Wilberforce and their horny dog. By the time Grace has undressed me, I've forgotten about the digital detox. And by the time she's undressed as well, I've forgotten what my own name is.

Later, Grace lies beside me, sleeping the sleep of someone who has accomplished what they set out to do – and was not going to be put off by anything, up to and including having to watch me get humped by a pug.

I can't sleep because I'm thinking back on something she said right before the evening took a dramatic turn for the better.

I have *fans*.

Grace is right.

Those people didn't just turn up to chat to anyone about detoxing. They turned up to see *me*. To meet *me*. I guess that's why I felt so uncomfortable about the whole thing.

And what makes me uncomfortable is that I have no idea why they'd *want* to be fans of mine – why they'd want to be part of Loggers Off.

What is it about me that they like so much?

What is it about poor little Andy Bellows that would turn a bunch of people obsessed with being online into his followers?

Followers.

Oh, Christ.

Followers.

That's what this is about!

If there's one characteristic of most people who spend way too much of their time on the Internet, it's that they follow a lot of other people – usually celebrities, from the very minor to the very major. Twitter, Instagram, Facebook – all of them are stuffed with famous people, selling their lifestyle and their brand to their legions of supporters.

And for those supporters, being allowed access to their favourite celebrities – no matter how manufactured that access might be – is exceptionally *addictive*.

I know. I've been there.

So has Grace.

So have Colin and Wilberforce.

And so have most of the people who have joined Loggers Off, I'm sure of that.

And what is it that they're doing now?

Following me.

Exactly the same thing they were doing on social media – only back out here in the analogue, real world.

'This isn't about *me*,' I say out loud into the darkened room, making Grace turn over in her sleep. 'This is about *them*.'

They need somebody to follow. I just happen to be that person.

And how have I let that happen?

By presenting a manufactured image of my own life, with all the bad bits taken out. That's what lying to that small crowd in Heirloom did that first time we all met there. It created the monster.

I created the monster.

Another stark and terrible realisation hits me at that moment: I've become Lucas La Forte!

OK, I didn't fake a load of photos of me sitting in sports cars and wearing Armani suits – but is lying to a bunch of people in a coffee shop really all that different, when you get right down to it?

Probably not.

And – just like Herbert – those lies have brought in more and more followers, and just made things even worse.

Oh, good God.

I am an *influencer*.

I am a Herbert Glerbett.

. . . I am in deep, deep *trouble*.

Chapter Eleven

Logging On

A week later, I wake up with my jaw locked for the first time in months.

It takes me a few minutes to work the damn thing free. I have to pop a couple of painkillers afterwards, because it hurts so much.

Then I spend twenty minutes in the toilet having a very painful poo.

Grace slept over again last night, and luckily she's a heavy sleeper, so she doesn't have to hear – or smell – what I'm up to.

As I sit on the toilet in misery, I try hard not to think about the nightmare I had last night – involving me running down a corridor naked with an iPad superglued to my left hand, while being pursued by Colin in his cagoule, a giant duck and an equally enormous Puggerlugs, this time dressed in an Armani suit.

I started awake just before they caught up with me. The last thing I heard was the dreadful sound of a snorting pug and the hideous quacking of the duck.

If I ever get around to writing a horror-movie version of my life, it will be called *The Quacking of the Duck* and will be banned in forty-three countries.

The reason for my current state of heightened anxiety is that last night was the second meeting of Loggers Off, and it was a *living hell*.

Nearly *a hundred* people turned up at Heirloom.

It was standing room only.

And I did exactly the same thing last night as I did that first time around – I lied.

Despite knowing what problems it would cause, despite being fully aware that it would probably just make things worse, and despite the fact it made me feel more and more like a complete Glerbett, I still maintained the fiction that doing a digital detox was the best thing ever, with no bad points whatsoever.

I answered the questions in that same cheerful voice, using the same cheerful words. I reassured the crowd that detoxing was great, and that they should probably all try it.

I didn't say anything negative to them at all as they downed their coffees and made their notes.

Because I just can't *let them down*.

Any of them.

And when I was finished, they clapped again. Hell, some of them even *cheered*.

Wilberforce was looking at me with nothing short of adoration by the time the meeting was over.

He bought a Loggers Off T-shirt. Colin bought two.

And Wilberforce has now started his own detox, alongside his partner. He says he's looking forward to seeing what comes of it a great deal.

I couldn't look him in the eye.

Grace and Fergus both agreed I did a very good job. I nodded my head and thanked them, while all the time I could feel my stomach churning at the horror and deceit of it all.

When Grace suggested she stay over at my place again, though, the stomach-churning was replaced by butterflies – which is a far more pleasant thing to experience.

I helped her clean up after the last of the Loggers Off had left, and we walked back to my car holding hands.

I should be as happy as a pig in shit.

Instead, I am a bag of nerves.

The revelation from last week that I have actual fans – and the subsequent massive increase in the attendance at the coffee shop last night – has ramped my anxiety right back up again.

I am not constitutionally capable of having fans.

I cannot bear the weight of that responsibility.

One of the reasons I started the digital detox was to stop being an online follower – and all the stress and anxiety that comes with it. But in doing so – and by encouraging people by lying to them – I have instead become the person *being followed* and have created a whole new level of anxiety and stress for myself, hitherto unexplored.

The irony is so thick, I keep expecting Alanis Morissette to jump out of the bathroom cabinet and hand me some toilet paper.

I have inadvertently come full circle.

I'm back to being stressed and in pain.

Only this time around, it's so much *worse*.

At least back then I only had myself to worry about – but now I have other people to think of. Other people who are watching what I do, and who want to meet with me on a constant basis. Folks who think I'm someone they can look up to.

Not least of whom is currently lying asleep in my bed. I have a responsibility to Grace. I started her off on her detox. She became the first person to follow my example.

And Grace has done so much for me. I would never have taken that day out in Bath without her. I would never have discovered the joys of the English countryside without her. I would never have been able to see the actual joy of being offline without her.

And now I'm in the first stages of a relationship with her.

I can't let her down. I can't *ever* let her down.

I can't let *any* of them down.

Not even Wilberforce and his horny pug. Going on a detox will probably improve his life no end – but would he do it if he knew I wasn't the shining example of detoxification that people think I am?

Probably not.

And that would be letting him down.

Hell, I don't even want to disappoint Fergus. He's been thoroughly enjoying the stories he's been writing about me, and the paper's sales figures have apparently gone up considerably because of them. OK, the bastard is responsible for the hideous situation I find myself in, but I went along with it all, didn't I? I never said no to any of it. And now he's kind of relying on me to keep the story going. To keep Loggers Off going . . .

Oh God.

It's all just too damn *stressful*.

'Are you OK?' Grace asks me as I pour her a coffee. The hand doing the pouring is shaking slightly.

'Sorry?' I reply, rubbing at my sleepy eyes with the other hand.

'You look like your dog just died.'

'Do I?'

'Yes. And it's not really the kind of expression I wanted to see on your face this morning. Not after what we got up to last night.' She suddenly looks very anxious, and starts to twiddle with the locket around her neck. 'Is there a problem? Are we . . . *OK*? Wasn't it . . . good?'

Oh crap.

'No! I mean, yes! Of course it was good! Christ, it was better than *good* – it was bloody amazing.' I reach out a hand to her. 'And *of course* we're OK. I couldn't be happier.'

Bloody hell. The tone in my voice is *awful*. I sound like I'm lying through my teeth. I'd better tell her what's actually going through my mind, before she gets the wrong idea completely and this relationship is dead before it gets out of the gates.

'It's nothing to do with you . . . with us,' I reassure her. 'It's the detox. It's Loggers Off. It's . . . all of it.'

Grace visibly relaxes. Thank God for that. I feel stressed enough this morning without having to think I've accidentally spoiled things with her.

'What's wrong?' she asks.

I put the cafetière down and try to compose myself a little. When I have, I tell Grace everything that's on my mind.

'Wow. I didn't realise you felt under that much pressure,' she says when I'm done. 'I'm so sorry to have put you through it.'

'It's not your fault!' I insist. 'It's not Fergus's either. It's mine. I should never have let things get so out of control. I should have said *no*. I should have told all those people the truth.'

'And *me*, Andy. You should have been a bit more honest with me. I had no idea the detox wasn't doing you that much good.'

'But it was! It has! The trip to Bath! Meeting you!'

'But it's not all been good, has it?' she replies. 'That's clearly not the case.'

I slump my shoulders. 'No. There's part of me that just wants it all to end. Especially now I've created this Loggers Off monster.'

'Oh, Andy,' Grace says, standing up and giving me a warm hug. 'Whatever am I going to do with you?'

I give her a forlorn look. 'I have no idea.'

She fixes me with a speculative look. 'I think we need to get you away from all this for the day. You need another Bath.'

I sniff one armpit. 'Well, possibly.'

She slaps me playfully, before returning to the hug. 'You know what I mean, mister. You could do with another big day out, doing something fun. Not just ambling around the hedgerows. Something a bit more *dynamic*. We could probably both do with it, actually.' Her eyes flash. 'And I think I have just the thing.'

Grace stops hugging me – which I am ever so slightly disappointed about – and goes over to her coat where it's hanging on the back of my front door. She delves into one pocket and brings out what looks like two tickets. 'I was going to mention this to you last night, but with all the excitement of Loggers Off and then what we did when we got back here . . .' She smiles as she says this. And no wonder. The sex we had last night was *meteoric*. 'I completely forgot. Here.'

She hands me one of the tickets.

'A theme park?' I say, looking down at it.

'Yep! It's a new one. Opening on Saturday. I got these tickets free from my coffee wholesaler's, for being their number one customer this month. All thanks to Loggers Off, of course.'

I screw my nose up. 'Not really one for theme parks, if I'm honest.'

The last time I went to one, I was seventeen, and was sick into a bin.

At least, that's the story I tell people.

I was actually sick on a four-year-old. Who was the same height as a bin, so I'm not being completely dishonest.

I've never been back to Chessington since. Not that they'd probably have me back. I can imagine a blurry photo of my seventeen-year-old self pinned up in every entrance booth, with orders to have me ejected if I am ever seen again.

Also, there's that whole thing about being around huge crowds of people to consider. Still not my thing – no matter how many coffee nights at Heirloom I might do with the Loggers Off.

'Me neither,' Grace responds, when I mention this, 'but . . . it might be fun – and exciting. And I think you could use something to take your mind off what's happening with Fergus and your new, merry band of followers. It'd be good for me too.'

While Grace is still enjoying her own detox, she is of course missing certain aspects of her online life, just like me. And filling your days can be a tricky thing to do in such circumstances. You can't walk around a field all of the time, especially with the British weather.

Grace has had all the fun and games of the increase in customers to keep her busy, but throwing yourself into work isn't necessarily the healthiest way to occupy your time. Sometimes you have to let off a little steam.

Outside of the bedroom, I mean.

And I concede that the last time Grace took me on a big day out, it ended pretty damn well.

I think we've reached the point where I'd follow this lovely raven-haired young woman into the jaws of hell itself.

A day out at this Thorn Manor place should be a breeze by comparison.

Parking isn't a breeze. It's a force-ten hurricane.

We spend a good forty minutes trying to find a spot in the expansive car park that sprawls to the south of the brand-new theme park. My anxiety levels rise constantly as we do so. All these parked cars mean that the place will be absolutely packed to the bloody rafters.

All those people. All those children. All those potentially awkward encounters.

Shudder.

We sit in a long queue of cars, all patiently (and in some cases, very *impatiently*) waiting for a space to open up. I've never been in a car park before where you're stationary and bumper-to-bumper with other cars before you've even had the chance to park up. It's hideous.

And I'm not even the one driving today. We're sitting in Grace's little Suzuki Swift, which is a tiny tin box with no air conditioning – on an English summer's day that is at least 27 per cent hotter than it should be.

We probably would have got parked a lot quicker had we arrived early, but without access to electronic satnavs, we got a bit lost and missed the motorway exit. It didn't help that no one has bothered to put up signs to the new theme park yet. I wasn't surprised in the slightest about this – this is England, after all – but my lack of astonishment at this oversight didn't stop my stress levels climbing before we'd even reached the damn place.

I'm just about to suggest we give up on the whole thing and try to find a nice pub somewhere when Grace spots a Hyundai SUV backing out of a space right in front of us. Inside, I can see the face of a very sickly looking child and deduce that she must be the reason for the early exit.

This earns us looks of hatred and jealousy from those behind us who are not parked up yet. If looks could kill, then Grace and I would be dead about two dozen times over.

Having actually managed to park, the queue to Thorn Manor is the next horror show to experience.

We both stand sweating in the morning sun for a good thirty minutes before Grace has the chance to hand over her free tickets and we get to walk into the jam-packed theme park itself.

I'm starting to think her coffee wholesaler's must actually hate the very ground she walks on, to offer her such a 'gift'. I can't think of anything worse I could do to a customer I despised than send them to this cacophonic maelstrom of sticky humanity.

Grace gives me a look that speaks volumes even higher than the ones being used by the countless small children around us. 'Hmmm. Maybe this was a bad idea,' she says, grimacing somewhat as we take in the barrage of noises and smells emanating from both the overheated crowds and the concession stands that ring the entrance plaza.

I hate to see that look of disappointment on her face.

Grace had the best of intentions bringing us here, and I don't want her to think she was in the wrong.

I wrap an arm around her. 'Come on, it's OK. Let's see what rides they have. Maybe we'll find one we like.' I am surprised by the enthusiasm I manage to inject into my voice. When I get home, I might contact a few talent agents. I obviously have a career on the stage ahead of me.

Grace offers me a rather dubious smile, but allows me to guide her towards a large map that stands in the centre of the plaza.

Everything on it looks awful.

I very much doubt the Mega Rapids are – and Mount Terror should probably be renamed Mount Mild Heat Exhaustion. Star Warriors sounds like the kind of *Star Wars* rip-off that they had to spend months working on to make sure it didn't break any copyright laws, and I'm not going anywhere near that thing called The Blitzer. It looks enormous, dreadful and the kind of ride that would have me yakking up over an entire nursery school of four-year-olds.

In one corner of the enormous sign is a splash panel that reads 'Don't forget to include the hashtag #ThornManorIsOpen in your social media posts!'

I roll my eyes. Because you can't enjoy a day out at a theme park unless you tell all of your friends on social media about it, can you?

I know I sound like a moany old bastard, but it's approaching thirty degrees on this unseasonably hot summer's day, and I am surrounded by sticky things.

And their parents.

I look at Grace, who is clearly as distressed as I am.

'Shall we get out of here?' I venture.

Grace nods. 'Oh yes. I think that would be a lovely idea.' Then her face falls. 'But I don't think I can face that car park again. Not yet.'

I shudder again. The traffic jam is probably still hideous out there. She's absolutely right.

'I tell you what, how about we go find a cold drink, have a sit down and decide whether we want to stay here any longer or not?' I suggest. 'If nothing else, it should give the car park a chance to thin out a bit.'

Grace nods. 'I am very thirsty. That sounds like a good idea, Andy.'

With that decision made, we take ourselves off in the direction of a small concession called Quench, which sits close to the ridiculous-looking monstrosity that is The Blitzer. Quench sounds like the kind of place you can pick up a very large cold drink, and that would be just about perfect right at this moment.

I pick us each up a Coca-Cola slushy and we sit down on a bench overlooking The Blitzer, which has a track that loops high over our heads in stomach-clenching fashion.

The ride has a very obvious arctic theme. The entrance is covered in a lot of large, pointy ice crystals and snow. It all looks vaguely ridiculous under this hot summer sun, it has to be said.

The Blitzer logo is *horrible*, as well. All silly jagged points and snowflakes. About as subtle as a half brick. They should have had me in to do it. I would have done a much more aesthetically pleasing job.

'Looks like they're gearing up for something,' Grace remarks as she unconsciously unbuttons the top of her shirt, letting it fall open almost to the top of her bra.

I would find this unbearably sexy in other circumstances, but my penis is far too sweaty and anxious right now to properly appreciate it.

The Coke slushy is rather glorious, though, and is managing to take the edge off my overheated internal workings.

I look over at where Grace is indicating and see that a section of the area in front of The Blitzer's entrance has been roped off, and a large queue is forming. 'Looks like it,' I agree, and continue to suck on my slushy as we watch proceedings unfold.

A young woman in a business suit emerges from the entrance to The Blitzer, with two old, rich-looking men standing either side of her. The woman begins to speak to the crowd in front of her, and while I can't hear every word she says because we're not quite close enough, I do pick up the gist of what she's saying.

'Looks like they're opening the Blitzer ride now,' I say to Grace as I take another grateful suck on the straw buried in my slushy. 'Those people have exclusive tickets for the first go on it. Lucky them.'

'I'd rather have angry hornets inserted into me sideways,' Grace remarks, also taking a gulp of cold, refreshing slush.

I nod in agreement.

The woman concludes her speech, and the crowd start to file into the ride's entrance. As they do this, I spot a guy who seems very nervous, walking alongside a pretty blonde girl. He looks like he'd probably rather have hornets inserted into him sideways as well, but his girlfriend looks very enthusiastic about the whole thing, so he's got no choice but to brave The Blitzer and hope to come out of the other side unscathed.

I give Grace a grateful look.

I'm very happy the lady I'm with today doesn't have that same kind of enthusiasm for such an awful-looking contraption. I'm not sure I could stand it. I'd probably let her go on it on her own, and stay down here, sucking on my slushy like the big coward that I am, to be honest.

The small crowd of lucky first riders have now disappeared into The Blitzer's bowels, leaving the plaza we're sitting in a little less crowded. From off to the left, close to where the ride lets its victims out after they've been hurled around for three minutes, I see a group of four men appear, all of them holding musical instruments and dressed in lederhosen.

'What on earth?' I remark, as they start to set up on a small stage just off to one side of the exit.

'That's not something you see every day,' Grace says, with a grin on her face.

'Absolutely,' I agree, also smiling. It's the first time either of us have smiled since we got in the car this morning.

This is a very odd turn of events, and no mistake.

Grace and I sit back on our bench a bit, to await developments.

Developments occur a few minutes later – as The Blitzer hurtles through the first of what will no doubt be millions of loops around its incredibly high track – when we see the woman in the business suit signal to the strange-looking band, who pick up their instruments. They are all of the brass variety and include a tuba, two trumpets and a trombone.

'Good grief. What kind of racket are they going to make with that lot?!' Grace exclaims.

'Not a bloody clue,' I reply – wishing I could ask Siri what she thinks. Siri would know. Siri knows all.

The band play a few warm-up notes on their instruments, and as they do, a crowd starts to instantly coalesce outside The Blitzer's entrance. No wonder – it's a little hard to ignore a tuba. A tuba is not a thing that can ever pass unnoticed when it is played in public.

Curiosity overcomes me. 'Come on, let's go and see what's going on.'

Grace nods excitedly and gets up from the bench with me.

We hurry over to where the crowd is really starting to get thick with people, most of whom are now holding up their phones and getting pictures of the band.

Usually I'd be extremely bothered by being in such close proximity to so many strangers, but I have to know what this business with the strange-looking Germanic band is all about.

Grace and I are jostled somewhat by the growing throng but are close enough to the front of it to see the nervous young man I noticed earlier emerge from The Blitzer's exit with his blonde girlfriend in tow. He's shielding his eyes from the sun, and still looks very nervous.

Funny. The ride's over. He should be a lot more relaxed.

He's not, though. If anything he looks more petrified than he was when he went in. Must have been a horrible experience. I'm glad I'm not doing it.

One of the trumpet players spots the nervous man and his girlfriend, and looks over at the woman in the suit. Now she's a lot closer, I can see that she wears a Thorn Manor name tag that tells me her name is Amy. Obviously one of the park's senior staff, from the looks of her.

Amy nods feverishly and points at the nervous man.

The large, red-faced trumpet player smiles, nods and draws in a deep breath. '*Eins! Zwei! Drei! Vier!*' he screams, and the band start to play what I can only describe as the sound of a large brass band falling down a flight of stairs.

Large stairs. Many, many large, hard stairs.

It's *awful*.

'Bloody hell!' Grace cries and puts her hands over her ears.

The crowd around us thickens even more as people come over to see what all the fuss is about.

The fuss is a cacophony the likes of which could cause severe mental distress if experienced for too long. If anyone ever has the desire to waterboard me, they can just play this hideousness on a loop instead.

I see the nervous man hurry over to the band and start pleading with them to stop. They eventually do, and he asks them who the hell they are.

There follows a brief conversation with the nervous man – whose name is Oliver, I think – wherein we discover that this is clearly not the band he wanted to see here today. He looks deeply distressed now, the poor bugger.

When his girlfriend comes over, Oliver tries to put a brave face on.

'Oh no. I think I know what's going on here,' Grace says, her hand going to her mouth.

'What?'

'He's going to propose.'

'Is he? How the hell do you know that?'

'The band. The set-up. All of it. He said it should have been a different lot of musicians. A jazz band. That's why he looks so upset. He was going to propose to his girlfriend.' Grace has gone a bit watery-eyed at this revelation. I would give her a hug were it not for the fact that we're packed into a tight crowd of people.

Then the trumpeter in the lederhosen hands Oliver a small ring box, and I know that Grace is 100 per cent right.

My heart starts to beat a little faster as I put myself in this chap's shoes.

To ask someone to marry you in such a public place is a thing I could never do. I absolutely admire his courage.

I'm truly hoping his girlfriend says yes.

He then drops to both knees – which is a bit weird. He must still be very nervous. And then he does indeed pop the question to the girl, whose name is apparently Samantha.

I hear the crowd around me all take an audible deep breath in. I do the same.

'No,' Samantha replies, in a deeply distressed voice, and we all let out a collective *ooooooh* noise as the shock of it hits us.

'Oh no,' Grace says, hand going to her mouth again.

My heart sinks.

Poor, poor chap.

I see his jaw go slack with absolute horror.

When Oliver eventually manages to speak, it's just a few nonsense syllables.

Samantha repeats that she doesn't want to marry him, and starts to back away quickly.

As she does, Oliver continues to make strange, unintelligible noises. His brain has clearly shut itself down.

I can sympathise. This happens to me a lot too.

Though never in circumstances quite as awful as this, I'm pleased to say.

Oh Christ . . . now Samantha is telling him that she thinks they should *split up*!

'Bloody hell,' remarks Grace, who looks absolutely horrified.

Samantha continues to back away from Oliver, and now I can see that she's more or less headed towards where Grace and I are standing.

The crowd around us, sensing that it's the right thing to do, start to part, forcing Grace and I to do the same. I hate been jostled like this, but I'm so wrapped up in this disastrous marriage proposal, I don't have time to think about it.

Samantha walks right past me and Grace, and starts to hurry away from the plaza as fast as she can. We watch her go, still gobsmacked by what's just happened.

And then, we all slowly look back at Oliver, who remains on his knees in front of us, looking like his world has just collapsed. Which, of course, it just has.

'Oh my, that poor man,' Grace says in a distraught tone.

I see her hand go to her locket – as per usual at times when she's feeling stressed or worried.

Her eyes widen in horror when there's no locket to be found.

'Andy! Andy! My locket!' she hisses at me as she starts to pat around her neck feverishly.

I instantly forget all about Oliver and his problems.

I have my own to worry about now.

'Where is it?' I cry, grabbing Grace's blouse collar and peering down her back. She frantically continues to pat around her midriff. To no avail, though. She's only wearing a thin white shirt and a bra. There's nothing else for the locket to have got caught in.

A high, forlorn trombone note plays across the plaza from one of the members of the strange German band as Grace and I start to frantically search around on the ground.

I begin to push other members of the crowd away, earning me a few dark looks and cries of outrage.

'My girlfriend's lost her locket!' I tell them. 'Has anybody seen it?'

I get a lot of head shakes, and my panic starts to rise.

We *have* to find the locket.

I've known Grace long enough to know that it's the most precious thing in her life. Losing it will be too much for her to bear.

'Andy! Where is it? Please find it!' she pleads with me as she continues to scan the paving slabs below our feet for signs of her heirloom.

The crowd thankfully start to spread out a little as we do this.

I look up to see that Oliver has disappeared as well. The show appears to be over.

That show, anyway.

Now there's a new one for everyone to enjoy.

The Disappearing Locket Show, featuring Andy Bellows and his highly stressed-out girlfriend.

'Has anybody seen a locket?' I call out again to the people around us. 'A locket? A gold locket? Quite small?'

Again, nobody answers me with anything remotely positive.

Oh God. Has someone *stolen it*?

Did somebody lift it off Grace in the crowd while we all witnessed Oliver's downfall?

That would be even worse than it just falling off! It means it's gone forever!

I look up at Grace's face and see tears in her eyes.

My panic levels spike higher.

'Excuse me! Has anyone seen a gold locket?!' I cry again. The stress in my voice has made it rise at least two octaves.

Nobody is helping!

Nobody has it!

Nobody can tell me what happened to the damn thing!

I start to move away from where Grace is searching, back in the direction of the bench we were sitting on. Perhaps it fell off earlier? Maybe when we were sitting down?

I go over and check around the bottom of the bench.

No dice.

No locket.

I comb the ground around me as I make my way back to where Grace is still searching. As I get back to her, I can see that her face is now stained with tears.

'Oh, Andy! I can't find it! I can't find it!' she cries in anguish.

'We will! I promise!' I reply, but with a sinking heart. We're surrounded by people. Any one of whom could have stolen the locket. Or picked it up and carried it away with them, not knowing whose it was.

But I can't tell Grace that. I can't let her think she won't see it again!

And so I start to search the ground once more, desperately hoping that the locket will appear and put an end to this horrible turn of events.

An hour later, and there's still no sign of the locket.

We've been back over all of our steps today. Right out to the car and back. We hadn't been in the park long enough to move around much, but we still covered enough ground for the locket to have fallen off somewhere I might not have scanned.

I went to the Thorn Manor lost property office, of course. The theme park is still so new, there was nothing in it whatsoever – including Grace's locket.

I asked at the nearby concession stands as well. Still nothing.

Everything I've tried has come up empty.

Grace has now gone from panicked and distraught to grey-faced and listless. She's sitting on the bench we first came to, staring at her feet.

I am sitting next to her, feeling absolutely useless.

We should *never* have come here!

Never have come to this stupid theme park, full of these stupid people!

I slam my hand down on the arm of the bench, making Grace start.

'We're never going to find it. It's gone,' she says in a defeated tone.

I open my mouth to argue – but it's been over an hour, and I'm terrified she's right.

Without responding, I look out at the milling crowds in front of us and curse them all.

This is entirely irrational.

It's not their fault this has happened. It's nobody's fault, in fact.

But I feel the need to blame someone – blame something. And the crowd are best placed to be the subject of my rage.

Look at them. Enjoying themselves. Having a *lovely* day. Moving around like the fucking sheep that they are, from one ride to another. Taking selfies of each other and tweeting all about what a fantastic day out they are hav—

Tweeting.

Selfies.

They have phones.

All of them having fucking *phones*!

And then I remember that splash panel on the sign in the theme park's main forecourt.

#ThornManorIsOpen, the hashtag said.

And I bet a lot of people are using it . . .

I stand bolt upright, making Grace start again. 'I need a phone!' I exclaim.

'Why?' she replies. 'Who the hell can we call? We've already spoken to the people who run the park and they don't know where it is.'

'No. I don't mean I need to make a call,' I say, scanning the crowd in front of me for a likely looking person.

Off to my right is a family consisting of two parents and a girl of about eight or nine years old. They are eating hot dogs and shading themselves from the hot sun under a large tree. The father is playing with his mobile phone – which looks exactly the same as the one I put in a box over two months ago, an iPhone XS.

Perfect.

I hurry over to them and attempt an ingratiating smile. This isn't easy, considering what a stressful day I'm having.

'Hello,' I say to the three of them, aiming myself more at the father than the other two, as he's the one with the phone in his hand. 'I'm so sorry to trouble you, but I need somebody's help with something very important, and you are the nearest people I thought might be able to help me.'

The man gives me a quizzical look. 'What's up, chief?'

I explain – in as much detail as I can, given the circumstances – what has happened.

As I'm finishing up, Grace has joined me, now looking as confused as she is upset. 'So, I just need to borrow a mobile phone, so I can put something out on social media about it,' I finish telling the couple.

The guy narrows his eyes for a moment. 'Yeah. I recognise you. You're that guy doing the detox, aren't you? I saw you on the TV news.'

'Yep, that's me! Andy Bellows is the name.'

Borrowing mobile phones for nefarious purposes is my game, my brain pipes up.

The man shrugs his shoulders and hands the phone over to me. 'Sure, no worries. Happy to help. You'll have to log me out of everything so you can log yourself in, though. Do you know how to do that?' He looks uncertain. 'I'm not all that good with social media stuff. We've got a Twitter account somewhere, but we haven't touched it in years.'

'Not a problem,' I reply, taking the phone and flicking through the apps with my thumb. 'I can use the browser interface. I won't have to touch any of your log-in details.'

As I say this, Grace's hand covers mine, obscuring the phone's screen from me. 'Andy? What are you doing?'

I look at her in surprise. 'I'm putting an appeal out on social media, Grace. To see if anyone has found your necklace. I'll use that hashtag we saw on the sign. That should get enough eyes on the appeal, with any luck.'

Grace looks distraught. *More* distraught, I mean.

'But what about your detox? What about *Loggers Off*?'

I stare at her for a moment, thinking silently, before answering in a resolute voice. 'What does that matter, Grace? Right now? Two and a half months of my silly life against your link to the people you love? What does it matter?'

'But you've been doing so well! I don't want you to . . . to . . .'

'To what? Watch you in any more pain, just so I can look good in the eyes of a bunch of complete strangers?'

'They'll be really *angry* with you!' Grace insists. 'Fergus will be mad, too.'

I shrug my shoulders again. 'Let them, if they want. This is more important.' I feel my lip tremble. '*You're* more important.'

And now I have to look back down at this man's phone – lest I get overemotional and lose track of what I'm doing.

I start to thumb at the iPhone's screen, and something very *fundamental* happens in my brain. Some connection – one that has been floundering around loose in my subconscious – reattaches itself deep down somewhere, and I feel a sudden rush of pleasure. Of excitement.

Look at it, would you?

Just look at it.

A tiny screen, no more than a few inches across.

And all the world beneath my fingertips, just waiting to be explored . . .

I pull up Google and navigate to the Twitter log-in page.

It all feels so natural. So normal.

So *right*.

When I log in to my Twitter account I let out an audible gasp.

The amount of people following @Andy_Bellows has *leapt up*. In fact, my follower count has nearly *tripled*.

That's comprehensively *insane*.

Fergus must have included my username in the tweets on the Loggers Off account. I don't feel brave enough to go and take a look at how many followers that has. Not right now.

While Grace chats with the couple and their small daughter, I compose a straightforward but heartfelt appeal about the lost necklace – including the #ThornManorIsOpen hashtag, along with any other hashtags I think that could be relevant.

I also include Thorn Manor's account in the tweet, because it can't hurt at this point.

A bolt of inspiration hits me, and I navigate over to the webpage of the *Daily Local News* and spend a few seconds searching for my name. Sure enough, I find all the online versions of the stories Fergus has written – which include photos. One of them is of me and Grace. I remember it being taken. We were both extremely awkward.

But yes! There it is!

Grace's locket is just about visible, hanging outside her blue work shirt. The photographer wanted it on display in the picture – to tie in with the name of the coffee shop.

I save the picture to the phone, zoom in on it and crop it so only the locket can be seen. Then I attach this picture to my appeal and hit the tweet button.

And I'm not done yet!

My thumb flies over the phone screen as my brain fizzes with energy.

Next I surf over to Facebook, copy and pasting the same appeal and picture on to my profile. I also post it on the Thorn Manor Facebook page.

And then I do the same on Instagram.

It's all so easy. It's all so quick.

It's all so damn *wonderful*.

My heart is going ten to the dozen when I'm done.

'That should do it,' I tell Grace and the couple. 'With any luck, we might get somewhere with it. Almost everyone here has a phone, and they'll all be using them to take pictures. With any luck, somebody will have either seen the locket or might have even picked it up.'

I'm not going to mention my fears about it being stolen. If that's the case, we're dead in the water, but I'm hoping and praying that isn't what happened.

I'm hoping and praying that today . . . people are better than that.

People *have* to be better than that.

The phone goes *ding* with a notification, and my pulse rises another notch.

It's Thorn Manor retweeting me.

Good.

That should help.

I don't have any of my accounts set up in apps, of course, so for the most part I have to constantly flick through each social media service in separate open tabs, searching for responses.

And it's not too long until they start flooding in.

Most offer commiserations about the loss of the locket and hope that we find it again.

Some are promises to keep a look out for it, and a few are the rather inevitable trolling criticisms about how we should have kept it more secure, so this disaster never arose in the first place.

All par for the course.

No one has seen the locket, though. Not yet.

A good twenty minutes goes by while I shuttle back and forth, primarily between Twitter and Facebook, replying with thanks to those promising to help with the search, and providing more details about the locket to those who ask.

And I'm enjoying every single fucking second of it.

I shouldn't be.

Grace is still very upset. We haven't found the locket yet.

But I'm *connected* again.

I'm plugged in again.

I'm logged on again.

'Andy?'

I ping off a reply to a woman who says she's in the queue for Mount Terror and will keep an eye out.

'Andy?'

I respond to a guy who suggested we contact the lost property office, letting him know we've tried that.

'Andy?'

I take a very quick look at what's trending on Twitter in the United Kingdom right now. Because I want to know. I *have* to know.

'Andy?!'

I cry out in surprise as Grace finally gets through to me – bringing me back out to the real world around me. I look up at her, blinking away the after-image of the phone's screen on the back of my retinas.

'Has anyone seen it?' she says, in desperate hope.

I shake my head. 'No. Not yet. But we'll see. Hopefully, it'll—'

And then it happens.

A notification pings on Twitter, and I look back to read it.

> Hi! I think I've got your locket! My little bruv
> picked it up!

It's from Sasha.

@SashTheMash to be exact. A fourteen-year-old girl, with bright eyes and a smile that you could probably launch ships with.

Sasha has taken a picture of the locket in her hand, and has attached it to her response. Tears of relief fill my eyes. It's the one.

My hand trembling more than ever, I hold the phone up to Grace to show her the picture. 'We've found it,' I tell her, voice a bit wobbly.

'Oh my God!' she cries with sheer joy, and it's the best sound I think I've ever heard.

'Great stuff!' the woman whose husband's phone I've been using says.

'Well done!' he adds excitedly.

'Thanks!' I reply. 'I'll just find out where this Sasha is, and I can give you your phone back.'

I send a reply back to Sasha, asking her where she is in Thorn Manor. When she tells me that her family are currently in the queue for Mega Rapids, I thank her profusely and let her know we're on our way over. She promises to hang around outside the ride waiting for us, as it's not one she's all that fussed about going on, because she doesn't want to get wet. Her mother will be waiting for us with her, because she's not keen on the idea either, as the skirt she's wearing is brand new and she only got it from Fat Face yesterday.

@SashTheMash likes to write long messages.

I tell Grace the plan and turn to the couple, whose day we have so rudely interrupted.

'Thank you so much for this,' I tell them, handing the man back his phone. 'I'm sorry, but I didn't catch your names?'

'I'm Jamie,' the man says.

285

'Laura,' the woman replies. 'And this is our daughter, Poppy. Say hello, Pops.'

The little girl gives me a wave.

'Well, it was very nice to meet you . . . and thanks again,' I say, looking at them properly for the first time.

There's something . . . *familiar* about them. I can't quite put my finger on why, but I definitely think I've seen them somewhere before.

'Thank you so much!' Grace remarks, breaking my train of thought. I feel her tugging at my hand. 'Come on, Andy, let's go and get my locket!'

I nod, give little Poppy a wave back and then follow Grace in the direction of the Mega Rapids, and a very important reunion.

Grace hugs the life out of Sasha as I offer my undying gratitude to her mother.

'Ah, it's nothing,' she tells me. 'You're lucky my girl here is never off her phone! I'm just sorry my son picked it up and took it away like that.'

'Oh, don't apologise!' I respond. 'Who knows what might have happened to it if he hadn't?'

She smiles and looks down at where Grace is still squeezing the life out of Sasha, who is giggling away to herself. 'Well, all's well that ends well, eh?'

'Absolutely!'

'And thank heavens Sasha is such a Twitter addict!' she adds. 'I don't go on it much myself. Don't like any of that social media stuff, if I'm honest. How about you? Do you use it much?'

It takes me a second to sort out what I think is a suitable response. 'I've been known to,' I reply, suddenly feeling very, very tired.

Much later that day, Grace and I are sitting on a riverbank.

We have left Thorn Manor far behind.

A walk in the peace and quiet of the countryside has calmed us both down magnificently. We've only seen two people in the entire time we've been here, and I can't express how happy I've been about that.

We bought Sasha a Thorn Manor season pass as a reward. It only seemed appropriate.

Grace clutched her locket tightly in one hand all the way back to the car. And has been checking it's still hung around her neck every minute since.

Until we reached the tranquillity of this riverbank, that is. Since we got here, I've only seen her hand stray to it once.

Mind you, once we get back, I'm going to take a close look at the clasp on that bloody necklace, and make sure nothing like this ever happens again. The lovely, ornate jeweller's pliers that Christos gave Grace will come in very handy with that little job.

'What a bloody day,' I remark, looking out at the pond skaters flitting about on the sunny surface of the water.

'It certainly hasn't been boring,' Grace says, nodding slowly.

I arch an eyebrow. 'That's one way of looking at it.'

She gives me a face. 'All right, it's been a *nightmare*, but the sun and the water have calmed me down fantastically.'

'Good.'

'How do you feel?'

'I'm OK. It was very stressful, but it all got sorted out in the end, didn't it?'

'What about . . . the detox?'

I shrug my shoulders again. I'm finding that's about the only thing I can do when thinking about the detox. I just don't know how I feel about having broken it.

I don't think I've ever once felt truly ambivalent about something before in my life. It's a very odd sensation.

'What's done is done,' I say, matter-of-factly.

'You don't feel bad about it?'

'Not in the slightest. We had to get your locket back . . . and it worked. It bloody well *worked*.'

Grace looks a little stunned again for a moment. 'Yeah. It did.'

And that's the thing.

I can't get away from the fact that without the Internet, without the ability to go online, to go on social media and put out an instant appeal, we wouldn't have found the locket. Without that instant connection to all of those people, it would have been lost. *We* would have been lost.

So, it's clearly not all bad, is it? All that tech? All those ones and zeros. All those websites and apps.

There are good reasons for having an online lifestyle. That much is very clear to me – despite all of the problems it can throw up as well.

Lots of ups and downs.

The good and the bad.

Advantages and disadvantages.

No wonder I feel so bloody ambivalent.

'What about Loggers Off?' Grace says, the hand straying again to the locket around her neck.

I look out over the water, continuing to watch the pond skaters go about their summery business. 'I don't know. With any luck, none of them would have seen what I was up to.'

'You mean you don't want to tell them you've broken the detox?'

'No. I can't lie to them. Not any more.'

'That's probably for the best.'

'But hopefully, I can let them down *easily*. I can break the news that I've broken the detox at the next meeting in a few days.'

'Are you going to stop completely now? Go straight back online, like you used to?' There's a sadness in her voice that makes me feel a little sick. I know she doesn't want me to stop. I think I've become as talismanic to her as I have to the rest of the Loggers Off.

I shake my head. 'No. I don't think so. I owe them that much before I see them. I won't go back until the next meeting.' I grimace. 'Besides, I think it's probably best if I do steer clear for a few more days . . . just in case the ones that haven't started their own detoxes yet did see what's happened.'

I'm used to the bloom of guilt that accompanies such thoughts these days.

And that's not the only reason for staying offline a little while longer, if I'm honest.

There *is* part of me that doesn't want to go back to that life again. Part of me that wants to stay here in the analogue world.

Because it is much *easier*. Much simpler.

. . . While at the same time being infinitely harder and more complex.

What on earth is the right thing to do?

Right now? Enjoy the sun, kiss Grace and maybe skim a few stones across the river, my subconscious orders me.

I decide that I'm going to listen to it, as those three things do sound quite marvellous.

There will be time to worry about the rest of the world later.

There always is.

Chapter Twelve

To Thine Own Selfie Be True

This, then, is going to be the final meeting of the Loggers Off.

At least with Andrew Bellows as the star attraction.

I can't go on.

It's not fair on them, and it's not fair on me.

I'm going to say some of the things I should have said the first time I appeared as the star – no matter the consequences.

And I'm *terrified*.

Terrified of that confrontation.

Terrified to tell the complete truth.

Terrified of letting people see me for who I am, rather than who they expect me to be.

But, let's be honest about this, I've been scared ever since the Loggers Off became a thing. Scared of letting them down or letting them in, and look where that's got me – a world where people are wearing Loggers Off T-shirts and drinking all of Grace's coffee.

Such is my fear and apprehension of this coming evening, I have pretty much hidden away in my flat for the past few days.

And it has felt like being right back at the beginning of the detox.

Much like those first few days, I have been *desperate* to go online.

I want to see if there's been any reaction to me falling off the wagon. I want to look at all those new people who have followed me on social media. I want to know what the web thinks of Andy Bellows.

I also want to know what the latest levels of *Candy Crush* look like, and what Keanu Reeves has been up to this week – but both things are rather beside the point.

I want all of these things – but am denying them to myself as a form of punishment. I could easily go online now, given that I've already broken my electronic fast, but am not doing so, because I don't deserve it.

That's not because I did break the detox. Not at all. That was the best decision I've taken in weeks. Without it, the locket would have been lost.

Rather, I feel like I need to punish myself because I have allowed everything to escalate the way it has. That I allowed myself to become the centre of attention. The Loggers Off deserved some-one better. Someone stronger. Someone more honest.

Sigh.

I could really do with Grace here with me right now, but she's at Heirloom, making preparations for tonight's crowd. I'm hoping she's going to use the caffeine-free coffee only. Everyone's likely to be riled up anyway, and the extra stimulus is not likely to help matters.

With constant nerves that are making my stomach do its famous clenching routine, and a head that feels thick with doubt and shame, I drive to the car park close to the coffee shop, as I do on a very regular basis these days.

As I climb out of the car, I have a sweeping sense of déjà vu. This is not the first time I've parked here feeling incredibly nervous about setting foot in Heirloom Coffee. That first time the Loggers Off was assembled is still very clear in my mind, and my digestive system bubbled away then much the same as it does now.

The café has become such a central part of my life, but I've never felt less like going into it than I do this evening.

If it wasn't owned and run by the woman I love, I probably wouldn't.

But that's why it is so central to my existence . . . because *she is*. In a very short space of time, the gravitational pull of my life has shifted from the online world to a beautiful girl and her coffee shop.

If I can just get out of this current mess I find myself in, then Heirloom will be a place of sanctuary for me once again – where the flat whites are tasty and the Wi-Fi is very fast (apparently). Everything might just work out OK.

I keep this positivity in mind as I walk down the street and past one of the windows of the coffee shop. I do this with my head down, deliberately not looking in through it, and arrive at the front door, which I go through still with my head low, as if trying to remain inconspicuous.

And then I walk into a giant wall of angry.

Word appears to have got around, all right.

You can tell by the way people have gone puce.

Puce, if you're not too sure, is a kind of purply brown colour. I used it once on a marketing campaign for a winery up in Suffolk. It's not a colour that human skin turns to easily. The people that the skin belongs to have to be very mad at something for it to happen. And what they're mad at tonight is yours truly.

Yep . . . there's Wilberforce, looking like Puggerlugs has crapped on his cornflakes. Colin looks like he wants to do unpleasant things to my person with the nearest Starfleet tricorder.

And Josephine – the large lady who asked me if I was happy all those weeks ago – doesn't look happy. Not by a long shot.

I have clearly gone from hero to zero with the Loggers Off, in one foul swoop of the touchscreen.

Dozens of angry faces stare at me as I freeze on the spot in the doorway. Many of them are wearing Loggers Off T-shirts – and a lot of them are people I recognise, but many are total strangers.

In fact, this is easily the busiest Loggers Off has been since it started.

I look over at Fergus, who has a look of panic writ large across his face, and Grace, who looks a lot more sympathetic, but no less worried.

It's clear they've borne the brunt of the crowd's displeasure before my arrival.

I am walking into the lion's den.

Or rather . . . I am taking one look at the lion's den, deciding that lions' dens are not the kind of places I want to frequent – given that I do not have a lion tamer's licence, or access to powerful weaponry – and am turning tail, back towards the street outside as fast as my stupid legs can carry me.

Many cries of astonishment and rage assail my ears as I do this. But I no longer care. This has all become too much for me to handle, and if I ever want to be able to unlock my jaw or take a comfortable crap again, I must get out of here! I must leave!

I scuttle off back in the direction of the car park, fishing for my car keys.

I have every intention of jumping in and driving away at Mach 5, when my progress is stymied by the arrival of my best friend and girlfriend, hurrying towards me with concerned looks on their faces.

Damn them for caring.

Why can't they just leave me be?

'Mate! What are you doing?' Fergus says as I arrive at my restored and pond-water-free Volvo. He comes to stand right by the driver's-side door, preventing me from climbing in and beating the hastiest of hasty retreats.

'I'm leaving!' I tell him.

'You can't do that, mate!'

'Just bloody well watch me!'

'Andy, it's really not that bad!' Grace says, coming to stand next to me on the other side. She then does the last thing in the world I want her to. She takes my hand.

Damn her and her seemingly supernatural ability to soothe my fevered temperament with just a hand-hold! If I'm ever going to get my way again in this relationship, I'll need to do something about that. Possibly chop the bloody thing off. Or constantly wear mittens.

'Not that bad?' I reply. 'Did you see them? Did you see what they looked like? They want to bite my head off!'

'I doubt they're that mad, mate,' Fergus remarks. 'And even if they are, it's not like you've shot their pets or anything.'

'I've let them down!' I cry in despair.

Fergus shakes his head. 'No, you haven't. You only broke the detox so you could find Grace's locket. None of them will be angry at you for that – if you just explain what happened properly.'

I let out a cry of frustration. 'That's not what I mean! I let them down because I *lied* to them!'

'What?'

'I lied to them, Ferg! I made out everything about the detox was *wonderful*, and so they all joined the Loggers Off . . . and now I'm Kim Kardashian!'

'I wish I could even begin to fathom what the hell that means,' he tells me, 'but I fear I am not nearly drunk enough.'

Grace gives him a look. 'Andy means that he thinks they're only following him because he made out the detox was a brilliant thing. That he's acted like all those celebrities online, talking bollocks to sell themselves to their fans,' she explains. 'He thinks that's why Loggers Off exists.'

Fergus looks at her for a moment, and then back to me briefly, before bursting out laughing and slapping his thigh. 'Oh, bloody hell!'

'What?!' I snap at him. 'Stop laughing!'

Fergus calms himself down a bit and puts a hand on my shoulder. 'Mate . . . you're nothing like Kim Kardashian. You don't have a massive bum, for starters. Or millions of pounds. Or a porno film . . . thank God.' Fergus visibly shudders at the idea of *Blowing Bellows 3: This Time It's Personal*. 'And you've done *nothing wrong*,' he continues, 'except tie yourself up in knots about all of this.'

'But I *lied*, Fergus!'

He shakes his head. 'No you bloody *didn't*. You just told them about the parts of your life that you wanted them to hear. And there's nothing wrong with that.' He points a finger at me. 'One of the worst things about that tech obsession of yours was the way it made you think you had to share everything, with everyone – all of the time. That's social bloody media for you – it's turned us all into people who think we shouldn't keep things private any more. And that doing so is wrong!' He stares at me. 'You're not *required* to let people into every aspect of your life, Andy! Not just because I wrote a bloody story about you for the newspaper!' Fergus looks off to one side for a moment, lost in thought, before returning his gaze to me. 'Living a happy life is about knowing how much of yourself you want to let people in on.'

I lean forward, a little shell-shocked. 'Fergus?' I whisper. 'Did you just say something *profound*?'

'Oh, fuck off,' he says in a derisory tone, and steps away from me a little.

I smile expansively.

It's rare I get to do that kind of thing to him. I savour each and every occasion.

But he makes a good point, doesn't he? One I hadn't considered until now.

Is my guilt at not being entirely honest with the Loggers Off more about how I've been conditioned to act online than it is about some problem with morality I've developed?

I've been cursing myself for not being completely open with them, but am I actually required to be?

The answer, I'm surprised to realise, is probably not.

'OK, you might be right about that,' I concede, 'but I still can't go back in there and talk to them. Not now. I won't carry on with this silliness any longer. And I won't keep telling them that everything about being on a detox is wonderful. It's quite clear to me that I can't give them what they want.'

'Andy,' Grace says, in a very serious tone, 'maybe you should stop worrying about telling them what they want to hear, and have a go at telling them what they *need* to hear.'

That sounds like a marvellous idea, but I don't think it's one I can countenance. I'm just not that brave. 'I can't do that, Grace. I don't have it in me.'

'Yes, you do! You're a lot braver than you think, Andy Bellows!' she snaps – emphasising her frustration with me by giving me a punch on the upper arm. I prefer the hand-holding as a motivational tool, to be honest.

'Am I?' I say, rubbing my shoulder.

'Yes! *You're* the one that started the detox in the first place. Do you know how hard it is to take a step like that? I couldn't do it on my own' – she points a finger back towards Heirloom – 'and those people couldn't do it on their own either. That's why they're all sitting in the café waiting for you to come and speak to them. They felt inspired by you, because you were brave enough to take that step all on your own!'

I let out a grunt. 'Well, they're not feeling inspired now, are they?'

'No . . . they're not.' She folds her arms. 'And what are you going to do about it?'

'Run away?' I hazard.

Her eyes narrow. 'You found my locket for me, Andy, without caring about the consequences. You're not the type of man who runs away.'

Oh dear.

I've got a horrible feeling she might be right.

Deep down, I don't think I am a coward.

Which is something of a shame, as cowards get to run off and hide, somewhere nice and quiet with a decent Internet connection.

Grace is right about the detox.

I *did* start it all on my own. I *did* make that leap into the unknown.

It *was* a big deal – and I am a big, brave boy who is going to march back into that coffee shop and tell all of those people the truth! Tell them what they need to hear!

My feet are carrying me back towards Heirloom before I fully comprehend what's happening. Best to just let them get on with it, and not ask too many questions.

As they propel me Heirloom-wards, something else occurs to me and I whip back around to face Grace and Fergus. 'Did you two cook up this little pep talk before I got here?' I ask suspiciously.

'No!' they reply in unison, before looking a bit guilty and shuffling their feet.

'Maybe,' Fergus says in a quiet voice.

'Yes,' Grace admits. And then she beams at me with a smile that I will probably never be able to say no to.

Fergus is also grinning at me – and I'm not so sure I know how to say no to him either.

God damn it all.

I make off in the direction of the coffee shop again, both of the cunning sods following behind me. I don't see them give each other a silent high five . . . but I know they do it all the same.

As I walk back inside Heirloom Coffee, all of those angry eyes turn to face me again.

Actually, not all of them are angry.

In fact, most people look relatively calm. It's just that there are a few in the crowd who most definitely are *extremely* mad at me, and those are the ones I concentrated on when I first walked in.

I take up my customary place in front of the counter in silence, and wait for Grace and Fergus to roll in behind me. I notice that both of them look quite happy to stand on the other side of the counter, where there is some protection from the horde.

Gulp.

'Good evening, everyone,' I say in a level tone, regarding the crowd properly for the first time. 'Thank you all for coming.'

'HOW COULD YOU DO IT, MR BELLOWS?' Wilberforce roars at me, making my heart rate skyrocket. Thus far I've only ever heard him speak in a shy, low voice. This is quite something else.

Everyone in the room shrinks back from the enormous volume and unbridled dismay projecting from the little man. Puggerlugs – who is today dressed as Harry Potter, glasses and all – growls at me from his customary position on Wilberforce's lap.

'Easy, Wilberforce!' Colin says. 'I'm sure Mr Bellows here is about to provide us with a decent and above all *believable* answer for his betrayal of the cause.'

Oh, good grief.

'I do hope so,' adds Josephine, looking at me daggers.

'Yes! I only started my detox yesterday!' a man at the back of the room cries. 'I want to know why you've ruined yours!'

When the man emerges from behind another couple of fuming Loggers Off, I recognise him immediately.

'Lucas La Forte?!'

'Yes!' he replies, moving forward so I can see him properly. I see the expensive suit has been replaced by a rather more casual T-shirt and jeans, and the hair is a little more dishevelled. It's like seeing the Queen naked. 'I've been following everything you've been doing!' he continues. 'After we met I had a good, long, hard think about my life, and I decided I needed to change! I decided to follow your example! So, why have you let us down?! Why aren't you who we thought you were?!'

I blink a couple of times. 'I'm sorry . . . are you actually mad at me because *you've* been following what *I've* been up to, and you feel let down because *I've* not lived up to *your* expectations?'

'Yes!'

'You? Herbert Glerbett and his mum's maxed-out credit card?'

That punctures his anger instantly, and the sheer gravitational weight of his hypocrisy forces Herbert to gulp a few times, go extremely red-faced and move back into the crowd again without another word.

Just as well. I don't want to have to call his mum to come and get him.

'Can we talk about why you broke your detox?' Josephine snaps, clearly impatient to get the character assassination back on track. A few grumbles and nods come from several members of the crowd in response to this.

I take a deep breath. Best to just get this over with. 'I broke it because *I had to*, Josephine. You probably all saw the message I put out on social media about finding Grace's locket.'

'There must have been another way to find it!' Colin chimes in.

I hold up my hands. 'I don't know, Colin. *Maybe?* But at that moment I wanted to get my girlfriend's locket back, and that was more important to me than anything else.'

'WHY?' Wilberforce wails. 'WHYYYYY?'

'Because I love her with all my heart, Wilberforce!' I snap at him.

I hear Grace gasp behind me.

I instantly go as red-faced as Herbert Bilch, as once again the crowd goes silent as they digest this latest revelation.

A lot of them seem to visibly relax.

Ah well . . . if love's involved, they seem to be indicating with their collective body language, *then it's probably all right.*

This is not the way I wanted to admit how I felt about Grace to her, but I've gone and done it now.

Thanks, Wilberforce.

'But what about us?' Colin pleads.

He doesn't quite go so far as saying *Don't you love us too, Andy?* but he's not that far away. You can tell by the look in his eyes.

'You're *fine*, Colin,' I tell him, and look around the crowd. 'You're all *fine*. You don't need me.'

'YES WE DO!' Wilberforce bellows.

'No, Wilberforce . . . you really don't.' I look to the ceiling for a moment, composing what I'm going to say next. I know it's going to be important, so I'd better get it right. 'Look . . . I never asked for any of this. But you guys needed something from me, and I tried to give it to you.'

'What was that?' Josephine asks.

'Someone to tell you that detoxing is the right thing to do, Josephine. Someone to tell you that yes – you should *definitely* change your lives. You *should* take that step into the unknown.'

'But we should, shouldn't we?' Josephine replies, looking a little stunned.

'I don't know!' I tell her in an exasperated tone.

Boy, it feels good to say that out loud.

'I just *don't know*, Josephine!' I repeat. 'And that's the absolute truth. The truth you all need to hear. You may not want to hear it, but you do *need* to.' I hang a quick look back at Grace, who still looks a bit shocked about the fact I've just admitted that I love her to everyone. She smiles and makes pushing gestures with her hands. *Carry on, Andy. You're doing well.*

'Detoxing has done me a lot of good, yes,' I tell them all. 'But it's not all been plain sailing – no matter what I may have made you think before now.' This earns me a few dark looks, but that's to be expected. 'I've felt . . . felt a lot of frustration. I've felt *disconnected*. I've felt out of my depth and a little lost.' I hold my hands up. 'I've made mistakes, and I've ended up in places I really shouldn't.'

'Then why the hell should we carry on doing it?' someone in a Loggers Off T-shirt asks. I don't recognise her at all.

'Because it *has* also done me a lot of good!' I say to him. 'I *did* learn to live a different kind of life. I *did* feel better about myself.' I look back at Grace again. 'And I also met the woman I have just confessed my love for in front of you all.'

'But that doesn't help us *decide*, Mr Bellows!' Colin points out. 'That doesn't tell us whether we should carry on or not! Which is it?'

'I don't know, Colin! You have to decide for yourself!'

He gives me a confused look. 'I can't do that.'

'Yes, you bloody well can!' I snap at him.

I then fix them all with a serious stare.

It's a good stare. I can feel it in my bones.

'You don't need to listen to anybody else to know what's right for you. You don't need to follow *me*. You don't need to follow *anyone*! You shouldn't look to me for answers . . . any more than you should look to the people you've followed on social media in the past.' I open my arms expansively. 'You can make your own decisions!'

Well, that's flummoxed them good and proper.

I am faced with a wall of incomprehension. This is somewhat better than a wall of anger, but not by much, when you get right down to it.

Silence temporarily descends as they let this strange concept sink in.

'So, are you saying, Mr Bellows,' Wilberforce pipes up, this time at a volume that doesn't knock the birds out of the trees, 'that detoxing has its good and bad sides? That it's different for everyone? And that we shouldn't necessarily rely on anybody else's opinion to help us decide what to do? That detoxing can only really be a success if the decision to do it comes from within?'

'Buh?' I reply incomprehensibly, completely knocked off my feet by this response.

Colin puts an arm around his partner. 'Sometimes Wilberforce here sees into the heart of the matter far better than you'd imagine, Mr Bellows. It's his greatest gift.'

I thought his greatest gift was the ability to stop his pug shagging furniture with badly constructed song lyrics, but this is probably much better, and is likely to prove more popular at dinner parties.

It takes me a moment to compose myself before I reply. 'Yes, Wilberforce. You're absolutely right,' I tell the little man. 'Detoxing comes with its bad points, and good ones too. You just have to take both on board and seek . . . I don't know . . .' The right word eludes me.

'Balance,' Grace says from behind me.

I throw her a grateful look. 'Yeah, that's it. *Balance*. That's what it's really all about.' I feel myself relax as I say this. My jaw starts to loosen. 'That's what I've learned . . . and that's about the only thing I can really guarantee you guys is the absolute truth.' I hold out my arms again. 'You just need to get a little balance in your life. And if that means detoxing for a little while to see what things are like on the other side, then fine . . . do it.' I shrug. 'Or not. The choice – as I really should have been saying to you right from the get-go – is yours. Find your own balance' – I look back at Grace one final time as I say this – 'the way I've found mine.'

And with that, I am done. Finally *done*.

I feel absolutely exhausted.

I lean back against the counter and rub my face with my hands as I let the audience fully digest what I've just said. I am very much hoping that when I take my hands away and look at them again, I will see something other than anger and recrimination on their faces.

. . . Oh, thank God for that.

OK, some people still look a bit unsure, but there's no anger there any more. None that's detectable to me, anyway.

Wilberforce is getting a lot of pats on the back, which he seems delighted about.

I am equally as delighted, as this means the attention has shifted away from me somewhat.

'Well done, mate!' Fergus says as he comes around one side of the counter and gives me a slap on the back. 'Couldn't have said it better myself.' He then thinks for a second. 'Well, maybe I *could*, but not by much.'

I give him a wry grin. 'I'm sure you'll make me sound much better when you write about this latest chapter of Loggers Off.'

Fergus looks thoughtful. 'No. I don't think so. I think I'm done with Loggers Off. I know you've blamed yourself for all of this, but let's face it . . . I pushed you to be the story for me. I think you've done quite enough now. And I've done quite enough too.'

I look over at Wilberforce and Colin. 'You know, if you want to write a story about interesting people, then why not go have a chat with those two? You'll have material to last you years, I guarantee it.'

Fergus raises one eyebrow and looks speculatively over at the eccentric twosome as they continue to happily chat with the other members of the crowd. 'I might just do that,' he tells me, and I am suddenly struck with the notion that Loggers Off will indeed be continuing on for a while yet – just without me as its figurehead. 'I think I'll go and see if I can make friends,' Fergus says, and saunters over to the pair with his most ingratiating smile slapped across his face for all to see, and be comforted by.

Grace hands two fresh cups of coffee over to a couple who offer me shy smiles, and then leans across the counter to put my hand in hers once they've moved away from us.

Ah . . . that's the stuff.

'How are you doing?' she asks, a look of sympathy on her face. She knows this hasn't been easy for me.

Actually, I'm fairly sure Grace knows *everything* about me – all the important stuff, anyway – even though we've only been together for a few short weeks.

'I'm OK. Tired, mostly. But also . . . er . . .'

'Free?'

'Yeah,' I reply with a smile. 'I'd say so.'

Grace gives me a speculative look. 'So, you just told everyone in this café that you love me, Andy.'

I suddenly feel very hot. 'Yes, I did. How do you . . . do you feel about that?'

She thinks for a second, and then I feel her hand squeeze mine just a little harder. 'I feel very happy about that, Andy . . . and very relieved too. Because I love you too.' The speculative look grows a little more pronounced. 'But I think you knew that anyway, didn't you?'

I smile. 'Yeah. I think I did.'

And I didn't even need Google to tell me.

Grace laughs, and then looks over at where Fergus is chatting amiably with Wilberforce and Colin. 'I think you're about to get replaced,' she says, perhaps changing the subject for the moment to cover our blushes.

I grunt. 'Yeah. Looks like it.'

I suddenly feel a bit downhearted. 'I hope . . . I hope they don't just all start doing the same thing with those two they did with me. I hope they all remember what I said about not needing to follow someone else. Do you think they will?'

Grace shrugs slowly. 'I have no idea, Andy. All you can do is give your best advice to people and let them make their own choices. You've told them the right thing to do . . . whether they choose to do it is their business.'

I grimace. 'That's not quite the ending to this I had in mind.'

She squeezes my hand. 'Cheer up. If nothing else, you've made two people who are used to being the butt of the joke the heroes of the moment.'

Grace isn't wrong. Just look at how popular they've almost instantly become with the rest of the Loggers Off.

The shift away from me as the centre of attention to Wilberforce and Colin has been incredibly quick. Enough to almost give me whiplash, in fact. The followers have moved on already.

It doesn't really feel like anything has changed – despite the things I've just said.

But . . . I have to *hope* it has. In the long run, anyway.

I have to hope that these people won't just fall into the same old trap with Wilberforce and Colin that they did with me – that they'll take my advice and look for their own path.

Will they look to Colin and his boyfriend to tell them what to do? Or will they find their own balance?

I really don't know what the answer is, any more than Grace does.

All I can do at this point is follow my own advice, and live my own life. Make my own decisions. And remember to always think for myself, instead of letting other people – or the Internet – do it for me.

Right now, I'm thinking about whether the rest of Grace feels as warm and lovely as her hand does.

And nothing else seems to matter very much.

Not the future of Loggers Off, not Wilberforce and Colin, and definitely not my bloody digital detox – which has most definitely come to its natural end here this evening in Heirloom Coffee.

If I only know one thing about the journey I've been on, about my time in the analogue wilderness, it's that all of it has been *completely* and *totally* worth it – because I met Grace.

I met the woman I love.

And I would follow her anywhere.

Including on Instagram and Twitter.

Epilogue

Balanced

Today is an important day.

It's the day Loggers Off meet at their new venue for the first time – a large community centre in town that holds about five hundred people. A lot of those attending will still meet up at Heirloom Coffee for the debrief afterwards, though. Wilberforce and Colin have promised to come along and continue chatting to those who are interested in hearing from them in a more informal setting. Puggerlugs has his own little Loggers Off T-shirt now. He looks very cute in it.

I won't be going along, for two very important reasons.

The first – and least important – is that I am no longer doing a digital detox. I am no longer a Logger Off. Haven't been for over two months now, in fact.

The second reason – which utterly *dwarfs* the first – is that today is Grace's birthday.

I'm taking her out for a meal tonight – at a Thai restaurant in the city.

I found it on TripAdvisor. It has a five-star rating, with over seven hundred reviews, so I'm very much hoping it's going to live up to expectations. The chicken with cashew nuts is meant to be particularly good.

I called the restaurant on the phone to make the booking.

I spoke to a very nice Thai girl called Preeda, who promised to sit us at a quiet table. She also offered to buy a birthday cake for Grace at a little extra cost, which she will bring to the table at the right moment. I don't know how embarrassed Grace will be when the whole restaurant starts singing 'Happy Birthday' to her, but I'm hoping she'll appreciate the gesture.

It's not lost on me that if I'd just booked the restaurant online, there would have been no friendly chat with Preeda, and therefore no birthday cake.

During the week I ordered a brand-new black short-sleeved polo shirt on Amazon, and a brand-new pair of blue jeans from ASOS. Both arrived yesterday. I liked the jeans, but the shirt didn't really fit, so I popped into town this morning to pick up a different one from M&S, which I love. It hides my small spare tyre quite nicely.

I paid for the polo shirt with cash, and spent five minutes chatting with the young guy at the till, whose name was Jarrod. He told me to wish Grace a happy birthday, and said he thought the polo shirt I'd bought was very nice.

Finally, this afternoon, I picked up a bunch of flowers from a local florist. It's one that has received rave reviews in the local community forum on Facebook. The bunch of red roses is enormous, very fragrant and does a good job of masking the slight odour of cigarette smoke in the Uber that takes me to Heirloom Coffee, where I am to pick Grace up at the end of her workday.

I tried to convince her to take the whole day off, but when you run a business it's not quite that easy to just chuck a sickie. Especially when that business is thriving – largely thanks to how much attention the coffee shop has got in recent months, and how many times it's appeared in the local paper.

I'd also like to think that its success is partially down to the new marketing campaign I put together for it. The new logo I designed – which features a stylised rendition of Grace's locket – looks rather fantastic on the front of the shop, even if I do say so myself.

Needless to say, I did that job for free.

I haven't had as much time to put into promoting Heirloom as I'd really like, though, because I've been inundated with graphic design work.

The coffee shop isn't the only thing that's done well from being in the spotlight – however temporary that spotlight turned out to be. Andy Bellows the detox guru may have died a suitable death – but Andy Bellows the busy graphic designer is very much alive and kicking.

No complaints, though. It means I get to take my girlfriend out for an expensive Thai meal on her birthday.

When I climb out of the Uber, I say goodbye to the driver with a broad smile on my face and turn to the café's front door with the roses clutched in my left hand.

I look every inch the man in love.

If you were to take an Instagram picture of me right now, you'd have to use the hashtags #lovedup, #deadromantic and #veryhappy.

Because I am all of those things.

I am also a man who has learned something very valuable.

A secret that really shouldn't be much of a secret at all.

And it's this . . .

Life is about finding your balance. No matter how long it takes. No matter how hard it is to get there. And no matter how many duck ponds you have to drive into.

Because you will get there, eventually. Trust me.

And if you don't trust *me*, then you can always google it, can't you?

But now it's time for me to walk into Heirloom Coffee, find my girlfriend, hand over these flowers and go for a lovely meal – where there will be five-star food and birthday cake.

The last thing I do before I venture inside is quickly rate my Uber driver on the iPhone app. I give him four stars, because the ride was quick and smooth but the car did smell of cigarettes.

And then, as I push the front door open with my shoulder and see Grace's eyes light up when she spots the flowers in my hand, I slide my phone back into the pocket of my brand-new jeans – where it will stay until tomorrow.

Because logging off isn't something you should only do once.

It's something you should do *every single day*.

ACKNOWLEDGMENTS

Logging Off is actually a book about people . . . don't let all that talk about technology fool you. And I have many people to thank for their help in getting this book into your hands.

First off there's my old agent Jon, and my new agent Ariella. Both of them are very good at stopping me from writing anything too weird or controversial.

Then there's everyone at Amazon Publishing. Without them you wouldn't have this book, and I wouldn't spend at least 80 per cent of my day online, feverishly refreshing my sales page.

Thanks to my family and friends, most of whom I actually speak to in real life sometimes, and not just on Facebook.

And, as always, thank you to my gorgeous wife Gemma – who I met online. This means that, in my book, the Internet is just about the best thing *ever*.

Finally, my thanks go to *you* . . . for buying and reading this latest Nick Spalding novel. You are the reason I keep doing this, and you're just about my favourite person because of it. Even if you don't follow me on bloody Twitter 🙂

ABOUT THE AUTHOR

Photo © 2017 Chloe Waters

Nick Spalding is the bestselling author of fifteen novels, two novellas and two memoirs. Nick worked in media and marketing for most of his life before turning his energy to his genre-spanning humorous writing. He lives in the south of England with his wife.